A CHILD'S
FEAR.
A WOMAN'S
TERROR.
THIS TIME,
SARAH'S
FIGHTING
BACK...

SOMEONE SHE CARED ABOUT
WAS BEING BEATEN

Sarah pressed her fingers to her brow and concentrated through the stabbing pain. "Where are you? Where are you?" Sarah reached out, and soon the scene began to emerge in her mind. As always, it came in a cloudy mist that slowly cleared as she forced her mind into the other realm.

"Oh, my Lord! He's found them!" Sarah could see Jack Simmons standing over Mary's body. One of her arms hung at a grotesque angle. Jack kicked her and pulled her to an upright position. Then he threw her against the wall. Sarah could see the look in Jack Simmons' eyes.

"He's going to kill her." Sarah watched in horror as Jack wrapped his huge hands around Mary's throat and began to choke the life out of her. Sarah felt the pain and began to push with her mind.

The blow seemed to hit Jack from nowhere. Jack felt his nose break and saw blood gush down all over his chest. . . .

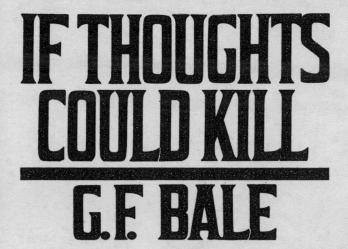

IF THOUGHTS COULD KILL

G.F. BALE

CHARTER/DIAMOND BOOKS, NEW YORK

IF THOUGHTS COULD KILL

A Charter/Diamond Book / published by arrangement with
the author

PRINTING HISTORY
Charter/Diamond edition / October 1990

ISBN: 1-55773-395-3

Charter/Diamond Books are published by
The Berkley Publishing Group,
200 Madison Avenue, New York, New York 10016.
The name "CHARTER/DIAMOND" and its logo
are trademarks belonging to Charter Communications, Inc.

PRINTED IN THE UNITED STATES OF AMERICA

10 9 8 7 6 5 4 3 2 1

ACKNOWLEDGMENTS

My thanks to Shirley Collins, Executive Director of N.E.W.S. in Kansas City for opening doors for me. To Lou Wade, former Assistant to Executive Director N.E.W.S, night staff shelter, for her invaluable help in showing me what life is like in a crisis center. To Judy Nienhueser for her knowledge of Kansas City. To Jim and Vicki Henley for opening their Kansas City home to me. And, most of all, to the abused women who granted me interviews. I wish they all had a "Sarah" in their lives to even the score!

For Ken
With Love

IF THOUGHTS COULD KILL

Chapter 1

ST. LOUIS, MISSOURI
May, 1953

The baby girl sat motionless, watching the afternoon sunlight filter through lace curtains and create moving patterns on the worn flowered carpet. Dancing rays of light touched upon the shiny, half-hidden object under the dust ruffle of the old re-covered chair. The metal nail file flashed and gleamed. Her small chubby hands slowly inched the new treasure from its hiding place.

She passed the file from one hand to the other, holding it high to examine its beauty from all angles. When she tired of that game, the toddler looked around the room for another diversion.

Leaning close to the electrical outlet on the wall, the baby's face crinkled into a smile as she jabbed the file at the small black openings. The first two tries missed their mark. She made another attempt.

When the intense surge of electricity entered

her body the girl was thrown through the air as
though she were an old rag doll. Her heart stopped
beating, but highly energized messages continued
to flash through her tiny brain. Currents rico-
cheted back and forth, short-circuiting, intensifying, dividing and multiplying. Working cells were
destroyed and dormant cells energized. Like caged
animals too restless to remain in confinement,
the volts rocketed against the sides of the small
cranium walls. The stilled heart was no match for
the electronically charged brain. Unable to resist,
the tiny heart returned to its rhythmic beating.

KANSAS CITY, MISSOURI
April, 1990

Sarah eased her Ford station wagon onto Ward
Parkway, automatically reaching for the radio
dial. A rock group whose name she didn't quite
catch was singing something vaguely obscene as
far as she could make out.

"I must be getting old," she muttered to herself
as she tried to find a station with a traffic report.
"Whatever happened to the Fifth Dimension?" It
was a forty-five-minute drive from her home in
Mission Hills to Kansas City's Northside Crisis
Center. She was running late—something she
seldom did—and a rush-hour jam-up would cost
valuable time.

The early-morning sun streamed across the
front of the windshield, half blinding her. With
one hand she groped through her purse until she
found her sunglasses, put them on, and settled
back.

"Good mornin', Big K.C. This is your buddy Traffic Jim comin' to ya from high in the sky and it looks like another gorgeous day in the Show-Me State! No problems on the highways so far—looks like smooth sailin' . . ."

Reassured, Sarah allowed Traffic Jim's voice to fade into a subconscious area of her mind. The two truckers who passed and offered appreciative whistles received the same treatment as the traffic reporter, relegated to a special compartment in her mind and filed under "indifferent."

Sarah was used to whistles, and while she was somewhat flattered, it occurred to her that men in their twenties ought to have better things to do than shriek out of vehicles at middle-aged women in station wagons. Tall and blond, Sarah Jamieson possessed the classic sort of beauty that defied years or fashions. The casual observer might think she was on her way to an early-morning tennis game at the country club, maybe lunch later with the girls. The observer would be wrong, because Sarah was on her way to a low-paying job at a battered women's shelter in one of Kansas City's less-than-fashionable neighborhoods. Several of her Mission Hills neighbors privately wondered why someone in Paul Jamieson's tax bracket would want his wife doing that sort of work. Surely Mrs. Jamieson could find something to occupy her time, which would not include dealing with the sordid side of the city. Fund-raising for the symphony would be a possibility. She'd be such an asset to Paul's law practice and political hopes if she'd make an attempt to move in the proper circles.

But fashionable circles had never been particularly important to Sarah. When every sorority at the University of Missouri rushed the straight-A blond beauty, she politely declined and remained in her old dorm with a roommate who had been one of rush week's unchosen. The University of Missouri social set dismissed her as an academic snob at best and went on planning the homecoming festivities. Even if Sarah had been interested in the sorority whirl, and she was decidedly not, her scholarship and student loan money would not have allowed such a luxury.

It's funny, she thought as she drove through the tree-lined Plaza district, *this job at Northside is really what all that scrimping and saving in college was for.* There was a special satisfaction that came with finding that exact niche in your own field, the perfect job.

Sarah lit a cigarette and sank deeper into thought.

There were so many tragic situations at the Center. Maybe her neighbors were right about one thing—she did deal with sordidness each and every day. But lately there had been something else bothering her. It was as though she was waiting and anticipating a disaster, unable to identify or stop it. It reminded her of the time just before three of the most vicious tornadoes in Missouri history tore through the campus in Columbia, wreaking havoc with an angry vengeance. Sarah had been closeted in the basement of the library studying for an Abnormal Psych test and had heard none of the weather reports. When she finally closed her notebook and climbed the back stairs, she opened the door to find a terrible, unearthly quiet. That day she'd been able to run back down the steps to the safety of the old stone building. This time she felt the storm was going to pull her right into it. No back steps to run down. A small ache began to spread across the back of her head.

By the time she reached the riverfront area and the last leg of her commute, she was so lost in thought that she missed the exit. *Space Cadet.* That's what her son called her when she drifted off like that. *Mom, you're starting to act like old Jimmy Preston again, and you know what a space cadet he is!* Dan would convulse with laughter at the very thought of his mother having any resemblance to poor old Jimmy Preston, the scourge of junior high. Her husband always accused her of having a computer for a brain, calling it her "down time."

Sarah had been thinking of Paul and his hopes of becoming the state's Attorney General. The office was something he'd wanted since he first began practicing law in Kansas City. She felt an invisible chain tightening around her stomach. *What if I ruin everything,* she thought as she finally pulled into the Center's parking lot. *What if it's like before?*

As she walked up the drive an inconsistency hit her. *Just like before.* "Why would I think that?" she wondered aloud. "I've never done anything that would hurt Paul's chances in the political arena." *Space cadet. Space cadet.* She could hear her son chiding her. Sarah shook her head and went into work.

"Mama, I made a new friend yesterday." Her daughter's timid voice cut into Mary Simmons' thoughts. "Today we're going to sit together at lunch."

"That's nice, Ellen." Mary glanced at her daughter sitting in the back seat of the dilapidated 1976 Volkswagen. "What's your friend's name?"

"Janie. She's new, like me. Maybe we'll be best friends."

"Well, Janie couldn't have a nicer best friend than you, honey." There was a distinct sigh of relief in Mary Simmons' voice. Barely five feet tall, with sandy red hair and a pale complexion, Mary Simmons was one of those women who would be attractive if she didn't look so worn out. Worry and fear had taken a big toll on the thirty-two-year old. She silently sipped the cup of instant coffee she'd hastily made while fixing lunches. It was long-since cold.

Maybe the kids would make new friends now. She'd felt enormous guilt about taking them from their old school, their old familiar neighborhood. But she knew that unless she buried the family deep in another part of the city, Jack would find them. Explaining to the school had been awkward. Only the principal knew why school authorities were never to acknowledge the fact that Billy and Ellen were enrolled. No information was to be given out on the Simmons children. Under no circumstances.

It had taken Mary fourteen years to fully comprehend that her husband was more than a man with a bad temper. He was a psychotic time bomb, fully capable of the kind of uncontrolled rage that can kill.

If a student had been assigned to paint a portrait of a fearful woman, Mary Simmons would have been a good subject. She was afraid of so many things. She was afraid of Jack and what he would do if he found them. She was afraid of the world and how she would manage to face it alone. She was afraid her old car wouldn't last another year.

As a matter of fact, Mary couldn't think of a single time in her life when she hadn't been afraid. Her father, Samuel Givens, had been a Reformed Pentecostal evangelist who looked for and found evil everywhere. He found it in the music playing on the radio, in the films in movie houses, and in the sitcoms on television. He found it in his pinch-faced mouse of a wife and their little pinch-faced mouse of a daughter.

When the Reverend Givens was felled by a fatal stroke during a particularly animated harangue at his congregation, he left little behind but a legacy of fear instilled in the hearts of Mary Givens and her mother. More than a few of his colleagues in the preaching business thought that God finally just got tired of being represented by a madman, and put Samuel Givens out of his misery and his ministry.

For Mary, the transformation from her father's

daughter to Jack Simmons' wife was natural and easy. Both men were about an inch away from complete lunacy.

Jack's high-school football career was lengendary, and based on one inescapable fact: he loved to inflict pain on other human beings. His coach knew it. The other players knew it. The college recruiters knew it and counted on a small alumni bonus check if they could sign the seventeen-year-old sadist.

The first time Jack took Mary on a date he knew she was his kind of girl. She kept her damned mouth shut and she knew when he told her to jump she'd better be putting on track shoes. Not like that whore of a cheerleader he'd taken to the Junior Prom—the one who'd told him if he ever twisted her arm again she'd have her two older brothers remove his balls with a jackhammer.

When a car accident involving a drunken Jack Simmons smashed both a leg and his college scholarship plans, several recruiters drowned their sorrows in bourbon, and Jack's father seriously considered shooting his ungrateful son for destroying the old man's shot at reflected glory. Al Simmons had already promised three or four guys complimentary tickets to a future Orange Bowl game, for Christ's sake. Jack was still on crutches when he hobbled down the aisle to wed his high-school sweetheart. And he'd just begun to think that she was probably the cause of a good share of his misfortune.

Lord, what a battle this has been, Mary

thought as she slowly drove toward the school. Sometimes she felt as though her life had only begun when Sarah Jamieson had walked through the door at Truman Medical Center. Mary trusted Sarah as she'd never trusted another living soul. The precious little strength on which she operated had come through that blond woman who looked like an angel to Mary. Sarah Jamieson had some sort of inner toughness that she was letting Mary draw from until she gathered up some of her own. That much Mary knew.

She no longer felt guilty about leaving Jack. But she still felt a twinge when she looked at the kids. They'd been through far too much. Ellen, with those trusting brown eyes and mop of curly red hair. It was so hard to change schools in the middle of the year, as if you're on the run. As if you'd done something wrong.

She worried the most about Billy. He'd seen and felt Jack's wrath far more than Ellen had. Old far beyond his twelve years, Billy had given up a great deal to escape his father's hellish temper. Billy was as much a natural athlete as his father, but without the underlying violence. He'd been on the wrestling team at his old school, and he was good. Mary had assumed he'd sign up for Greyson's team, but Billy pulled her aside in the principal's office.

"Mom," he said with a frown. "I can't be on the team. They'd put the match results in the paper."

Jack would be checking the sports page for just that information. Mary alone knew what that decision cost her son the previous season. No matter how poor they were, how many hand-me-down jeans he had to wear, Billy Simmons was a champion wrestler.

Mary half turned in the car. "How about you, Billy? Are you making friends?"

"Sure, Mom. Some of the boys I helped during wrestling—they've been pretty nice." Billy's voice trailed off.

Tears stung Mary's eyes. She knew what he'd felt, and how badly he'd wanted to be on the team. The coach had been stunned that such a natural wrestler was not allowed to participate. If only she'd allowed the principal to explain. But Mary believed the fewer people who knew anything, the better. So the coach allowed Billy to help with some of the novices. "I promise you that by next year we'll have enough money to move away from Kansas City, Billy," she said with a lump in her throat. "We'll go so far away that you can be on any team you want."

"Don't sweat it, Mom. I like helping Coach Novak out."

Mary bit her lip and vowed she'd figure out a way to make enough money to get them out of the city. Away from Jack Simmons.

His Blazer was parked two blocks from Greyson Elementary School. He stood under the branches of a large elm and watched with a cold, steady glare. From his vantage point he could see both entrances the students used. It was the tenth school Jack Simmons had staked out.

"They have to be somewhere, by God," he swore under his breath.

That stinking little bitch. Who did she think she was? Five months now, they'd been gone. He'd called schools and checked the sports pages for news of Billy. They seemed to have vanished off the face of the earth. She had to be somewhere in the city. She didn't have enough money to eat, let alone move away. But so far nothing had turned up.

The morning sun hurt his eyes. If Mary hadn't walked out on him he might not have had to drink so much last night. His head hurt and he was enraged that he'd been forced into this early-morning ritual, searching for his scum of a wife.

All women were alike. Whores, every one of them. That dame he'd picked up last night, for example. Threatened to call the police—hell, what did she expect? She'd been sitting there in the bar, just waiting to be picked up. She'd wanted it all right. Bitch tried to act like she didn't once they got to her van. But he'd put it to her anyway. He'd shown her how rough it could be if you messed with Jack Simmons. He couldn't remember how many times he'd hit her, but when he finally spent himself, she was just lying there in a pool of blood. Once he regained his strength, he grabbed his pants and left.

Jack stared at the school. Quite a line of cars now, and he had to concentrate on finding his. When he saw the Volkswagen he almost mistrusted his own eyesight. He stepped closer to get a better look, and saw Ellen and Billy jump from the car and start up the walk.

Jack just watched, making no move to follow Mary as she pulled away. She'd be coming back after school and then he could get his family back where they belonged. Jack smiled and knew he was going to teach them a lesson they'd never forget.

Chapter 2

ST. LOUIS, MISSOURI
July, 1955

The Hamilton Institute for Psychic Research was housed in two huge, unimpressive brick buildings in the rolling hills outside St. Louis. Tom Hamilton, steel magnate and amateur philosopher, had endowed the Institute to the tune of ten million dollars in 1946. Hitler's war had been extremely good to Tom, and in return he hoped to give something back to the world that had endured so much through the long dark siege. For years Tom's fascination with paranormal phenomena had been but a hobby, but in 1946 he sought to bring respectability to a subject shrouded in mysticism.

"It's a science, you see. Just like chemistry. Physics," Tom was fond of explaining to skeptics. "There's an entire dimension that flourishes in a largely uninformed and patently unintelligent modern civilization. One day the world will wake

13

up and realize that it's only been living up to a minute bit of its potential. Mark my words."

Tom Hamilton had not built his empire on empty words. He donated land, erected two gigantic—if unimaginative—buildings, and funded the entire project out of his own pocket. Then he proceeded to find the best people he could to staff the center that bore his name. It was Tom's opinion that any scientist in the world could be enticed to come to St. Louis if offered enough money, and he was correct. In the nine years since the Institute had been in operation it had established itself as one of the most thorough and progressive research centers in the world. By the time a young St. Louis widow phoned the Institute about her toddler, Hamilton was in the enviable position of having to turn subjects away.

"Yes, sir," she spoke quietly into the phone. "My daughter has some sort of powers. I—I just don't know what to do with her anymore."

The strain was beginning to wear on her. Months of living in fear someone would find out. Afraid they'd come and take her baby away.

She sighed. "I was hoping you'd have some pamphlets or something. Anything to help parents of these—uh—these children. I want her to lead a normal life. She'll be starting school soon. Then what will I do?"

An emotion between sorrow and relief overtook her. It was inevitable. The baby had to be turned over to someone who understood these things. To people who could do something about her powers. The woman listened as the condescending voice on the line explained that hundreds of people were turned away each year. He droned on and on.

"Yes, I understand all that." She was exasperated. The decision was made as far as she was concerned. "We'll come next week." She listened a moment, then shook her head. "No. I don't think that will be a problem. You won't be turning my little girl away."

KANSAS CITY, MISSOURI
April, 1990

Sarah entered the large, sunny sitting room and smiled. It certainly wasn't a room she'd have chosen for her own home, but there was such a nostalgic charm and Victorian elegance to the old Jennings house that she couldn't imagine the Northside Crisis Center being anywhere else. Antique velvet curtains fastened with tasseled cords and brass rosettes framed the large open doorways on the main floor. A tufted chintz chaise sat to one side, with tiny pillows carefully crafted from needlework designs. An elegant framed calligraphy was placed on a burled walnut table. *Quem colorem habet sapientia? St. Augustine.* "Tell me, what color is wisdom?" Sarah stared down at the small framed quote. What a fascinating woman Margaret Jennings must have been. The house was filled with books, all worn from reading and rereading. She'd been interested in everything, from the great philosophers to better farming methods. Sarah reached down and ran her fingers over a fringed leather slipper chair. They were lucky, she knew, that Margaret's last will and testament specified that most of the furnishings remain when Northside moved in. Somehow the decor gave everything a solid feeling. It was a refuge of simpler, hopefully more idealistic times.

The house sat on Bluff Drive, a once fashionable street where the years had not been particularly kind. Many of the once-proud homes had been sectioned off into apartments. It was not a slum, but then, it was not what it once was, either. With the single exception of the still-unvanquished Jennings house, the area was a sad testament to the ravages of time.

Elizabeth Evans, director of Northside, had reacted with disbelief when she was notified that Margaret Jennings, a local widow, had left her home to the Crisis Center. The Center had been operating out of an old storefront on Brighton Avenue, and federal cutbacks made their existence more and more precarious. The Jennings gift was a godsend.

Sarah, deep in thought, was slightly startled when she realized she was not alone in the room. "Good morning," she said softly to the girl sitting on the hassock by the window. "I didn't see you there, Kathy. Feeling any better today?"

"I'm okay," the girl answered, managing a slight smile.

"Just okay? Is that all?"

"Oh, it's starting to itch. Mother says that means it's healing."

"I brought you a present," Sarah said, changing the subject to something less painful. "What did you tell me your favorite color is?"

"Blue," Kathy answered in a voice that was barely audible.

Sarah unwrapped the blue iris she'd clipped from her flower bed that morning. Dew still glistened on the perfect petals. "It's the first one this year." Sarah held out the flower, careful not to move too quickly.

Kathy stared at the blossom for what seemed to be a very long time. "It's beautiful," she whispered, taking the flower and beginning to back away. "Thank you."

Kathy never turned her back on an adult.

Damn, Sarah thought, lighting her second cigarette of the day and staring at the doorway through which the girl had vanished. If she could get her hands on Kathy's stepfather she didn't know what she might do. The bloody carnage that had occurred the night Kathy and Julie, her mother, were first referred to the Center would long be etched on the little girl's mind. Kathy's mother had become so accustomed to the beatings that she took them stoically. At least she had someone, even if he knocked the devil out of her. The years since Kathy's father's death had been lonely, and Sam Thomas had filled that void. The fact that Kathy seemed to retreat more and more into herself worried the girl's mother, but she put it down to a difficulty in adjusting to a new father.

The fourteen-year-old girl was too terrified and guilt stricken to tell her mother about the nights her stepfather crawled into bed with her.

The pattern might have gone on forever, or until Kathy became another runaway wandering the streets, if Julie Thomas hadn't come home from work two hours early one evening. As soon as she walked through the front door she heard her daughter's screams and started running up the stairs to the bedroom. She expected to find Sam spanking Kathy for some childish prank. What she found was something entirely different.

"No, no! Stop! It hurts!" Kathy's screams had turned to hysteria by the time Julie threw open the door. Sam Thomas' naked body was on top of the screaming child. "Mama, help me!" Julie threw herself at him, jerking at his arm and pulling him up by the hair. Sam wheeled around, slammed his fist into Julie's face, and jumped from the bed. He picked his wife up off the floor and began hitting her again and again.

Breathing hard, Sam pulled on his pants and turned to Kathy. "You little tease! Whore! Look what you made me do to your mother!" he snarled, working himself into an insane rage. "I ought to kill you for this."

Sam picked Kathy up and heaved her at the wall with an inhuman strength. Even through the pain-filled haze, Julie could hear the bone snap.

Both mother and daughter would no doubt have been city morgue statistics if not for Mrs. Garcia next door. The old woman had heard all the screaming she could take from that house and had called the police. The two patrolmen who were sent to investigate found the front door standing wide open and heard shouting coming from the second floor. They burst through the bedroom door just in time to see a child sail across the room and crash into a large framed picture on the wall. Glass shattered over her as she slid to the floor.

"Christ almighty!" Bill Wilson had been on the force ten years and thought he'd seen everything. The woman and child looked dead or close to it. Bill's partner ran to the girl.

"Please—help . . . " The woman was moaning and trying to pull herself along the floor toward the girl. Somehow, though Bill would never understand how, she'd managed to rouse herself. He hesitated for a split second, and that gave Sam Thomas all the edge he needed. He bolted out the door and down the stairs. By the time Bill hit the bottom step Sam was out the back.

There was no way the patrolman could have known that Sam Thomas kept a car parked in an old garage down the alley, and there was no way he could have anticipated the two Dobermans in the backyard. The dogs paid no attention as their master charged through the weeds, but they damn sure weren't going to allow a stranger in a blue uniform to trespass into their territory. Bill cut around to the front of the house and through Mrs. Garcia's yard, but Sam was already to hell and gone.

Julie Thomas lapsed into unconsciousness and didn't come around for three days. It was only then that the police learned of an old unregistered car Sam Thomas kept in the alley and that he had friends—Julie didn't know them, but had heard him talk about poker buddies—and those friends would no doubt help him. As long as Sam remained at large, Kathy and her mother would remain in seclusion at the Center.

Sarah sighed and put out her cigarette. She wondered what would happen to the Thomases. Mrs. Evans had already bent the rules by allowing them to stay longer than the one-month limit. But Elizabeth was known to make her own rules when she saw old ones not working.

In her office Sarah sat down heavily in the chair. "You look like you need this," Elizabeth noted as she followed Sarah through the door and handed her a steaming cup of coffee. "I heard you talking to Kathy."

Sunlight caught the silver beauty of Mrs. Evans' short hair, making it sparkle like diamonds. Under perfectly arched eyebrows her china-blue eyes widened expectantly as she waited for Sarah's assessment of Kathy's progress.

"I'm worried. She's still so very frightened of adults. It's hard to picture her ever having anything close to a normal life."

Elizabeth paused before answering. She'd been the victim of sexual abuse herself as a child. Though there had been none of the violence Kathy experienced, the years of being handled by her mother's youngest brother had left scars on Elizabeth. Not until she met Martin Evans had Elizabeth trusted a member of the male sex. As his graduate assistant at Stanford University, and later as his wife, Elizabeth worked through her personal anguish and eventually became one of the most respected scholars in the clinical psychology field. When Martin retired to his native Kansas City, Elizabeth opted to leave the isolation of academic life and founded Northside.

"It may take years of professional help, but it's certainly possible. The important thing now is to apprehend Sam Thomas. I shudder to think what hostilities are building in the man now that he's running from the police."

Sarah nodded. "Anything happen last night?"

"Nothing we couldn't handle. I stayed late—Martin's working such long hours on his book that I like to stay out of his way. Two women came in, neither of them was hurt badly, thank God. One is going home today—she spoke with her husband. The other is staying awhile. She's pregnant. Cindy Lou Merit is her name. Originally from Kentucky. I think you're really going to like her, Sarah. She's already made friends with Kathy."

Sarah's eyes opened wide. "That's wonderful! Kathy needs every friend she can get right now."

"I knew you'd like that development. Cindy Lou has a matter-of-fact way about her that I think will be good for Kathy. There's not even that much difference in their ages. Cindy Lou's only seventeen, though she looks older. I've asked her to stop by and talk with you later this morning. She seems to want to help. Kathy had a bad time last night. The dreams again."

"Have any of the board members questioned the Thomases being here so long?"

"No, but I'm ready for them if they do. By the way, have you seen the paper this morning? More cutbacks, and we're operating on a shoestring already. I don't know how those idiots in Washington think we can exist like this—who do we turn away?"

"I know." Sarah looked thoughtful. "It looks as though we both will have to twist a few more arms in the private sector."

"We? Do you want to get involved with fund-raising?"

"I've been giving it some thought. I feel like I've been passing the buck long enough."

"I didn't hire you to raise money, Sarah. You're one of the best counselors I've ever worked with." She paused. "But if you really want to help, it would be wonderful. You have access to an entire new segment of the moneyed public."

Sarah laughed. "You mean Paul's business crowd. That's why I started thinking about it. They seem to give enormous amounts to the Philharmonic and the museums—the 'in' charities around town. I think it's time they started developing a bit of a social conscience, starting with Northside."

"And you don't mind approaching them?"

"No. But Paul may die when I tell him I want to attend the next soiree at the Country Club. He usually has to drag me."

Elizabeth stood to leave. "I just don't want you to burn out with any extra loads. You're too valuable. And I don't want Paul to burn out either. You take too much of this home with you as it is."

Sarah laughed and assured her employer that Paul Jamieson wouldn't have it any other way.

At forty-one, Sarah's husband was still as much in awe of her as he'd been the first day he'd seen her in the university library. The legs alone would have hooked him—they seemed to go on forever. But when she turned that serious gaze on him, with those cool green eyes, Paul realized that she was one of the most astonishingly beautiful females he'd ever seen. In the months that followed she continued to astonish him. He kept waiting for the fatal flaw to show up. Somewhere under all that wonderfulness there had to be a strain of bitchiness, or something. He didn't believe in superwomen. As it turned out, with two exceptions—she smoked too much and didn't care for Paul's progressive jazz records—Sarah was Paul's idea of the perfect woman. She was a knockout, smart and funny, and Paul figured he must be the luckiest man in the world.

After seventeen years of marriage he still figured it exactly the same way. Therefore it would never have occurred to him to ask Sarah to fit in with his law partners' social set. She outclassed any woman he knew, and he took pride in the fact that his wife was incapable of falling for the trappings of being Mrs. Corporate Law.

Sarah knew Paul understood her devotion to her job. Knew that she couldn't help feeling personally involved with many of the women at the Center. She reacted on a gut level to their problems. So great was her empathy that Elizabeth once asked her if she, too, had been a battered child. But Sarah said her father had died when she was but a baby and her widowed mother was gentle beyond belief. Mrs. Evans had warned Sarah when she took the job that she might become far too involved with the clients. *Clients.* What a term for the emotionally and physically wrecked women Sarah talked with on a daily basis. When Elizabeth first used the term, Sarah had chided her for an academic regression.

Elizabeth had just smiled and shook her head. "One of these days you can write a paper introducing a new line of jargon."

Thinking back on that conversation, Sarah vowed to get started on just such a paper—as soon as things settled down a bit. She pulled her morning appointment sheet from the desk drawer and took a sip of coffee. On the side of the page she'd made a note to herself: "Call about Sat. nite—Jason and Alison."

Talk about sordid, Sarah thought. *The Center probably seems like Sunday School compared to what Jason sees every day. Being a captain of Homicide must be grim.*

ST. LOUIS, MISSOURI
July, 1955

June Carver looked at the small girl sitting across the table from her. Blond and fluffy, the child was the youngest the Institute had ever dealt with. Mrs. Carver smiled.

"Now, Sarah, this first test is a guessing game. Do you like games, sweetheart?"

Sarah nodded, warming to the woman.

"I have five different symbols on these twenty-five cards. A cross, a star, a circle, a square, and wavy lines. I'm going to hold up the cards one at a time. I'll show you the blank side and I want you to guess which symbol is on the other side. Okay?"

The child nodded again.

Mrs. Carver held up the first card. It was a cross. "Which one is this, Sarah?"

The three-year-old screwed up her face and stared at the card. Finally she gave up. "I can't tell you."

"Just guess, honey. This is just a guessing game."

"I don't remember."

Mrs. Carver chose a different card. This time it was the wavy lines.

"Can you tell me what this card is, Sarah?"

"No," Sarah answered apologetically. "I don't remember."

June Carver went through all twenty-five cards. Sarah guessed ten times. Five stars and five circles. The other times she refused to answer. June was astonished. Why did the little girl keep saying she didn't remember? And how in God's name did she get so many of the same symbols correct? The woman thought a minute, then held up a card with a square on it for Sarah to see.

"What is this card, Sarah?"

"I don't remember," Sarah said and hung her head.

Mrs. Carver nodded. Of course. The child was only three years old. She was unsure of the proper names for all of the symbols. She couldn't remember.

"Let's change the game a little, honey. I'm going to hold up some cards and you tell me what they look like to you."

She held up a card.

Sarah thought a minute. "It's a box."

Another card. The wavy lines.

Sarah wrinkled her nose. "Yuk. Worms."

"Then worms it shall be." Mrs. Carver smiled. "How about this one?" she held up the cross.

Sarah just looked blank.

"I know," Mrs. Carver said. "Why don't you just make a sign like this." She crossed her fingers and made an X sign.

Sarah grinned and nodded.

Mrs. Carver was getting excited. "And you know about the circles and stars."

Sarah brightened. "Oh, yes. I remember them!"

Something about the child was very different. The fact that she refused to guess, that she seemed to know exactly what the symbols were— just couldn't remember the names.

She held up the first card, a square.

"A box! It's a box!"

The next card was a circle.

"A circle—I already knew that one." The child was obviously proud.

The pattern continued. A star. A box. A worm. (Yuk!) And every time Mrs. Carver held up a cross Sarah giggled and crossed her fingers into an X. One hundred percent correct.

A perfect score was unheard of. Even a 9.9 percent correct showed psychic ability. Mrs. Carver wondered if the testing would lose credibility because she'd broken standard procedures and methods. *Only to a fool*, the woman thought. *The child is too young to be tested normally.*

"You did very well, honey. Would you like to play this game again?"

Sarah looked surprised. She liked this big, happy woman.

"Okay, but . . ." Sarah's tone became conspiratorial. "I'm not guessing. I can see the cards."

Mrs. Carver held up one of the cards to make sure the ink was not showing through somehow. She looked at the little girl and noticed the simple confidence she conveyed. "How do you see them, Sarah?"

"On the back of the card, and in your head."

"All of the time or just part of the time?"

"When I want to."

In all of June Carver's experience she'd never met anyone who claimed they *knew* what was on the other side of the card. They had no special feelings about which cards were correct guesses. And the child was a mind reader. That might change things a bit. But June had the feeling it was much more than mind reading. She had a feeling that this child was going to amaze them all.

Chapter 3

KANSAS CITY, MISSOURI
April, 1990

"Yes, of course I'll speak with you for a few minutes," Sarah reassured the woman on the other end of the telephone line. "As long as you want to talk. That's what I'm here for."

"I'm so very frightened." The voice was cultured, melodic. "I don't know what to do or where to turn for help."

"Do you have family?"

"Only his family nearby, and they would never believe me. I can hardly believe it myself. I—I'm sorry. I never should have called."

"Please, wait a minute!" Sarah's shoulders sank as she heard the tiny sharp click and the dial tone. Damn. It had been one hell of a day. The only bright spot was Cindy Lou Merit. No sign of a typical victim personality about her! Mrs. Merit would be one of the lucky ones. All she needed was to get back to Kentucky to the safety of her family. From what Cindy Lou had told Sarah,

Johnny Merit would never have the nerve to follow her there. He'd never stand a chance against the girl's father and brothers. She'd be just fine.

Mary Simmons maneuvered her Volkswagen into the long line of cars waiting in front of the school. She unwrapped her Snicker's bar and started nibbling at it. Since leaving Jack she'd made a conscious effort to gain weight. Her nerves had been so strung out over the past couple of years that she was down to under one hundred pounds. It was too thin even for her small frame. *Fifteen more pounds*, she thought. *That's what I really need to gain. I look like a mouse. Just like Daddy always said.*

She was beginning to control her nerves a little. *You have to take control.* That was one of the first things she'd learned in her counseling sessions. "I'm all right. I will remain calm." Mary spoke aloud to herself, as if she needed to hear a human voice for reassurance. She took a deep breath. Something was causing her to be edgy right now. She glanced around. There was nothing out of the ordinary.

"I've got to get out of this city," she said to herself for the hundredth time. "I can't go through life looking over my shoulder. The kids have to have a normal life. I've just got to get away from here."

But it took money to get away and money was something she didn't have.

She glanced over her shoulder once again,

watching as the line of cars grew longer. Just people waiting for their children. *Just like me*, she thought. *They're just people like me. I am getting more paranoid by the day.*

Mary started her deep-breathing exercises. "I'm all right. I will remain calm."

Jack's angry eyes were glued to the lone occupant of the Volkswagen. Boy, how he'd like to walk over to that car, tap on the window, and watch Mary's face when she turned toward him.

Nobody walked out on Jack Simmons.

He loved those kids. She had no right taking them from him like that. Sure, he had to discipline them. He had to make up for his stupid wife's lax standards. By God, you had to show kids who was boss or they'd end up dope addicts, or holding up liquor stores. His dad sure as hell showed him who was boss, and you never saw Jack Simmons take any drugs. None of that hippie shit for him.

Jack took another swig from his flask. As for Mary, he knew he'd hurt her pretty bad that last time. But hell, she never could get anything right. Look at her—skin and bones and that haggard look he hated so much. Shit, he could barely stand the sight of her. Just watching her made him want to smack her in the face. His father had been right. She wasn't good enough for him. Looked a little like pictures he'd seen of his old lady. Not that he really remembered her. Took off as soon as she got the chance. Left him and the old man high and dry. Some women stuck with their men. Not anybody he knew though.

Well, she'd pay for it. Only this time he'd be careful not to lose his temper. Couldn't risk putting her back in the hospital. There was still a court date set for that last time. But he'd figure out something. He'd fix her ass.

Billy and Ellen came running down the school steps, waving goodbye to their new friends. They piled in the car, both talking at once. Mary kept her eyes on the traffic, waiting for a chance to pull out. The uneasy feeling was back. Even the incessant chatter coming from the back seat couldn't take her mind off the growing tension.

Jack's eyes filled with tears when he saw his children's smiling faces. *Damn them all*, he thought as he eased into the traffic and followed.

It was after six when Sarah pulled the car down the curved drive in front of the sprawling home on Mission Road. She parked in back, looking longingly at the tiled pool as she walked through the courtyard. Maybe they could fill it next month; the weather was almost warm enough.

What a day. She could feel the muscles in the back of her neck tightening and a headache building. Seemed like she'd been busy all day, yet got nothing accomplished. It was a relief to get home. Everything here was sane and right. Blessedly normal. Paul's car was in the garage. Good. Maybe he started dinner.

She walked in and tossed her jacket on the nearest chair. Paul's sport coat lay on the long leather couch. Sarah smiled to herself at how the two had grown so alike in their habits. It was a good thing Mrs. Albertson came in three times a week.

Kicking off her shoes, Sarah could feel the cool terra-cotta tile under her feet. The sensation somehow soothed her nerves. She and Paul had found the tile in Mexico City over ten years ago. They'd just bought the house and were in the process of redecorating when a case required Paul's going to Mexico. Sarah went along and they spent an extra week haunting the stores of the old city. They not only found the precise tile they wanted, but several artifacts they now considered a part of the family. An exquisite carved conch shell graced the mantel over the fireplace in the den, and an Owl Warrior they'd named "Fred" sat on the coffee table in the living room. The Ned Jacobs paintings came from a small gallery in Taos. Both Paul and Sarah loved the Southwest, spending most of their vacations in New Mexico or Arizona. Their home reflected the clean, earthy feeling so common to the region. Sarah wondered what she'd have done if Paul had been a Chinese modern aficionado, or been enamored of Italian provincial.

"That you, honey?" Paul was in the kitchen. She walked in to find him unpacking small containers of food from a shopping bag.

"Glad to see the chef is at work." Sarah grinned and slumped in a chair.

"Thought you might like to try my old family recipe for Chinese food," Paul said. "Taught to me by my Irish grandmother who trusted no one who wasn't named Chin when it came to ethnic dining."

"Your grandmother was a wise woman. How was your day?"

"The usual. Saved a man from the electric chair. Made a fool of the D.A. The Governor called and said he needed me for Attorney General next term. Usual stuff."

She laughed easily, knowing full well that her husband was indeed being considered for that position, and that he wanted it very much.

"How about your day?" he asked.

"Kathy's still pretty bad. She barely communicates with us. I'm afraid it's going to be a long haul."

"Christ. I hope the D.A. locks him up for good when they find that creep."

"The same D.A. you enjoy making a fool of?"

"Yeah, that's the guy," Paul said with a chuckle. "By the way, where are the kids?"

"Janet called and said her art class is meeting later tonight. A film or something. The teacher's dropping them off around seven. Dan had baseball practice. He grabbed a sandwich and took off just as I was walking in the door."

"Does that mean we actually have the house to ourselves for a change?"

"That's right, sweetheart," Paul said in a miserable Bogie imitation. "Got any ideas?"

"You know me," she answered. "I don't believe in wasting anything—especially time."

She beat him to the bedroom door.

ST. LOUIS, MISSOURI
September, 1955

"Sarah, I want to play a game with dice today. Do you know what dice are? They are little cubes that have six sides. There is one side that has one dot on it, one side that has two dots—all the way up to six. Can you count up to six?"

The child nodded.

Dr. Peterson was anxious to begin testing Sarah. So far she'd amazed everyone. Her test results were perfect, and the amount she'd learned in general knowledge from Mrs. Carver's tutoring would stagger any educator. But the testing was questionable as far as Peterson was concerned. There always seemed to be extenuating circumstances. Because of her age, standard procedures weren't always followed. Peterson was not a man who liked bending rules for anyone.

"Sarah, I want you to call a number between one and six. Then throw one of the dice on the table. I want to see if you can guess what's coming up."

"Okay."

Sarah picked up the dice. "Five," she called. The dice rolled and settled on six. She picked it up. "Three." It stopped at one. She tried to look into Dr. Peterson's head, but he didn't know what was coming up either. She tried to look into the dice, but the numbers flashed by too quickly.

Dr. Peterson watched her intently. These fools must have been wrong—he knew the findings were too good to be true.

"Try some more, Sarah. See if you can do it."

Sarah threw the dice over and over, and the results were no better than chance. Suddenly she turned red. Dr. Peterson was thinking about Mrs. Carver. *Her* Mrs. Carver. That wonderful fat lady with the friendly eyes. "Idiot." She heard him say it as plain as day. He was mad at Mrs. Carver and it was because of her! Because she couldn't see what would happen with the dice. Sarah could not let that happen. She threw the dice. "Three." Concentrating hard she moved the dice on the table until the number three came up. Then she let it go.

"Fine, Sarah. See if you can do it again." Dr. Peterson was still uninterested.

On she went, until Peterson's attitude began to change markedly. Fifteen correct answers in a row.

"Sarah, that's wonderful! Continue."

An overwhelming feeling of shame enveloped the little girl, and she burst into tears. She was cheating. Mrs. Carver wouldn't want her to cheat. It was wrong.

"I can't do it right," she said in a small voice. "I'm cheating."

"There's no way you could be cheating."

"Yes there is. I'm making the dice go to the number I call. I didn't want you to think bad things about Mrs. Carver."

Peterson looked at her a long time before answering. "Sarah," he finally said. "You could tell what I was thinking about Mrs. Carver, so you flipped the dice to make it come up correctly?"

"Yes." Sarah was burning with shame.

"Let me see you move that." Peterson pointed to one of the cubes on the table.

Sarah concentrated, and the cube began to shake.

"Make it turn to the number two," Peterson instructed.

Slowly the cube began to rotate. It finally came to rest at the number two.

Dr. Peterson was breathing hard. "Keep on, Sarah. Keep calling numbers and then make them come up. Don't even touch the dice."

Sarah was confused. Dr. Peterson wasn't mad. He liked what she was doing. Did he *want* her to cheat?

Over and over the cube rolled, always stopping when Sarah made it stop.

Dr. Peterson pulled out a handkerchief and wiped his face. "Sarah, can you move the dice off the table?"

"Where?"

"Can you make it go across the room to the wall."

Sarah shrugged. "I guess."

The cube lifted up about a foot off the table and went flying across the room. The sound of it hitting the wall reminded the scientist of a rifle shot. Peterson inhaled deeply, trying to stop the shaking in his hands.

KANSAS CITY, MISSOURI
April, 1990

Dan charged into the house clutching his glove
and baseball bat, leaving the front door to slam
with a thunderous bang.

"Guess what?" he yelled from the foyer. Sarah
figured the neighbors down the street could probably hear him as easily as she and Paul. "I hit two
over the fence at practice. It was *great*! The coach
moved me up to cleanup batter."

"Dan, that's wonderful!" His parents answered
almost in unison. Paul widened his eyes and
looked at his wife.

"I bet he's going to tell us all about it. What do
you think?"

"No kidding around, Dad. It was great!" Dan
repeated himself. "It was between that jerk Leonard and me and I got the spot. Remember him,
Mom? The kid who was such a turkey back when
I couldn't play very good? The jerkface who
wanted me kicked off the team?"

Sarah shook her head in amusement and shot a
knowing look at Paul.

"I remember how bad you felt when he made
fun of you," she reminded her son. "You might
remember that, too. Don't rub it in now that
you're the better player."

"Nah. I didn't. But it was great, anyway."

Paul looked at Sarah and grinned. "I'd say it was
great."

Not quite fourteen, Dan had overcome tough
odds to win a place on the league team. When he

started playing ball he was small for his age, and so clumsy that his parents despaired of his ever being any good at sports. They knew he'd get his height someday. Both parents were tall, and Dan had been a big baby. His oversize feet indicated that he'd be a big man, but in the meantime all they did was trip him. He reminded Sarah of a newborn colt trying to run on gangly legs. Legs that comprised almost half of his small body. It was almost comical to watch him try to coordinate the top half with the bottom half.

But Dan was a worker. He wanted to play ball more than anything in the world, and Paul pitched to him so much that he developed a constantly sore arm those first few years. If determination counted, Dan might someday be playing for his favorite team, the Royals. But back then, determination couldn't quite make up for the legs and feet.

As Sarah looked at her tall, athletically built son she thought back to that day three years earlier, when his sports career had really begun.

He came home from practice and went straight to his room that day. Sarah listened through the door and heard muffled sobs.

"Dan?" She knocked lightly. "Dan, honey, what's the matter?"

"Nothing."

Sarah stood there a moment, then opened the door.

"Come on, kiddo. Something's wrong. Tell me about it." She sat down on the bed beside her son.

"They don't want me to come tonight. Leonard

talked to everybody and said I'd lose the game for them."

It was the night of the League Championship. Dan always struck out, and a group of his classmates had approached the coach with the suggestion that the boy be left off the lineup on this, the team's most important night of the year. The coach had said no. Under no circumstances would he remove a player from the lineup. God love Coach Samuels. A former minor league player, Samuels had told Dan's parents over and over that the youngster had great potential, if he could just build up his confidence. The legs and feet would eventually take care of themselves, the coach had said with a short laugh. The confidence was the main thing.

Damn everything, she thought. *It's not fair for him to have his spirit broken so young. By the time his body catches up with his legs, he won't have the nerve to pick up a bat.*

She reached over and stroked her son's hair.

"Kids can be pretty cruel sometimes. But, honey, you can't let that stop you. You go out there tonight and play baseball with your team. Your dad and I will be proud of you no matter what. Look how many times Babe Ruth struck out. And what about your hero, Bo Jackson? He certainly strikes out! The main thing is that you try. You know how I feel about quitting, about giving up."

Dan finally agreed to go, and both of his parents were in the stands to cheer him on. Two times up to bat and two strikeouts. Dan slunk back to the bench as though he'd been caught shoplifting.

It was the top of the ninth inning. Dan's team was up to bat with one boy on base and two outs. The opposing team led five to four. Dan came up to bat, and an audible groan could be heard from the bench. The boy hung his head and trudged up to the plate.

Leonard Watson's voice could be heard above all the rest. "Shit, we might as well quit right now. *Jamieson* is up to bat. I *told* that freak not to come."

Dan took a few hesitant practice swings and stepped up to the plate.

First pitch. He swung and missed.

Sarah prayed he'd hit the next ball.

The next pitch was wide. Ball one. Then came a perfect throw. Dan swung and missed again. Strike two.

Catcalls from the bench caused Dan's face to turn a deep red. Sarah knew he must be fighting back tears. She made her decision.

The moment the next ball left the pitcher's hand, Sarah concentrated on it. She pushed the baseball straight into Dan's swing and then carried it high into the air and over the back fence.

The crowd went wild as Dan and his teammate trotted around the bases.

"Jesus! Did you see that? What a hit!" Paul grabbed her arm.

Sarah nodded. She'd seen it all right.

As the team crowded around Dan, his old nemesis Leonard watching in amazement, Sarah wondered if she should feel guilty for what she'd just done.

The game wasn't over yet. In the bottom of the ninth, Dan's team led six to five. There were two outs, and the bases were loaded. The other team's power hitter was at the plate. The boy swung and sent the very first pitch sailing out to left field. Dan started running, but Sarah could see he'd never make it in time. *Just once more*, she thought.

She turned her eyes on the ball, and it began to lose speed. Dan reached out his glove, and the ball seemed to drop right into it. Three outs.

They'd won the championship. As Dan was carried from the field, Sarah felt a wave of satisfaction. She seldom used her powers. God knows she'd been instructed not to enough. Certainly her family knew nothing of them. What would Paul say if he knew she could send objects flying through the air, or read his mind if she wished. Not that she ever did. Rarely did she wish to get into another person's mind. No, her mother had been right. It was best to keep this part of her existence to herself. Private.

"What on earth did you say to him this afternoon, Sarah?" Paul was still jumping with excitement.

"Not much," she said quietly. "I just tried to give him a little self-confidence."

Jack circled the block three times, parked, and settled down to study the house his family had just entered. He pulled out his bottle of Old Charter and twisted off the cap.

Even the kids had turned against him. *She* had done that. It was her fault. It seemed to Jack that every injustice he'd ever had to face was somehow connected to Mary. As a matter of fact, if she hadn't insisted on going to church with her fool of a mother that night back in high school, he wouldn't have been out drinking with his buddies, wrecked his car and ruined his whole life. If she'd been a real wife instead of a whining little weakling, none of this would have happened.

Damn her. Damn them all. He was head of his family, and no damned court could tell him to stay away from what was rightfully his. The radio played on and on, caught between two stations and squawking in an irritating manner. Jack glared at it, but made no move to change the dial. Who cares about the stinking truck. He figured the finance company was looking for it anyway. Probably had at least a couple of repo men on his trail. He shifted in his seat and spilled Old Charter down his shirt. Looking in the rearview mirror Jack saw bloodshot eyes staring back at him. Surely they couldn't be his.

His emotions were starting to get to him. Maybe they could make it work this time. He'd give Mary another chance. She was such a pretty little thing once, back before she turned into such a bitch.

Darkness settled in and lights started coming on in the nearby houses. Jack fumbled for the door handle, took another swig from his bottle, and lurched off into the cool spring evening.

Billy stood in the living room, trying to decide between homework and a quick ride on his new/old bike that Dan Jamieson had outgrown and given him. Mary and Ellen were clearing dishes away from the table. Things seemed pretty normal to Billy. Like a real family. Not so long ago meals had been nightmarish.

Billy felt sorry for his mother. She worked so hard trying to make ends meet. She was getting a raise down at the Qwik-Shop, but even that wasn't enough. He knew the manager allowed Mary to bring home unsold deli food, and that was mainly what they ate. When they could afford a lawnmower, Billy would try his hand at grass cutting this summer. He'd seen the tight, worried look on his mother's face when she looked through the mail and sorted out the growing stack of bills. But things could be worse. At least they were safe from Dad.

Billy sometimes thought about his father, but he didn't love or miss him. How could you love someone who beat up your mom all the time? Not to mention the welts he always had to hide. How many times had he insisted on wearing sweatpants to gym instead of the regulation shorts? He used to wonder what it would be like if his dad quit drinking, or saw a doctor, or something, but it never happened. Dad was always drunk, hitting Mom, and breaking furniture. He turned on Billy if he got in the way. The last year had been the worst. Billy couldn't count the times he and Ellen huddled in the corner of the room, praying their father would forget they were there. Praying Jack would pass out before he really hurt their mother.

The little radio on the end table announced the day's news and weather. The temperature had hit 68 degrees in the afternoon, but would drop to 45 during the night. Fog had contributed to three highway deaths the night before. Toronto had beat the Kansas City Royals 1–0. Billy figured Dan Jamieson would hate that fact.

The knock on the door interrupted his thoughts. Billy couldn't tell if it was just his imagination, but it seemed like someone had tried the locked handle first.

"I'll get it, Mom. It's probably the guys. We talked about riding bikes tonight."

"It's a little too dark now, don't you think," Mary called back.

Billy opened the door and the smile on his face dissolved into a look of stark terror.

"D-dad," he stammered. "How did you—uh, what are you doing here?"

Jack Simmons reeked of whiskey and stale sweat. He stood unsteadily in the doorway and sneered at his frightened son. "Is that any way to greet your old dad, Billy boy?" Jack staggered past his son and into the tiny house. He walked around, eyeing the room his family shared apart from him. He dropped into an old chair and pulled out his whiskey, draining the bottle.

"Where's your mom, boy? We need to talk. Get things straightened out."

"There's nothing to straighten out, Jack," Mary said as she walked into the room. Her voice was steady, but the white face and clinched hands told Jack she wasn't quite as calm as she was trying to appear.

"You've got to leave. The court ordered you to stay away from us, Jack. And I called the police the minute I heard your voice. You better be gone when they get here."

Billy looked at his mother in surprise. He'd never seen her actually stand up to his father.

"So you called the police, did you? Well, you're getting pretty damn good at that. Just call the cops and have them haul your old man off, when all he wants is to see his kids. Where's Ellen? Where's my little girl? Ellen! Come out here and say hello to your dad before the cops get here and take him away. The damn cops that your bitch of a mother called."

"Ellen, stay where you are." Mary's firmness startled Jack.

"Damn it, kid, I said get out here!"

Ellen poked her head around the corner of the kitchen. Her big brown eyes looked questioningly at Mary.

"Get the hell out here," Jack roared. "You don't need Mommie's approval to come to your own father." He started toward the kitchen, shoving Mary to one side.

"Get out of here, Jack. You're drunk." Mary's voice was shaking and she was as close to anger as

Jack had ever seen her. "You've shoved us around for the last time, do you understand me? Get out!"

Fury welled up in Jack. "Why you miserable slut! How dare you talk to me like that?" He took a step in Mary's direction and Billy jumped in the way.

"Just go, Dad," he pleaded. "Please go."

"You stinking brat. You're a poor excuse for a son! If you even *are* my son—considering what a whore your mother is! I'll show you what I think of you *and* your stinking mother!"

Jack smacked Billy in the face. "This is my family, and *I won't be thrown out of here!*"

Mary tried to reach her son, but Jack grabbed her by the hair and twisted. "And now, *you! You* are going to call the police and tell them you don't need them after all."

He dragged Mary to the kitchen and yanked the phone off the hook. Through bleary eyes he read the number Mary had scribbled on the wall calendar, and dialed.

"Screw this up and those brats are dead, got that?"

"Hello," Mary spoke softly into the phone, praying that somehow the dispatcher could tell she was being forced to make the call. "Hello, this is Mrs. Simmons on Green Street."

Jack pulled Mary's arm behind her back and twisted.

"I, uh, called a few minutes ago. I thought someone was breaking in the house. I was mistaken."

Jack twisted her arm a little higher.

"No, no. Everything's all right. You don't need to come."

Mary was sure that the dispatcher couldn't tell she was lying. Jack took the receiver from her hand, slammed it down, and twisted Mary's arm.

"YOU BITCH!" Jack was wild-eyed and raving. Mary could see something new in his expression. Jack Simmons had the look of some creature the devil himself had created. She knew he was going to kill her.

Sarah was cleaning off the kitchen table when she felt the first blow. A pain shot through her arm with such intensity she nearly passed out.

"God, no!" She gasped and fell back against the wall, thinking she was having a heart attack or a stroke. Then she felt a fist ram into her stomach. Breathing heavily, she staggered to her feet and down the hallway to the bathroom. Sinking to the floor, Sarah felt the blows raining down on her body. There was no question in her mind now. Someone she cared about was being beaten. It was like the time when Janet had been bitten by a dog on the way home from school. Sarah had felt the pain as if it had been she who had been attacked. And she'd been able to stop the dog.

She pressed her fingers to her brow and concentrated through the stabbing pain. "Where are you? Where are you?" Sarah reached out, and soon the scene began to emerge in her mind. As always, it came in a cloudy mist that slowly cleared as she forced her mind into the other realm.

"Oh, my Lord! He's found them!" Sarah could see Jack Simmons standing over Mary's body. One of her arms hung at a grotesque angle. Jack kicked her and pulled her to an upright position. Then he threw her against the wall. Sarah could see Billy lying unconscious and hear Ellen screaming from somewhere in the house. She saw the look in Jack Simmons' eyes.

"He's going to kill them." Sarah watched in horror as Jack wrapped his huge hands around Mary's throat and began to choke the life out of her. Sarah felt the pain and began to push with her mind.

The blow seemed to hit Jack from nowhere. He felt his nose break and saw blood gush down all over his chest, and tried desperately to ward off his unseen attacker.

Mary lay dazed on the floor, her swollen eyes not believing what she was seeing. It looked like Jack was fighting with himself, or else having some kind of a fit. The blows stopped as suddenly as they had begun.

With an unholy scream of terror and rage, Jack lunged toward Mary. "I'll kill you for this," he gurgled through the streaming blood. He tried to grab the limp body on the floor, but found himself hurtling backward. The blows began again.

Jack felt a searing pain in his sternum, his belly. It shot through his kidneys, so severe that he lost control of his bladder. He fell to the floor, feeling his jaw snap in midair, arms flaying out in vain as he tried to stop whatever was battering him.

The viselike grip the thing had on his chest

tightened, cutting off his air. Then in one awful moment, Jack Simmons knew he was going to die. He could hear his heart pounding in his ears, and from somewhere far away Jack thought he could hear bees droning on and on. Finally the muscles of his heart could take no more and the organ called it quits.

Sarah unclenched her fists. There were drops of blood on her hands where the nails of one hand had dug into the palm of the other. Her hair and face were wet with perspiration. She sat there alone in the bathroom, shaking.

Slowly she forced herself to her feet. She had to call an ambulance for Mary and the kids. Sarah thanked whatever powers that existed that her own family had been watching television in the den.

Her body ached as she made her way down the hall to the telephone. She had to make the call. Then she had to sink into a hot bath and come to grips with what she'd just done.

Chapter 4

ST. LOUIS, MISSOURI
January, 1956

Tom Hamilton stood watching the snow slowly falling outside his office window. One by one his board members and directors arrived and took a seat around the conference table. There was a tense excitement in the air, a sense of anticipation that had been growing ever since Sarah Livingston had arrived at the Institute. Finally, Tom Hamilton spoke.

"Ladies and gentlemen, we have here at our research center a child with the greatest degree of psychic ability ever recorded. Every department head has now had the opportunity to test Sarah Livingston, and I feel the results are conclusive. This child is going to make history."

He picked up a pencil from the table and nervously tapped it on his stack of notes. "We now face a twofold problem. We must test her on grounds the world will accept, and we must keep both the child and her mother happy with what we are doing. The second issue is vital. I do not want this girl leaving here and being tested elsewhere."

Dr. Peterson shifted in his chair, quickly glancing at June Carver.

"Peterson." Tom turned to the doctor. "Do you have the compiled results of her tests?"

Dr. Peterson rose and opened a thick file. "The first tests were done by June, as you all know. She took Sarah through the Zener cards, but had to deviate from standard procedures somewhat because of the child's age. Once June devised a way for the girl to remember each symbol, Sarah has never missed another identification. Not once."

June Carver interrupted him, "Dr. Peterson, I only worked with Sarah a few times before she could remember the correct symbol for each card. No scientist in the world would question the results of these tests. Certainly no one at Rhine would find fault with our procedures at this time."

Tom Hamilton nodded grimly. "Rhine is just what I'm worried about. What are the chances of them trying to convince Mrs. Livingston to take her to them?"

Peterson sighed. "The chance might be very good if we jump the gun and release anything too soon."

"Rhine is better known than we are," Tom added, addressing his remarks chiefly to the visiting board members. "They just might be attractive to the girl's mother. We have to move very cautiously now."

June rubbed her temple, frowning. "But the thing is, Mrs. Livingston doesn't want any publicity. She wants her daughter to live a normal life—that's one of the primary reasons she brought her here in the first place. She wanted us to teach the child to control her powers, not become some sort of freak."

"June, do you honestly believe that child will be able to have anything even remotely connected to a normal life?" Peterson asked with an air of impatience, glad that June Carver was so close to retirement age. He removed a sheet of paper from his file and began to read. "In general, from our testing thus far, we've established that Sarah scores higher than anyone ever before tested in clairvoyance, telepathy, and psychokinesis. So far there is no evidence that Sarah has any special ability in precognition. Of course, she's only four years old and we haven't devised an adequate testing situation to see if she can foretell events. I will say this—I've never seen anything like her psychokinetic ability. Jerry, that's your field. Can you elaborate on it?"

Jerry Wilson stood. His voice shook a little and he appeared bewildered. "It's still unbelievable to me. I started with something simple, a little rubber ball. I put it on the table and asked Sarah if she could roll it to the edge without using her hands. She looked at the ball and it started to roll. I reached down to catch it when it rolled off the table, and it suddenly stopped. Right at the edge. She has control over the objects. Most adults we've tested came nowhere close to the degree of control this little girl has."

Peterson spoke up. "Tell them about the dolls."

Wilson leaned on the table. "This is one of the reasons I'm against releasing any information until we study this child further. We were in the children's wing, and up on a shelf was a Raggedy Ann doll. I asked Sarah if she could make the doll come to her, and immediately the doll sailed right through the air and into her arms." He wiped his brow. "Then the door to the room opened and two more Raggedy Ann dolls sailed in and dropped into her lap. They had been in another room, *but Sarah didn't know that!*"

Peterson's eyes narrowed. "You see, we have here an individual who could sense where the identical requested items were, and make them come to her, even if it meant opening doors to do it."

"If we expose her to publicity now, we run the chance of this child's mother being offered immense amounts of money," Tom Hamilton added. "She could end up little more than a sideshow freak, and our Institute a footnote in the matter."

June shook her head. "None of you have spent much time with Mrs. Livingston. She'd never allow that to happen."

"June," Peterson began. "At some point we are going to have to go public with Sarah Livingston—whether her mother likes it or not. We owe it to the world."

June Carver was not a woman who gave in easily. "As head of the Children's Clinic, I want you all to understand one thing. If I see that the testing or any plans for publicity are exploitative, or harm Sarah in any way, I will insist that we stop. We have a charming, loving child in our care. I intend to see that she stays that way."

KANSAS CITY, MISSOURI
April, 1990

Detective Max Killen leaned back in his chair and stared at the clock slowly ticking away. Half an hour to go and he could call it a day. Paperwork was finished. No loose ends to worry about for once. It would take him exactly fifteen minutes to drive to his West Port Square apartment, maybe half an hour or more to shower, shave, and slip over to the Plaza where the sexiest broad in Kansas City was waiting for him. Killen had only known Sally Merril two weeks, but her bedroom prowess was already about to drive him to an early grave.

It would not be a bad way to go. There was an additional plus in that she was the first woman he'd met in the two years since he'd been transferred to homicide who hadn't stifled a laugh and commented on his name. "Killen in homicide?" He'd just as soon stayed in Vice for Christ's sake. Saved himself a lot of ribbing. It had not yet occurred to Max that Sally's IQ was about ten points lower than his golf score, and therefore she never remarked on his name or anything else that required much thought.

Eight thirty-five. With a little luck he'd be in Sally's bed by ten.

The call came in at eight thirty-six.

"Killen, you'd better get over to 312 Green, fast. There's an ambulance driver who says he's got a dead man, a woman in critical condition, and a badly beaten boy. Says it looks like somebody went on a rampage."

Shit, there goes the night, Max thought angrily, then shouted to his partner, "Steve, get a move on it. We've got troubles."

The police car pulled away from the old brick police building at 1125 Locust. In front of headquarters the statue of an officer holding a baby stood proud and erect, reminding anybody who cared to look that Kansas City's finest were doing more than just issuing traffic tickets.

Max turned on the siren and the two men sped through the night.

Joe Turner, the Medical Examiner, was already there when they pulled up in front of the shabby little house on Green Street.

"What have we got, Joe?" asked the tall, lanky officer in charge. "This had better be good— ambulance driver made out like it was a massacre."

"What's the matter, Max? You got somewhere better to go?"

"Damned right I do."

Turner rubbed at his chin as though there was a deep itch he couldn't quite isolate.

"You better call Links. This isn't any ordinary homicide. Something pretty wild here."

"The woman and kid still alive?"

"Yeah. I think she'll pull through. She revived long enough to tell the driver that the dead man is her husband, and he beat up both her and the kid. The boy was still unconscious. Plus there was a little girl locked up in the closet. Scared half to death. She said the same as her mother—that the dad did the beatings. Guess he's not going to be hurting anybody else."

"Nice guy, huh?"

"Yeah. Real nice. Looks like somebody gave him a taste of his own medicine."

Turner looked at the body lying on the floor. "I wanted to let you do your job first, but I want another real close look at this guy."

"Right. Hank, get on the phone to Links and then get started. Blood samples. Don't miss any— God knows there's enough of them. Steve, get some photos. We'll need overlapping shots of the entire room. Get some of the guy's face."

Max turned to the fresh-faced uniformed policeman standing in the corner. "Not a pretty sight, huh, Tommy? Guess you better get this room dusted."

He almost forgot about Sally Merril's soft double bed.

He watched as the men set about their tasks. It was a good team. Whatever clues the killer had left behind would be found.

Almost a shame, he thought. *Dead guy must have been a wacko. World was probably better off without him.*

• • •

When Jason Links arrived the room had already been turned over to the Medical Examiner. Max was sitting at an old wooden table in the living room, filling out a report.

"What's going on, Max? They tell me I need to see this for myself."

When Jason Links entered a room he dominated it, making everybody else seem slightly less alive. He was tall, and even with a slight paunch he was still an extremely handsome man at age fifty-four. The graying at his temples added a dignified air that had been missing in his youth. The raw energy he'd exuded at twenty-five had turned more sophisticated, more refined. But there was still a jagged edge just under the surface, and it caused every woman he met to fall under his spell just a little. It was an energy women saw as sexual and men viewed as strength, and both sexes tended to give the man their complete trust.

The opportunity to work with Links was the only thing that kept Max Killen from asking for a transfer back to Vice.

"Well, it looks like the husband was beating up his family—put two of them in the hospital. Then someone killed him. Beat him to death. I'm pretty sure there's no gunshot or knife wounds. Seems kind of strange though. You'd better talk to Joe."

Links' stomach lurched as he knelt down beside the body. There was blood everywhere, but that wasn't what shook him. He'd seen blood before. It was the victim's eyes. They were fixed in a frozen look of terror.

"Christ. What happened here, Joe?"

"I don't know, Jason. I can't figure it out yet. I was just getting ready to wash off some of this blood so I can get a better look."

The Medical Examiner carefully wiped the misshapen face, shaking his head as he worked.

"No abrasions."

"What's that supposed to mean?" Links frowned.

"Not a damned mark on his face. He has a broken nose, a broken jaw, and his face is caved in. But there isn't a scratch on his face. And look here at his chest. It's been crushed—but the only mark on him is where this rib came through the skin."

"So what are you trying to say? Was he beaten to death or not?"

"I'm saying this is weird as hell. I can't wait to do an autopsy on this one. Somebody worked him over, but good. But as to how or with what, your guess is as good as mine."

Steve Jeffries came in from the squad car parked outside.

"Got a rundown on our friend here. Three arrests for battery, plus a couple of DWIs. According to Rodriguez, he's also a good candidate for some rape cases. His size and that mole on the left side of his nose fit descriptions given by four different women."

"What's his name?" Links continued to stare at the contorted face of the victim.

"Simmons. Jack Simmons."

Max Killen lit a cigarette. "Maybe we ought to

give a medal to whoever did this. Simmons sounds like one sorry excuse for a human being."

"Right. Then we can all quit the force and turn law enforcement over to vigilantes." Links turned to Joe Turner. "What did the ambulance driver say about the wife? Did she give him any clue as to who did this?"

Joe shook his head. "She was barely conscious. Guy said she just mumbled about Simmons trying to kill her."

Links nodded. "Well, we'll talk to her later. The killer was probably somebody she knew. Maybe a family member."

"Captain, some reporters are here." A young officer stuck his head through the partially open front door. "Do you want me to handle it, or should I tell them we don't have a statement at this time?"

Links cursed the day the newspapers started chasing ambulances.

"I'll take care of it. Max, let me see that report."

Flashbulbs popped as he stepped outside.

"Captain Links! Is it true that there's been a massacre here?" The man was short and thickly built, a tape recorder in one hand and a camera in the other.

"What's the matter, Charlie? Can't the *Star* afford to send a photographer with you these days? Sorry you got your hopes up, but there's no massacre. I'll tell you briefly what we have so far. The victim is Jack Simmons, age thirty-two, white. He was not a resident of this address. Simmons was killed somewhere between six-thirty and eight P.M. according to the M.E. He was severely beaten by a person or persons unknown. That's it."

"Come on, Links. You got more than that." Charlie strained to see inside the house. "What's the story on all the other bodies the ambulance driver was talking about?"

Jason sighed. "All right, Charlie. Prior to Simmons' death he beat his wife and son into unconsciousness and locked a daughter in a closet. We have no leads or witnesses."

"What about the wife?"

"Unable to make a statement at this time. Both the woman and the boy were in critical condition when the ambulance arrived."

"Could the wife or the kid have done it?"

"Impossible. Both were hurt severely."

"Think the killer will be able to claim self-defense?"

"Anything's possible, Charlie. I'm not a lawyer."

Charlie Kaufman bit his bottom lip and looked wistfully at the front door to the house. "Did the guy have a criminal record?"

"Battery and some drunk driving arrests," Links answered impatiently.

"How old are the kids? Got their names?"

"The boy is twelve, girl is eight. And you know I can't release the names right now."

"What's the condition of the wife?"

"Numerous abrasions, broken arm, and internal injuries."

Charlie stood watching Captain Links. "Whoever

did this probably saved the lives of the woman and kids, right?"

"It's possible," Links reluctantly admitted.

"So what we have is a wife-beater who got the tables turned on him?"

Links could see it coming. A murderer made out to be a hero. Christ, these press guys were full of it. "What we have is a murder."

"Where were the woman and the kids taken?"

"I can't give you that information." Links turned on his heel and walked back into the house.

Joe Turner was waiting for him. "They buy that?"

"The esteemed defenders of the public's right to know were more interested in the 'wife-beater-gets-his' angle than in what weapon was used to kill the guy. I can see the headlines now. GOOD SAMARITAN KILLS THEN SLIPS AWAY."

Max Killen finally remembered that he was exactly one and one-half hours late for a date. "We're finished here, Captain. Okay if I take Steve and head back? I've been off duty since nine o'clock."

"No sense in half the force being here now," Links growled. "I guess you can go—but there's a couple of things I want to know. First, what did the neighbors have to say?"

"No one saw anything or heard anything." Max pulled out his notebook. "Not regarding the actual attack anyway. Two kids across the street saw a man enter the house sometime around dusk. They thought it might have been around seven. From the description, it must have been Simmons. They said nobody else came in."

"How long were they out there?"

"One kid said he thought it was around eight when his mother called him home. They'd been waiting for the Simmons kid."

"So as far as the kids know, nobody else entered the house unless it was after about eight?"

"That's what they said. They were riding bikes—who knows if they were really paying attention."

Links nodded and stared at the dead man on the floor. "They noticed Simmons come in. If they were expecting the kid to come out they might have been paying attention."

"Could be. That's all they knew."

"Of course, someone could have come in through the back and they might not have seen."

"No. There's no alley, and the people next door were grilling hamburgers in the backyard. They didn't see anything."

"Then the killer must have been here when Simmons arrived." He looked around the room. "We'll sort it all out down at headquarters. Max, you go ahead. Leave a couple of guys here, though. I want this place sealed up tight. Some teenager is sure as hell going to want to say he got in and checked out the scene of the crime. Look tough for his buddies."

Links watched as the Medical Examiner and a crew of men in white uniforms loaded up Simmons' crumpled remains and left the little house on Green Street. Finally he turned back to Max.

"By the way, why was Joe Turner here before you guys?"

Killen laughed. "You know Joe. Thinks he's goddamned Quincy. He was in a shopping mall near here and his office beeped him about the 'massacre' report. He wouldn't miss a massacre for the world."

"Damned near was a massacre," Links said, staring again at the congealing pools of blood on the floor. "Tell Hank I want him to get down to the hospital and see if Mrs. Simmons is awake enough to give any kind of a statement. Tell him to talk to both the kids, too. Turner is trying to make this out to be some big mystery. Simmons' wife probably had a boyfriend. That's about as mysterious as it's going to be." He followed Killen to the door. "From the sound of it, couldn't say I'd blame her if she did."

Chapter 5

She sat back in the steaming water and stared fixedly at the mist gathering on the deep green mosaic tile, numb except for the throbbing in the back of her head. The accusing voice seemed to come from far away.

You killed a man, Sarah.

What else could I do! He was going to kill Mary and the kids.

You don't really know that, do you?

He was a psychopath.

Are you God, Sarah?

Mary won't have to hide anymore. They'll all be safe.

You killed a man so she wouldn't have to hide? Does life mean so little to you?

No! He tried to kill them!

The battle raged. She turned the hot water on and again bent forward to inhale the steam.

If I'd been in the house I'd have picked up a gun and shot him, she rationalized, but the voice wouldn't buy it.

It wasn't that hard, though, was it? It was easy.

As easy as helping a boy hit a homerun. As easy as it was before.

Stop it! I've never hurt anyone before! Never.

A shudder crawled down the back of her spine, and Sarah Jamieson crawled out of the tub.

Jason Links slapped his hand down on the morning papers spread across his desk.

"What did I tell you?" He looked at Max Killen, whose bloodshot eyes and slumped shoulders indicated he'd slept little in the past twelve hours. Links hadn't slept well himself, but, he suspected, for different reasons then his subordinate. "They're making this guy out to be some kind of folk hero. Kansas City's own Charles Bronson. The *Star* almost indicates the police force could use a few more guys like him to help out. I knew damned well Charlie would take that angle."

He walked to the window and stared at nothing in particular, finally turning back to the men seated in the squad room. "Just so we don't lose sight of our priorities, let me say this. In all my years on the force, I've never seen a corpse in that shape because of a beating. If the guy—or guys—who did this just wanted to protect the people in the house, the broken jaw and the ribs would have done it. I suspect this guy—if it's just one person—has to be huge. Simmons would have been in no shape to fight back once that jaw cracked. But the guy didn't stop. This isn't any ordinary passerby who stopped to help a lady in trouble. Keep that in mind. Now. Let's go over what we have so far. Prints?"

The officer cleared his throat. "Uh, sir, there were fingerprints all over the room. No attempt to wipe anything clean. But they're all accounted for. They belonged to either Simmons or his family, with the exception of some small child-size prints, old ones. Probably those kids who were waiting for the Simmons kid. The guy must have worn gloves."

Links folded up the newspaper and tapped it against the side of his desk. "Then the guy probably wasn't there when Simmons arrived. And he probably didn't stop in by accident. It's too warm for somebody to be running around in gloves. I don't want any 'probablies'—fingerprint those friends of the kid and see if they match what you found. I want to know every person who's been in that house. Check around the neighborhood for someone trained in martial arts. Okay—what about blood samples?"

"Three types of blood found in the living room, Captain. Mrs. Simmons', the kid's, and the victim's. We figured the victim's hands might have some of the killer's blood on them, but it came up negative."

"Hair samples?"

"Same thing. Nothing to give us a clue to the killer. Simmons had a lot of his wife's hair on him—looks like he must have jerked her around by her hair, as a matter of fact. That's it, though."

"According to this report, she gave a short statement last night. Said he'd pulled her from the kitchen by her hair. But she said she must have been unconscious when the killer entered. She must be protecting someone." Links frowned. "I can't possibly believe this. Are you guys telling me that you couldn't find one *shred* of evidence to indicate that another person was in that room? None? Simmons was a big man. I can't believe that he didn't put up some kind of fight."

The young officer looked uneasy. "He did, sir. We could tell by the scuff marks on the linoleum. But the marks were all from the victim's shoes. Not even any from Mrs. Simmons'—so that definitely lets her off the hook."

"No kidding," Links said sarcastically. "The report says she weighs less than one hundred pounds. Anybody who saw Simmons last night would rule her out." He ran his fingers through his hair and wished he hadn't quit smoking. "Well, you've got to be missing something." It was physically impossible to leave no trace. A stone was being left unturned. Someone must have been sloppy.

"Killen, were you too interested in a late nighter to give this a hundred percent? Or maybe you didn't take this seriously. Maybe you figured this guy deserved what he got?" Links regretted it the minute he spewed out the thoughts. Killen may be living in the fast lane, but he was one of the best detectives he'd ever seen.

Killen scowled. "Let's get back over to the house and scour the room, *again*."

"Good," Links said in an almost apologetic tone. "Take extra men with you. Get somebody over to where Simmons was staying and scour that place, too. Start checking out the family and friends of Simmons and his wife. Shit, who knows—it may even be a professional hit. Check out all the women we suspect Simmons might have raped. And get a policewoman over and check out Mary Simmons again. See if we can find out if she was really unconscious or if she's covering for someone. I have to believe that she is."

"There's one more thing, Captain." Max was still touchy, but he was beginning to loosen up. "I went back over the police log, and Mrs. Simmons called a squad car at seven-twelve. Then at seven twenty-two she called and canceled it. Car was already on its way, but the dispatcher called it back. She says she was forced to make the second call. Then, at eight-ten someone called an ambulance. It was a female voice. Mary Simmons says it wasn't her."

Links' mouth dropped open. "Who the hell made the call, then? I thought you said the neighbors hadn't heard anything at all."

"That's what they said. Nobody will admit making the call. Mary Simmons was covered with blood, and there's no blood on the phone. Plus, the ambulance driver says she wasn't coherent enough to have made it. The operator who took the call remembered it. She said the woman was whispering, but entirely sure of herself. The woman said that an ambulance was required at the Green Street address. Said someone might be dying. The way I figure this, we can pinpoint the time of death between seven twenty-two and eight-nineteen. That's when the ambulance arrived."

"Question all the neighbors again. Make it clear that if anybody's withholding evidence they'll be held as an accessory. I suppose we can't ignore the possibility that the killer is a woman. She'd have to have gone somewhere else and made the call."

Max's eyebrows raised in unison. "A *woman*? Shit! I'd hate like hell to meet the woman who could have taken on Simmons and made that kind of mess of him."

"My wife would call you a chauvinist pig for that remark, Max." Links stifled a grin. "Of course, you're right. Get me a complete rundown on the wife. Boyfriends. Uncles. Who the hell knows, maybe her brother is Andre the Giant."

Max Killen shrugged. "Sure. So far she says she didn't see anything. Says she was in and out of consciousness the whole time. We've got a taped statement from her. She swears she didn't see anybody come in the house. Says it was almost like a dream to her. Said she heard a scuffle, but it seemed like it was coming from far away. I was at the hospital early this morning." He turned serious. "Captain, you've got to meet this woman. She doesn't seem the type to have any homicidal boyfriends lurking in the background."

Links grunted. "Don't make any assumptions. She sure had a killer of a husband. What did the little girl have to say?"

"We haven't talked to her yet. She's at Northside Crisis Center. I spoke with the director there, a Mrs. Evans. Dr. Evans, to be precise. She asked us to wait until this afternoon. Says the little girl was pretty shook up."

"Why was she taken there?"

"Ambulance driver says the Simmons woman kept mumbling about calling the Center. They stayed there after the last assault. The doctor at Truman called this Dr. Evans and she drove over and picked the little girl up. Evidently it was the Center that helped the family relocate on Green Street. They were hiding from Simmons."

Links nodded. "Okay. Look, Max—pull yourself together and get out and talk to those rape victims. I keep wondering if one of them had a friend who was looking for Simmons. And I'll handle the Crisis Center. Paul Jamieson's wife works there. Maybe Sarah knows something that will help."

Sarah's high heels clicked out a staccato beat on the long hospital corridor. Room 362, the patient information clerk had said. She'd had no sleep the night before. Just sat in the kitchen and stared at the wall, smoking cigarettes and thinking. Justifying. If there had been any alternative, she wouldn't have killed Jack Simmons. If she'd only hurt him, he'd have come back. And then he'd have killed Mary. The kids too, probably. He was crazy, damn it. She'd done the only thing she could do. Thank God Paul was a sound sleeper. By the time he awakened and checked on her whereabouts, she could honestly say that the Center had phoned her about the incident at Mary Simmons' house. She was worried sick about it.

Softly opening the door to Mary's room, Sarah peered into the darkness. Mary's small frame was barely visible under the blankets. The drapes were pulled tight, and Sarah longed to throw them back and introduce Mary Simmons to the world of sunlight. The world she could now enter without fear hanging over her head. She looked down on the swollen, battered face.

Mary blinked her eyes and looked up at Sarah through a drug-induced haze.

"I'm glad you came," was all the woman could get out before the tears started streaming down her puffy cheeks.

Sarah leaned over and smoothed back Mary's matted hair.

"It's going to be all right now. You don't have to worry. Everything is going to be all right."

"Sarah," Mary said in a thick whisper, as though something evil was still hanging over her and listening to every word. "Sarah, it was awful. Jack wanted to kill us. I could see it—he wanted us dead. He hurt Billy so bad. I thought he'd broken his neck. I tried to stop him—"

"Don't try to explain." Sarah picked up the cold rag lying on the stand beside Mary's bed and began wiping her brow. "It's all over now. He can't hurt you anymore. Don't think of anything but that."

"Sarah, they keep coming in and asking me who killed Jack. But I don't know. I swear I don't know. I kept nodding out. Who could it have been?"

Sarah took a deep breath. "I don't know. Someone was probably passing the house and heard you scream. They must have come in and stopped him, then got scared and ran away. Don't worry about it. Whoever it was, it was a friend." Sarah frowned. "They, uh, don't think you had anything to do with it, do they?"

"No. They don't seem to think I could have— killed him. But they think I saw something. But I *didn't*, Sarah. There wasn't anybody there."

Sarah bit her lip. "Now, you can't be sure of that. Somebody had to be there."

"I didn't tell the police everything, Sarah. They'd think I was crazy. I saw Jack fly backward when he tried to grab me. Like I'd thrown him. Only I didn't. I couldn't have thrown him like that. Then he flung his arms up like someone was hitting him—like he was protecting himself. But nobody was there. He looked just like a puppet, dancing by himself." She shook her head painfully. "Then I must have passed out."

"You were in shock, Mary. Someone must have pulled him from behind and you just didn't see them. That's how it had to be."

"Yes," Mary rasped, still questioning. "Yes, I guess that's what must have happened." She turned her head away from Sarah. "I'm not sorry he's dead. I should be, but I'm not."

"I know. Just don't think about it. Think about getting well and the life you'll have. No more hiding, Mary. It's a terrible thing, hiding. A terrible, terrible thing."

A long-forgotten memory started to surface in Sarah's mind. Then it was gone again, floating into that vast area she couldn't comprehend. Her down time.

When she looked up she saw a man standing outside Mary's room holding the biggest bouquet of roses Sarah had seen since Janet was born.

"Excuse me, but are you a friend of Mrs. Simmons?"

Sarah nodded. "I'm Sarah Jamieson."

"Sorry to bother you," the man said with a soft, but self-assured voice. He was solidly built, wearing an ancient college letter jacket and Levis. "I'm Tom Novak. I coach wrestling at Greyson Elementary. I came as soon as I saw the morning papers. Is Mrs. Simmons going to be all right? And Billy?"

"They'll be fine. It's going to take a while though."

"Thank God. When I saw the name in the paper, I couldn't believe it. Simmons must have been a lunatic. That's what this has been about all the time, isn't it? The fact that Billy couldn't be on my team. They were hiding out from Simmons. I just figured she was afraid Billy would get hurt. He's good you know. I'm pretty high on that kid."

"Me, too." Sarah smiled and glanced at the flowers. "Are those for Mary?"

Tom Novak looked thoughtfully at the bouquet. "Yeah, yeah they are. I owe that woman an apology. I had her pegged all wrong. She's one hell of a lady. I've got something for Billy, too."

He pulled a small gold pin from the side pocket of his jacket. "It's a coach's pin. Billy's helped the beginners a lot since he came to Greyson. I'm going to make him my official assistant coach until he's well enough to get on the team."

He stared at the pin a moment, then looked back at Sarah. "Tell you the truth, Mrs., uh, Jamieson, is it? Well, to tell you the truth, when I read about what happened I was glad that bum got his. 'Course, I'd never say that to Billy or his mother. Sounds terrible to condone a killing—but that man got what was coming to him."

"Don't apologize, Mr. Novak. I agree. Jack Simmons got exactly what was coming to him."

Jason Links glanced at the clock hanging off-balance on his wall and realized he'd better hurry if he was going to meet Joe Turner for lunch. Funny Joe was so insistent about it. He probably had some exaggerated theory about the Simmons case. Links hurried through the precinct room and out into the breezy spring day.

Links was glad Joe Turner had suggested Houlihan's for lunch. If he got to the Plaza early enough he could wander around a bit, clear his head. The case was shaping up to be a bitch. The press was going to turn it into a circus, and if his men were missing anything vital, it would probably end up on the front page of the newspaper. Lots of things worried him about this case.

Even Links' closest friends, friends like Paul

Jamieson, would have been astonished to know that the captain of Homicide was uncertain, apprehensive. The facade of confidence was seldom missing.

Jason Links' career had started in Kansas City, and he'd never had any desire to leave, even though he'd been offered more money in both New York and L.A. He'd been a rookie detective when one case got him the national attention that resulted in countless job offers and a fame of sorts.

The case had been unusual from the start, since it involved the Attorney General of Missouri, Bob Richards. One week after announcing his plans to run for Governor, Richards' wife's nude body had been found in a wooded area five miles from their home. She'd been shot twice in the back, apparently the victim of an attempted rape and robbery.

The newspapers had a heyday with stories of the devastated Attorney General and the ineffectual Kansas City police force that allowed murderers and rapists free reign. When Richards fell apart on nationwide television following his wife's funeral, he probably could have run for God and been elected. The talk was already beginning. Richards might be good presidential material after a term as the Governor of Missouri.

There was one person who would not have cast a ballot in Richards' favor. That person was a rookie detective named Jason Links. He thought Richards was lying through his teeth.

According to the Attorney General, his wife had driven to the city from their suburban Kansas City home, planning on doing some last-minute

Christmas shopping. They'd only returned from the state capitol, Jefferson City, three days prior to the fateful shopping trip. Richards knew she'd made it all right, because she'd phoned about a shirt size from the downtown Hall's store. When she still hadn't returned home by midnight Bob Richards called the police and reported her missing. Her body was found the next morning, about fifty feet from the family car. Apparently she'd been forced to drive to the isolated spot where she'd been robbed and killed. The killer had obviously escaped on foot.

Links thought the theory was dead wrong.

Pat Richards had been shot in the back, with her clothing still on. Then the killer had disrobed her and made a halfhearted attempt at rape. That part alone caused Links to raise his eyebrows. The killer took the time to disrobe a corpse, then merely stuffed some leaves between her legs. The killer might be a complete mental case, but Links didn't think so. The scene of the crime felt staged. The area in which her body was found was two miles from the nearest house, so no one would have heard her screams. There was nothing to indicate that the killer had been frightened away. That bothered Links, but it wasn't what concerned him most. The thing that stuck in his mind was Pat Richards' makeup. It was still perfect. Everyone who was even remotely connected with the Attorney General's office knew that Bob Richards' wife was a highly emotional woman, driven to tears easily. In fact, she was considered the one detriment to an otherwise perfect political future for Richards. Links didn't believe the woman had been kidnapped and taken to a deserted part of the countryside and stayed dry-eyed through it all. Her makeup was so perfect it appeared masklike.

As far as Links was concerned, everything pointed to the fact that she'd known and trusted her killer. His attention shifted to the woman's husband. He was fully aware that his career could come to a screeching halt over this investigation. But he also knew that if Bob Richards were not the Attorney General of the state, somebody would have suggested checking him out. Links ignored the warnings of his superiors and began putting a case together.

Little by little a damaging picture emerged. One of Richards' most carefully guarded secrets was that he had a girlfriend. She was from the moneyed set, an old Kansas City family with strong political connections. Just the kind of wife a man running for political office might want. Then Links found a newspaper boy who had dropped by the Attorney General's home that evening looking for his weekly payment. No one appeared to be at home. Motive and opportunity.

Then Links got lucky. An old-timer at the police vehicle lot called and wanted to show Links something. The car Mrs. Richards had been driving contained a vital piece of evidence. Evidence so obvious that the initial investigating team had gone right past it. There was a sticker inside the door. The date was the day before Pat Richards' death, and it showed that the car had only been driven six miles since it had been serviced. One mile from the garage to the Richards' home and five miles to the field where the wife of the Attorney General had drawn her last breath. By claiming to have spoken to his wife on the phone from downtown that evening, Bob Richards had drawn the noose around his own neck.

Links tried three judges before he found one with enough nerve to issue a search warrant, but once he had it the case was as good as wrapped up. Richards had been so confident that no one would suspect him that he'd placed the murder weapon right back in his gun collection.

The next day, Bob Richards once again fell apart on nationwide television, only this time it wasn't an act. Yes, he'd killed his wife. He'd driven her to a wooded area on the pretext of looking for Christmas greenery, shot her in the back, and torn her clothing off. That done, he couldn't bring himself to simulate rape. It sickened him. He jogged the five miles home and waited to report his wife missing. The previously sympathetic public was offended at having been taken in, and responded by making the investigating detective, Jason Links, a media hero.

When a local television station sent a reporter to interview Links, he made a statement that was to be repeated to rookie cops throughout the country: "Don't get hung up on theories. If you stick to the facts, the truth will emerge. I've always thought that if the facts don't jive with your theory, you better look for a new idea."

Alison Johns hadn't been with the station long when she was sent to question the young officer. In fact, she would not have been sent at all if the senior reporter hadn't been out with the flu. But sent she was, and as a result of her direct, pointed interview and expert thoroughness, Alison became somewhat a celebrity herself. She was even considered for a promotion to the station's New York affiliate, but by the time the offer came it was too late. Impressed with the candor and presence of her subject, Alison invited Officer Links for a drink following the interview. Within six weeks they were engaged, and the day before Jack Simmons was killed, Jason and Alison Links had celebrated their thirty-first wedding anniversary.

Links had no time to wander on the Plaza. By the time he arrived, Joe Turner was already sipping a glass of white wine at the bar.

"Let's get a table in the back, Joe," Links said as he started past the bar. "The noise level in this place is enough to drive me crazy."

"I called and got a reservation," Joe offered, hastily grabbing his bar tab and following. "Same table as last time."

Links grunted. "The last time you got me down here for lunch you had some wild theory about the West Port killings. Some kind of out-of-state involvement. Does this mean you've solved the Simmons case?"

Joe took a long drink of his wine and settled in his chair. "No. It means we've got a problem.

Several problems, as a matter of fact. But I'm going to give you the worst up front. I think tomorrow's *Star* is going to print information you aren't going to like. And before you start raising hell about it, let me tell you what happened.

"I've got a college intern working with the department. He's a bright kid—usually. One of these days he'll be an asset to us." Turner pulled out a pack of Winstons and lit one.

"Last night the kid ran into Charlie Kaufman at an after hours joint near the medical center, and Kaufman bought him a round of drinks. I think you know Kaufman wasn't there by accident. I found out later that he'd tried to get in and see Mrs. Simmons. He didn't manage that, but he knew damned well you were holding something back. The kid doesn't remember what all he said, just knows he ran his mouth too much. We'd just been talking about the condition of the corpse, so he knew everything I knew as of that conversation. Plus a couple of things you don't even know."

A young waitress arrived, as if on cue to save Joe's ass. Links waved her away.

"Let's talk about the kid later, Joe. Tell me exactly what we did know last night. I'm not so sure myself."

Joe handed the report across the table and watched as Links scanned the pages and jerked his head up.

"What's this supposed to mean? As far as I can

see this man died of a ruptured heart. Do you mean he had a heart condition?"

"I mean it exploded. The heart was still beating when it happened." Turner put out his cigarette. "And no, he didn't have a heart condition. His heart was perfectly healthy."

"How can that be?"

Joe shook his head. "I checked for some abnormality—any weakness that could cause the heart to rupture during the fight. Nothing. The tissue was strong. I've gone over it a thousand times and it doesn't make any sense. Whatever killed him was quick. It couldn't have been much more than five minutes from the time he was first hit. And he was hit from all directions. Crushed, actually. It wasn't just a blow on one side."

Links started to speak, but Joe interrupted him.

"Imagine someone putting a steel band around Simmons' chest and tightening it. That's how the pressure burst his heart. Whatever it was broke his back into pieces, shattered it. Bones, muscles, ligaments—all crushed. That's as far as I got last night, and that's probably what Charlie Kaufman knows. That's what will probably be in tomorrow morning's *Star*."

Links picked up the menu. "I think I'd like to order now."

Both men settled on the club sandwich, and Links ordered a glass of tea.

"I don't think you want me to even start on your intern and his boozing with Kaufman, Joe. If one of my men had done it he'd be off the force right now. Plus, why didn't Kaufman get this in his story this morning?"

"It was late. The *Star* was probably already printing."

"Well, aside from that. *Was* a vise placed around Simmons' chest?"

"The lab boys say no. There's no evidence that anything was put around the man's chest. As a matter of fact, there's not a particle of evidence to show that *anything* crushed him."

"Joe, has cutting up bodies started to affect your brain? What about karate? Or some kind of strongman—a bodybuilder maybe. Could someone have crushed Simmons with his bare arms?"

"Well, the strongman theory is better than anything else. Karate wouldn't force everything in the body upward, and that's what happened. But if a man put his arms around Simmons and crushed him, he'd have to have incredible strength. And even then, the pressure wouldn't be even. Keep in mind, there's not a mark on Simmons' body. Nothing. Bruises, sure. But there's not a cut anywhere except for where the rib came through the chest."

"It has to be a bodybuilder or some kind of weight lifter. I don't see any other way it could have happened."

"Jason, if I were to put my arms around your chest and squeeze, the pressure would be different on the sides then on the front and back. It would be impossible to apply pressure on all sides. And that's the condition Jack Simmons' body is in."

Their sandwiches arrived, and Links took a

small bite of his club. Tentatively, he offered another thought. "Then it has to be two people. They both applied pressure at once."

Joe downed his drink and ordered another. Links shook his head.

"How the hell can you smoke and drink so much after you see what it does to the human body?"

Turner snorted and lit another Winston. "I don't think you paid any attention to what I've been telling you. No matter what crushed Simmons, we should have found some physical evidence. Some foreign particle that didn't belong there. We found absolutely nothing."

"You're just missing something."

Turner shook his head and finished his sandwich in silence. When the bill came, he grabbed it. "I owe you this one for the department leak. Sorry."

"Straighten the kid out, Joe. Unless you want me to come over there and talk to him myself. I can't have this kind of thing happening while I'm investigating a murder."

Driving back to headquarters Links tried to make some sense out of what he'd been told by his men and by Joe Turner. No physical evidence. Not a shred. Well, whatever had happened, he was going to find out. The key was Mary Simmons. She must know more than she admitted, probably knew exactly who killed her husband.

Chapter 6

Sarah got back to Northside at one forty-five. Even though she knew the police were coming to interview Ellen, she was taken aback when she saw the patrol car parked in front of the house. Elizabeth Evans hurried out the massive front door to meet her.

"God, I'm glad you're back. There's a policeman here who wants to interview Ellen. I think you should be with her." Elizabeth started to open the door, then turned back to Sarah. "How's Mary? The floor nurse didn't give me much information."

"She's going to be fine." Sarah braced herself to meet the officer. "Just fine."

They went inside to where Max Killen stood waiting.

"Sarah, this is Officer Killen. He wants to talk to Ellen. You've spent so much time with the family, I thought you could fill him in."

"Good afternoon, ma'am." Max smiled and extended his hand. *What a looker*, he thought.

He'd figured on meeting a bunch of sour dames here.

"Hello. I'm Sarah Jamieson. Let's go into my office and talk, then you can see Ellen. I'll help anyway I can."

Sarah Jamieson. She was Paul Jamieson's wife. "Oh, well," he said. "You're the second reason I'm here. Captain Links wanted me to ask you some questions."

"Me?" Sarah sucked in her breath. "Why?"

"The captain tried to call you earlier, and they said you were out. He thought you might be able to help us—tell us something about the family. Whether Mrs. Simmons had any boyfriends, or any family who might have gone after her husband. We think she knows who killed Simmons. Probably protecting the guy."

Sarah relaxed. Of course Jason would remember that she worked at Northside. She'd be the natural person to talk to. Nothing was wrong. She couldn't possibly be linked to the killing.

"Officer Killen—"

"Please, call me Max, ma'am."

She laughed. "Only if you drop the 'ma'am'— makes me feel like your grandmother. All right, Max. I'll tell you all I know, starting with what Mary told me at the hospital this morning. She knows absolutely nothing. She saw no one. She was barely conscious, and with the exception of feeling like someone had pulled Jack off her, she can't tell you a thing. I believe her.

"On top of that, Mary had no men friends that I know of, and I'd know if anybody would. You see, she and the children had only been gone from their home for a few months. Part of that time Mary was recovering from a terrible beating, and the rest of the time she's been trying to get started on a new life. She was in no condition to meet anyone—mentally, physically, or emotionally. She was too busy trying to salvage three lives."

"How often were you in contact with her?"

"I try to call every few days. I was worried— they were so scared of Jack finding them. But when I talked to Mary day before yesterday, nothing seemed out of the ordinary."

"Mrs. Jamieson—Sarah. Is it usual procedure for a counselor to phone people who have been here months earlier? I mean, the constant contact you've had with her. I'm just wondering if you had a feeling something was wrong. Maybe she wasn't telling you something."

"Something was very wrong. Mary Simmons was afraid for her life. In answer to your question, no. We don't keep in close contact generally. I consider Mary a friend, and I might add, one who is probably incapable of lying. So if I were you, I'd look elsewhere for information on the killer."

"You can't remember any visitors or phone calls she had while she was here?"

Sarah frowned. "No. I don't think Mary had any close friends. That's often the case with a battered wife. She's so afraid people will find out her horrible secret that she cuts ties at the very time she needs friends most. I don't think Mary has any close relatives. She was an only child and both parents are dead."

Sarah nervously lit a cigarette. "Let me reiterate one thing. If Mary Simmons knew who killed Jack, she'd tell you. No matter how thankful she was for being saved. In the first place, I can't imagine a jury in the world who would convict the man. He did save three lives, after all."

"Well, you're probably right," Max said, standing. "I guess we better talk to the little girl now. I'm sure Captain Links will be going over all this with you later anyway."

Sarah escorted Max to the sitting room, where Elizabeth sat waiting. She held Ellen on her lap. The child reached out for Sarah, her lower lip trembling.

"Come here, sweetheart." Sarah reached down and picked her up. "Ellen! You've gotten bigger since I saw you! I can barely lift you now!" As Sarah spoke, a faint smile began to cross the child's face.

"Mama says we need to fatten up. Sometimes she brings us treats from work."

Sarah smiled. "Well, I wish I had that problem. I have to hide the treats or I'll get big and fat." She sat down on the chaise with Ellen beside her, motioning for Max to take a chair. The child scooted in close to Sarah.

"Ellen, honey, this is Max. He's been helping your mother and he wants to ask you some questions."

The girl watched Sarah closely. "Is Mama okay—"

"She's just fine," Sarah said firmly. "She's going to be fine and so is Billy. I went to the hospital this morning, and the doctor says not to worry.

Now, you just tell Officer Max what happened last night. Just the way you remember it."

Ellen turned to the officer. "I already told Mrs. Evans. Daddy put me in the closet. He was beating up Billy and Mama." She moved closer to Sarah. "I was scared he was going to come and get me."

Max felt a lump in his throat. "Ellen, did you hear anybody actually say anything?"

"Mama screamed."

"Anything else?"

The little girl was solemn. "Daddy said he was going to kill us."

Max figured whoever killed Jack Simmons had done the world a favor, no matter what Captain Links had to say. "Did you hear your dad say anybody's name—after he put you in the closet? Did it sound like anyone came into the house and surprised him?"

"No. He was just yelling at Mama. Then he didn't yell anymore."

"Did it sound like there was a fight?"

Ellen frowned, shaking her head. "I don't know. There was crashing."

Sarah opened her mouth to say something, then changed her mind. She'd been about to comment on the possibility of an attacker coming from behind. *Shut up, stupid*, a small voice in the back of her head was saying. The less you say, the less chance you have of messing up.

"Did you want to say something, Sarah?" Max was looking at her, unable to get a make on the woman. At times she seemed casual and he felt fine on a first-name basis. But on the other hand, there was a stone wall around the woman. Still waters running deep. He'd have to ask Links what her story was.

"No. No, I was just thinking how awful it all is."

A phone rang and a volunteer motioned to Sarah from the door. "I'm sorry," Sarah said with quick relief. "It seems I have a phone call."

"This is Sarah, may I help you?"

"I called yesterday," the quiet, refined voice began. "I'm so very sorry—I know I sounded rude, hanging up that way. It's just the strain of these past few months. I guess it's caused me to forget my upbringing."

"I'm glad you called back," Sarah said quietly. "And please don't apologize. I understand completely. It must be very hard on you. Now, tell me. Are you in any physical danger right now?"

"No. My husband is at the office. But I'm afraid when he gets home it will start all over again. It was terrible last night."

"Is this a case of physical or mental abuse? I'm concerned about your immediate safety."

"He hits me. It started about a year ago. At first he just got angry, sometimes he shoved me. But over the months it's gotten much worse. I can't seem to do anything to please him anymore."

"So the abuse is intensifying. Have you suggested he see a counselor?"

"He would never do that. If I even suggested it—" She sighed, and Sarah could almost visualize her shudder. "If this got around it would damage his business, his name. He says it's just the pressure, but it's got to be something more."

"Hasn't anyone noticed the bruises?"

"No. They're never anywhere anyone could see. He never hits me in the face or anything." She paused. "He just completely loses control."

Sarah thought a moment before responding. "It doesn't sound to me like he really loses control. After all, he appears to be taking care that you're not marked or bruised for anyone to see."

"Oh, my God. Yes, I see. That makes it worse. He wouldn't want any of the servants to notice."

"Servants? Are there people in the house who could come to your aid if necessary?"

"Not when he's home. We used to have live-in help, but about a year ago my husband said they made him nervous."

"That sounds calculated. You realize that you are the only one who can break this cycle. It won't go away by itself."

"I know. I shouldn't be covering for him. But he's—he's always so sorry afterward. He's so upset, and then he promises it won't ever happen again."

"But it does happen again, doesn't it?"

"Yes," the woman said. "Yes it does. I know I have to do something. I just have to think. I—I have to hang up now. I'm afraid some of the servants might hear me."

"*Please* call if you're in trouble or if you need a place to stay. We can help you, and I guarantee there won't be any publicity."

"Thank you. Thank you so very much. It helped just to talk about it. I never have before."

Sarah hung up the phone and looked up to find Cindy Lou Merit standing in the door.

"Hello, Mrs. Jamieson. Could I talk to you a minute?"

"Of course, Cindy Lou. Sit down. As a matter of fact, you're a welcome sight."

Cindy Lou came from the hills of Kentucky, where the Garrison family lived on Stone Mountain in a three-room log house, more like a shack. They farmed a little, but primarily, Butch Garrison was a moonshiner. In those three rooms resided the two parents, one great-grandmother, eight children, three dogs, and a banty rooster named Slick. On the whole, it was a happy home.

By the time she was twelve everyone on Stone Mountain knew Cindy Lou was destined for better things than Stone Mountain had to offer. She was a special child. It wasn't just that she was growing up a beauty, the mountain had produced other beauties. But Cindy Lou was a rarity—a good-hearted, good-natured hard worker who was the delight of young and old alike. She'd inherited the huge blue eyes from her father, who would have been a handsome man if he'd sampled a little less of his moonshine. Her black hair was thick and shiny, just like her great-grandmother Samples' hair had once been. She had spunk, too. The time a town boy had tried to slip his hand under her shirt after Sunday meeting, she'd blacked his eye before he could blink it. Old man

Garrison had chuckled about the event for weeks.

Butch figured his girl could do just about anything she took a mind to do. Even get into the moving pictures. Maybe marry the damned President of the United States. None of that silly mountain courting for his girl. It would prove to be a dangerous way of thinking.

"Just you wait, child," Butch would say. "You're gonna do something big. Don't you get tied up with none of these no-count hillbillies. They ain't near good enough for you. Remember how I told you about them fancy ladies up in Loui'ville? You're gonna be just like 'em. Maybe you'll be smart, read books just like your ma here."

Cindy Lou just grinned when her father talked like that. Her mother had taught her to read when she was five, but after a few nips her father never remembered that. But Cindy Lou listened to his stories of Louisville and wondered about a world where people had toilets in their houses.

And if Cindy Lou couldn't go to the city, the city was bound to come to her sooner or later. It came sooner, and in the person of Johnny Merit, insurance agent. Driving a white Buick, he stopped by the Garrison place to ask directions to the Widow Spriggs' house. Said he had some money for the old woman. When he saw Cindy Lou standing in the yard, looking for all the world like an untamed goddess of the woods, he wanted her more than he'd ever wanted a woman in his life. And he'd wanted quite a few. This one he hoped to have with no strings.

Old man Garrison was nobody's fool. Johnny

Merit's lusting heart was no match for a man who had been outsmarting government men for over forty years, and Cindy Lou was kept very close to her mother's side. Johnny soon found that the widow's insurance matters were going to take a little longer then he'd anticipated and graciously accepted the old woman's offer of lodging, and settled into the spare room for a few weeks. When it finally became obvious that Butch Garrison wouldn't leave him alone with his seventeen-year-old daughter for more than five minutes, Johnny asked for the girl's hand in marriage. He figured a man could do a lot worse. True, she was strictly backwoods, but she just might come in handy in more ways than the one in which he was currently interested.

Johnny didn't get around to telling anyone that he'd been married three times, and that his last divorce wasn't exactly final. Nor did he mention that there were warrants out for his arrest in Arkansas where he was charged with child abuse, wife-beating, and passing bad paper. He certainly didn't let slip that the Buick was owned by a widow in Little Rock who firmly believed Johnny was coming back for her as soon as he got down to Georgia with her $850 and paid for his poor dead mother's Christian burial.

No, Johnny Merit kept many things quiet, including the fact that the insurance company he represented had fired him two months prior to his visit to Stone Mountain. The only good that job had done him was the knowledge of a widow in Kentucky who was getting an unexpected settlement. He figured he could cash in. Butch Garrison pegged him as a hotshot city businessman, and if he had any misgivings, they were assuaged when the widow Spraggs mentioned that the boy had done everything possible to help her get the money due her, and even paid a few dollars room and board while he was there helping out. Johnny decided that Cindy Lou was worth more than the widow Spraggs' settlement in the long run.

When Mr. and Mrs. John Merit drove off the mountain that day there was much that Butch Garrison didn't know about his new son-in-law. Before the wedding night was over, Cindy Lou Garrison Merit, seventeen years and one month old, had developed considerable insight into her new husband's nature. He liked sex only when it was violent, and her inexperience only seemed to spur him on. Cindy Lou's mother never talked about sex to her daughter, so she had no idea what was normal and what was not. Somehow Cindy Lou could not see her good-natured pa ravaging her mother the way Johnny Merit did her.

When Johnny finally fell asleep that first night, Cindy Lou lay awake a long time, just going over things in her head. Her body ached, but her soul was what hurt the worst. The Garrisons were poor, and for the most part uneducated. But they were good people. Cindy Lou had heard her pa talk about men who knocked their women around, and he had no respect for that sort of behavior. She wondered what her father would tell her to do.

Cindy Lou gave her husband the benefit of the

doubt, and thus began a nightmare journey through several states, numerous scams run by Johnny, and a slow realization on Cindy Lou's part that she had married a liar and a crook. She was two months pregnant when she found out Johnny Merit was trying to wheedle money out of an old man in Kansas City, claiming his young wife needed an operation. After explaining to their elderly landlord—who saw Cindy Lou as the granddaughter he wished he had—that she certainly needed no operation—she walked out. She had a telephone number to call, a number she'd seen on television ads. With a baby on the way, Cindy Lou knew she couldn't risk another beating. Twenty minutes after making the call she was safely riding in a car toward Northside Crisis Center.

"Mrs. Jamieson," Cindy Lou continued. "I can't just stay here without helping out. I can cook and clean—anything to help earn my keep. And I'd like to help look after Kathy. She reminds me some of my baby sister." Her face turned dark. "My pa would make short work of the man who hurt her so bad."

Sarah smiled. Cindy Lou was a breath of fresh air. Maybe she could help Kathy. Who knew what it would take to crack the shell the child had built. If Cindy Lou could get some training, she might just be an excellent counselor.

For the second night in a row Jason Links hadn't slept well. On top of the puzzle connected with

Simmons' death, everyone's attitude irritated him. Even Alison agreed with Charlie Kaufman's newspaper article. The killer was a hero. But everyone hadn't seen the state Jack Simmons was left in.

Links crept out of bed, hoping to not disturb his sleeping wife. Maybe the morning paper was here, and he could see what distortions Kaufman had come up with. Links had tried to call Charlie twice the previous day, but he was always out and never returned his calls. *Kaufman knows damned well what I'm going to say to him. Bastard,* Links thought as he stumbled down the stairs of the turn-of-the century home.

Alison had found the place fifteen years ago. West Port was beginning to get quite fashionable, and she'd been sent to do a story on the renovations being done in that part of town.

"Jason, I've found the house I want to die in," she'd said breathlessly over the phone.

It seemed to Links that it had taken the better share of their lives, but the ramshackle place was finally fixed up. Maybe since Alison found she couldn't have children, she diverted her nesting instincts to the house. Sure seemed like she'd given birth to it. Jason knew he was only kidding himself, though. He loved the place just as much as his wife did. Maybe more.

He turned the coffee maker on and went out to get the newspaper.

MYSTERY AVENGER KILLING MYSTIFIES POLICE. It was obvious to Links that Kaufman got far less information out of the drunken intern than he was letting on. All he really knew was that the heart had burst and the M.E. couldn't explain it. There was nothing about the lack of physical evidence. No mention of the lack of abrasions on the body. The article pissed him off, anyway.

"Well, what did your friend Charlie have to say?" Alison stood in the doorway and yawned.

"Take a look." Jason held out the paper and Alison scanned the story. "You're the news director, Alison. Wouldn't you consider this irresponsible journalism? Read all those speculations. 'The avenger must be a giant of a man. Wife-beaters throughout the city should be nervous today.' Christ!"

"I think it's kind of funny," she said with a quick grin. "I wonder if anybody is nervous. And I can tell you that we'll probably quote some of Charlie's article on the noon news today. Sorry."

"Well, at least you aren't on camera anymore, so the wife of the man heading up the investigation can announce that her old man is mystified."

She laughed. "That's one consolation, I guess. When I was twenty-five it never occurred to me that all it took to get promoted was a few gray hairs and a couple of wrinkles. They couldn't afford to have me on camera, so they had to make me the boss!"

Links smiled for the first time since he'd awakened. He pulled his wife onto his lap and for a moment wondered just where all the years had gone. "That broad you hired for the anchorwoman slot can't hold a candle to you on her best day."

• • •

Paul Jamieson was already showered and shaved when he came downstairs to find his wife reading the newspaper. He still had the look of a graduate student, with his thick dark hair falling in unruly waves on the back of his neck, and his horn-rim glasses constantly slipping down the bridge of his nose. Sarah continued to wonder at the amount of food he ate and the fact he remained pencil-thin. Nervous energy, she guessed. He glanced at the front page headline and chuckled.

"Bet Jason's fit to be tied over *that*. I ought to call him today and suggest he hire a psychic."

Sarah kept on reading.

"Hey, honey—I'm sorry. I shouldn't be joking about this. I considered canceling last night's meeting—got to thinking how this must be affecting you."

"No," Sarah said, finally looking up. "No, I'm glad you didn't. I was in bed by eight-thirty."

"I'm surprised Jason didn't come by the Center."

"He called," Sarah answered, folding the paper carefully and laying it on the counter. "I was at the hospital and one of the girls took the message. When I got back he'd already sent an officer over to talk to Ellen. Killen was his name."

"Max? Good man. Jason seems to think so anyway."

"He's nice, but he seems kind of laid back for that line of work. He's certainly nothing like his boss."

"You've been watching too much television. Links is the exception, not the rule. The only time I see him get his mind off his job is when we play bridge, and even then he's intense. Are we playing this weekend, by the way?"

"I forgot to call Alison. I'll do it this morning." She glanced at the clock. "Paul! Look at the time! I'm going to have to step on it."

"Go ahead and shower. The kids can fix their lunches." Paul slapped his wife on the backside and turned to the refrigerator. He paused, then said, "Sarah, don't let this whole thing get you down. Jack Simmons was a lunatic. This is all probably for the best."

Mary Simmons lay staring out the window of her hospital room. The young nurse who had given her a sponge bath and her morning's medicine believed in sunshine for the spirit. She'd pulled open the curtains, propped Mary up in bed, and brought in a cup of coffee. Only when Mary asked for the morning paper did the girl hesitate.

"We'll see about that later, after breakfast. Just enjoy the pretty morning for now."

There was probably some horrible story in the paper, Mary thought. She wondered if she should call the police and tell them again about the way Jack jumped around just before she passed out. It all seemed so unreal.

In another city, across the state, an old woman reread the *Star's* account of the mystery avenger and Simmons' exploding heart. Her gnarled hands smoothed out the paper and her mouth curled into a private smile. Slowly, ignoring the constant pain from the cancer that daily consumed her body, the woman got up and walked across the tiny room. She sat down at her little desk and took a piece of paper from the drawer. In spidery, spiked handwriting she began, "Dear Mr. Kaufman."

Chapter 7

Sarah was getting tired of the games. She'd been at the Center almost a year now, and it seemed to her that they did the same things over and over. *Bend the spoon, Sarah. Concentrate. Move the chair, Sarah.*

For a short time she'd been allowed to participate in games with other children. They were older than Sarah, but they seemed to like her, accept her. Then Mrs. Carver retired, and things changed. The woman who replaced Sarah's beloved teacher was tall and skinny, not at all like chubby Mrs. Carver, whose stomach was always rumbling.

"Listen to that, Sarah," she'd say. "That's my tummy grumbling—telling me it's time for milk and cookies." Then they'd sneak off to the kitchen for treats.

Sarah knew that Mrs. Crawford would never let anyone sneak anywhere, especially if it involved a treat. Since the day Sarah pushed her, Mrs. Crawford had made sure she didn't even get to play with other children. *Well*, Sarah thought, *Mrs. Crawford deserved pushing. Shoving Jimmy like she did. Yelling at him. He hadn't done anything so bad—just made a face when he didn't think the teacher was looking. After she'd already yelled at him for not concentrating.* And so Mrs. Crawford shook him, and Sarah pushed her.

Charlotte Crawford was astonished when it happened. At first she thought she'd stumbled, but when it happened a second time she knew one of the children was pushing her. There was only one in the group with that kind of potential. Sarah Livingston. Something was wrong with the child, that much was clear to Charlotte. She'd noticed the girl staring at her at odd times, in odd ways. She knew it had been stupid to allow Sarah to develop her powers, to become even more of a devil than she already was. Charlotte had reported the child to Dr. Peterson and had sent copies of her complaints to members of the board. But to no avail. Peterson was besotted over the girl. Once he'd realized the girl's potential he'd started acting as if he'd personally discovered her. And the board was completely dominated by Tom Hamilton, who believed Sarah was a gift from God. Charlotte Crawford knew better. A messenger from hell, more likely. But she also knew her position at Hamilton was precarious, on shaky ground since she'd let her dislike of the star attraction be known. She'd have to be careful if she was to deal with the child. But deal with her

she would. Before the little monster hurt someone.

KANSAS CITY, MISSOURI
April, 1990

Sarah sat up in bed and stretched, wishing she'd
never offered to help with the Center's fund-
raising efforts. Why didn't she remain in the
background, a behind-the-scenes worker, as she'd
done in every job she'd taken. But the Center
needed money, and she'd promised. The monthly
meeting of the Fountain Head Country Club's
ladies' group was today, so there was little she
could do at this point. She had to go ahead with
her talk. Elizabeth Evans said stage fright was
normal.

Normal. Sarah felt the word had dictated her
life story. Above all else, she had to appear absolutely, categorically normal. She understood why,
or at least partly why. Her mother first, then old
Mrs. Carver—both had told her over and over
again what would happen if the world found out
about her. Found out what she could do. She'd
wind up a freak, or worse. The State Department
might even step in and get control of her in some
way. Try to harness the power for some govern-
mental purpose. Or so June Carver had said. All
Sarah knew was that her mother was terrified, all
the time. And it was because of her.

God help her now. If anybody found out, if they
started to suspect. Everything Paul had dreamed
of would be down the tubes. And once again it
would be because of her.

Stop it! She had to quit thinking about it, if only for the time being. *Think about the speech.* She'd been trying to write a speech for the past three days, and it wasn't happening. She was prepared with all the statistics, all the specifics, and it sounded as dry as last week's toast. She glanced at the clock radio beside the bed and saw she had ten more minutes before the alarm went off. She was an early riser, and in reality needed no morning reminder. Setting the alarm was just an old college habit that stuck.

Paul was already downstairs. He was also a morning person. This was their time. Before the kids were up and the rat race on. It was their time to talk, make love, or simply sit comfortably, drinking coffee, and lost in separate thoughts.

She could smell the aroma of the coffee now. Thanks to the automatic coffee pot she had set the night before.

"Morning, gorgeous," Paul greeted her from his favorite kitchen chair. "Ready for your speech?"

"Don't ask." She bent down and kissed him. "It sounds like a TV commercial. I wish I could make it more personal or something. These women could give a lot of money if I can just convince them. But if they don't feel like it has anything to do with their lives—"

Paul nodded. "One of the secretaries at the office told me that if a woman allows herself to be beaten more than once she deserves everything she gets."

"I hope you straightened her out."

"Well, I tried to make her think about it. About

the difference in physical size, about not having any money or anyplace to go."

Sarah thought about it. Maybe that was what was missing in her speech. Maybe she could make them walk a mile in someone else's moccasins, so to speak. She had a glimmer of an idea.

She parked her station wagon between a Mercedes and a BMW in the Fountain Head parking lot, took a deep breath, and got out of the car. She'd been to the club with Paul on several occasions, but they were by no means regular members. They paid the dues that kept them on the active roster for only one reason: Paul's career. They both preferred quiet, out-of-the-way restaurants. She went inside, walked down the long hallway on plush carpeting, and wished that her extraordinary powers could make her give an effective speech.

Locating an attorney's wife with whom she was slightly acquainted, Sarah seated herself at a small table toward the back of the room. After a lunch of lobster bisque, caesar salad, and the most exquisite chocolate hazelnut torte Sarah had ever tasted, Mrs. Norris, acting president of the group, stood.

"Ladies, Sarah Jamieson is with us today. She's going to tell us about a project she's involved with. Sarah?"

Sarah's stomach lurched and she was afraid she'd lose the bisque at any moment. Hoping that sheer bravado would carry her through, she walked with what appeared to be confidence to the front of the room. She took the microphone and hoped that the short introduction was not an indication of the reception she'd get.

The room looked like a sea of Dior, Chanel, and Bill Blass. Sarah decided she'd better get started before the money spent on clothes began to intimidate her.

"Good afternoon. First I'd like to thank you for giving me this opportunity. This is the first time I've given a speech since college, so please bear with me." She glanced around at questioning faces. A few offered smiles of encouragement. "I'm here on behalf of the Northside Crisis Center. For those of you who aren't familiar with Northside, we provide a safe home for women and children who are victims of domestic violence. It's a refuge where husbands or boyfriends cannot harm them.

"I know the whole idea of physical violence may seem alien to most of you sitting here." Sarah paused and looked at her typed notes. She put them aside. The long list of statistics were not going to impress anyone. "I, uh, I have a lot of numbers here—statistics about how many women in Kansas City are beaten every day. How many children. But that's not really what I want to say. What I want to say is this. Someone you know is an abused woman. Some child your child knows is an abused child. Maybe the whole idea of physical abuse is not so alien to some of you. But if it is, let me ask you to try something. Try and put yourself in a very different situation than the one in which you are in. Please imagine that you have none of the usual support systems. Imagine that your parents are dead, or that they are physically or financially unable to help you. You have no money of your own. Now picture yourself in a bad marriage, with a husband who gets violent. You want to protect yourself and your children, but you have no means to make a move. I guarantee you, you can't check into the Hyatt. You don't even have cab fare." She leaned forward on the speaker's podium. "And even if you did, your husband would bring you back. Then he'd probably beat you within an inch of your life. You can call the police, but your husband won't be kept very long. When he gets out, he'll be half crazy with hostility, all built up against you. Then you'll really be in trouble. So where do you go?"

She let that soak in a minute, pleased that the women seemed to be paying close attention. "I do want to share one of my statistics with you now. Every eighteen seconds a woman is abused. They need someplace to go. Northside is one of those places. We provide a support system and a safe place to live. We provide counseling and, when we can, financial assistance. Think about your own daughters. What if some terrible tragedy left them without you and your help. What if they were trapped in a violent situation? They would need someone to turn to. The women we work with need help, and we provide it."

She glanced around the room. "I'm here today to ask you for money. Moreover, I'm here to ask you to contact women within your circle of friends. Try to get them involved. Maybe some of you would even like to volunteer to work at the Center one morning a week. We need all kinds of help. If each of you in this room would make helping battered women and children your cause for just one year, you could make a difference like this city has never seen."

She walked around the room to the front of the podium. "I really wish you wouldn't let it end with a donation. I know that most of you"—she laughed—"no, *all* of you, are far better at fundraising than I am. I'd love to help you organize some small benefits. We could show Kansas City that this club is interested in much more than tennis and golf."

The warm applause told her what she wanted to know. She'd struck a chord. As women crowded around, checkbooks in hand, Sarah relaxed. One by one they pressed donations into her hand, until suddenly a cold chill covered her. Sarah's breath grew shallow and her smile fixed. *She's* here. It's the woman who called. She's here in this room. Sarah gazed at the perfectly coifed elegance. One of these women had spoken with her just days earlier and in terrible trouble.

"So the speech was a success?" Paul dealt the cards, smiling at his wife as she told them of her triumph. "You stuck the ladies for a bundle, huh?"

"A bundle." Sarah looked at Alison Links and rolled her eyes. "And there's more where that came from."

Paul finished dealing and picked up his cards. "Of course, now that we've got the mystery avenger out on the streets, we may have little need for you and your kind, Sarah." He bit his lip to keep from snickering and stole a look at Jason Links' face.

Alison roared with laughter. "Especially now that all of Kansas City knows the police are mystified. Right, hon?"

"Cute." Jason picked up his cards and started separating them into suits. Then he put them back down on the table. "It is mystifying, Paul. I can't even come up with an intelligent theory. We just don't have anything to go on." He shook his head and picked up his cards again. "Absolutely nothing."

"You mean Joe Turner doesn't have a theory? I'm stunned." Paul grinned. "I thought he usually had your cases solved within forty-eight hours."

"Oh, he's got theories all right. One of them involves men in plastic suits. You don't even want to know about it." He looked at Sarah. "You're absolutely sure Mary Simmons didn't have any boyfriends or hard-ass relatives?"

"No. It's like I told the young policeman you sent to Northside. Mary doesn't have any family, and abused women tend to isolate themselves. Mary had locked herself up in a private little hell. She told me that I was the first real friend she'd ever had."

Paul chuckled. "And you can't pin this on Sarah, Jason. She was home with her attorney at the time."

Sarah began sorting her cards.

Jason rubbed his thick fingers across his brow. "Well, what do you think about—"

"A spade," Alison interrupted.

Sarah passed and Jason Links bid four spades.

"Damn!" Alison looked at her hand, horrified. "You just took me to game! You'd better have one hell of a hand."

Paul doubled and Jason put his cards on the table.

"Well, that's just great, Jason! You barely had enough count to answer me, let alone jump to four." Alison glared at her husband. "Maybe you better get the avenger off your mind and start thinking about your bridge game."

Jason looked down at his cards as if he'd just noticed them. "I know. But this case bugs me. And, Alison, I wish you'd stop calling him 'the avenger.' That makes him out to be a good guy, and a good guy is one thing our killer isn't."

Sarah lit a cigarette and led a small heart.

"I don't know, Jason," Paul said thoughtfully. "It seems to me that this guy saved Mary's life."

"That's right," Sarah added, still staring at her cards. "Jack Simmons was an awful man. No one should be allowed to get away with the things he did to Mary and the kids." She finally looked up at Jason Links. "I think he deserved to die."

"I agree," Alison chimed in. "Whoever killed Jack Simmons is a hero as far as I'm concerned. Why don't you just close the case and get on with something else? Then maybe you can play a decent game of bridge."

Jason raised his eyebrows in mock horror. "My own wife? My partner all these years, and you think I should just look the other way?"

They laughed and picked up the game again. When Alison played her last card, Paul promptly trumped it.

"Down three, you jerk." She glared at her husband.

Sarah's hand shook slightly as she wrote down the score. She knew Jason Links better than that. There was no way he'd ever look the other way. But it wasn't going to make any difference. There was no chance of them ever tying her to that killing. No chance at all.

Chapter 8

ST. LOUIS, MISSOURI
July, 1956

Sarah was sick of it all. Sick of being told what to do. Sick of Charlotte Crawford and her meanness. Sick of the Hamilton Research Institute. She knew Dr. Peterson was watching her through the two-way mirror, waiting for her to bend the metal rod.

"Now, Sarah," Mrs. Crawford said. She was speaking in a soft voice, and Sarah knew it was for Dr. Peterson's benefit. "Concentrate on the bar. Try to bend it."

She sat there, defiantly. This time she wouldn't bend it. She wanted to go outside and play with the other children, or go home and play with her friends. She'd do anything to get out of this building.

Mrs. Crawford's voice took on an edge. "Sarah, pay attention. Concentrate on the rod. Remove all other thoughts from your mind."

"I don't want to do it," Sarah whined. "I want to go home."

"Now, Sarah." Mrs. Crawford's there-are-other-people-listening tone was back, droning on. "You are not being a nice little girl. What do you think your mother would say if I told her how you're acting? She'd be very disappointed in you."

"She would not!" Sarah yelled at the woman. "She doesn't care if I bend that dumb rod or not."

Mrs. Crawford's face was set in cold fury. "You will do as I say!" She leaned close to Sarah and the girl could smell her sour breath. The woman spoke in a low whisper. "You miserable little brat. Dr. Peterson is watching you." She took hold of Sarah's arm and squeezed down, digging her fingernails into the girl's skin.

Sarah jumped away from her. She turned her face to the metal rod and clinched her teeth. The bar began twisting and turning. It rose in the air and seemed to come alive under Sarah's steady gaze. The bar curled and changed shapes, wriggling like a snake. Suddenly it flew toward Mrs. Crawford and landed at her feet. It appeared malevolent as it continued to change shapes and glow white-hot. Charlotte lunged at Sarah and the bar flew at her, grazing her forehead.

Dr. Peterson rushed in. "Pull back, Sarah." He held her gently by the shoulders. "That's enough. Think of something else."

His voice jarred her back to reality. She closed her eyes and thought about playing outside with her friends.

The mass of metal smoldered, burning into

the oak floor. Sarah began sobbing, and Dr. Peterson took her in his arms. "It's all right. Don't worry about it. The bar just got away from you."

Mrs. Crawford felt the welt across her forehead. What was the matter with that fool Peterson? Couldn't he see that the brat had tried to kill her? That she was dangerous? Well, the Institute would pay for this. They'd pay all right.

Dr. Peterson's thoughts weren't even in the same ballpark. As he held the crying child all he could think of was the incredible feat he'd just witnessed. He knew they'd only just begun to tap Sarah Livingston's powers.

KANSAS CITY, MISSOURI
May, 1990

It had been three weeks since Cindy Lou had walked out on him, and Johnny Merit was just beginning to realize how much he missed his wife. He missed her incredible body, the beautiful, honest face. Just thinking about her made him break out in a cold sweat. He had to find her.

He hadn't meant to hurt her. She had to understand that. Using his fists had always been his way. It was the only way you control a woman. And she'd made him so mad. How could she possibly refuse to help him with his scam? If she'd just played along, they could have been rolling in money. The old geezer she'd spilled the beans to would have popped for lots of cash. Old lech. Cindy Lou thought he was just a nice old man, but Johnny knew better. Old fart probably wanted to get into her pants. Johnny took a drink of his vodka and thought. Well, why not? With his know-how, his ability to spot a pigeon, and her looks, there'd be no stopping them.

He stared at the television. *I Dream of Jeannie* was on. It made him miss her all the more. She always watched this channel. Wouldn't miss an episode of *Beverly Hillbillies*. Said Jed Clampett reminded her of her father. *Her pa*. That's what she called the old man.

Yes, he could make a fortune off Cindy Lou. If only he knew where she was. This marriage could work. And there'd be no snot-nosed kids to louse it up, either. Crying little bastards. God, what they did to a woman's body. Sagging breasts, flabby stomach. It made him sick to think of Cindy Lou without that creamy, smooth body. He'd have to convince her to get that operation women got. He sure as hell wasn't going to have one. Getting "fixed" like some damn dog.

A commercial rolled on the screen. A woman's voice screamed out and two children huddled in bed, listening. "Don't let the violence in your life continue," the announcer said. "If you need help, a place to stay, call the Crisis Hot Line."

Johnny sat up and looked at the screen. He'd seen the same commercial three times now. Could that be it? Cindy Lou sure as hell kept this channel on day and night. Would she have had the balls to call that damned hot line? The commercial was over and he'd missed writing down the telephone number. Damn rattrap only had a pay phone outside the front office. If Cindy Lou had kept her mouth shut, he'd still have the little apartment. Actually he didn't mind not having a telephone. That way it was hard for people to track you down.

He walked to the front office, then stopped. Maybe he'd better get some more vodka. He'd just call from the liquor store. He sauntered up the street toward Mickey's, positive he'd solved the mystery of his missing wife. He bought a pint, then walked over to the pay phone. There in the front of the Yellow Pages it was. The Crisis Hot Line. He dialed the number.

"I'm sorry, sir." The voice at the other end of the line sounded pleasant, but firm. "We can't give you the addresses of any of the shelters."

Johnny slammed the receiver down.

"Stella, hon—" He eased over to the middle-aged woman behind the counter. "How's my girl today?"

"Just fine, Johnny. Same as always."

"Listen, darlin', I need some information. I got this friend, a lady. She keeps getting knocked around by her old man and needs some place to hole up awhile—"

"I ain't takin' anybody in, Johnny." Stella scowled.

"That's not it, babe. She wants to go to one of those shelters. Where the hell are they? I just called and they won't tell me how to get there."

"They don't work that way. If they did that, any asshole in the world could come and start something."

Johnny grinned knowingly. "Smart thinking.

But in the meantime, what can I do about my friend?"

"I ain't sure, honey. They probably come pick the women up or somethin'. Call and tell 'em the problem—see what they say."

Johnny walked back to his room and got the keys to the Buick. He drove to a busy Wendy's, went in, and approached a waitress.

"Sorry to bother you, ma'am. But there's a lady in the parking lot. Had a pretty bad fight with her boyfriend. She asked me to have someone call that, uh, Crisis Hot Line, I think it's called."

"Oh, dear—is she hurt badly?"

"Just shook up. Better call those people now, though. Guy might come back."

Johnny returned to his car and waited. Fifteen minutes later a car pulled up and two women got out. They searched through the small parking lot until they were sure the woman was not there. Finally they gave up and returned to the car. Johnny followed them back to Northside Crisis Center. He had no idea whether this was the right place, but the call had been placed in the same vicinity where Cindy Lou would have called. He figured it was worth the shot.

He settled back and waited.

Bingo. There she was. Walking in the yard with some bratty kid. Her long hair flowed down her back and she was wearing a tank top. She looked damn good.

Another woman left the house and started walking with his wife and the girl. It was an old broad, short gray hair, wearing a business suit.

Johnny continued to watch. They'd never allow him to waltz up and take her away. Probably had some big bodyguard there, who the hell knew. Place was probably like a prison. He needed a plan, a way to get her away from the house long enough to talk some sense into her.

Elizabeth Evans walked back into the house and Kathy continued on the walk with her new friend. The only time the child ever stopped thinking about her stepfather and what he had done to her was in the company of Cindy Lou Merit. For some reason the dark-haired young woman could take Kathy's mind off the horror of that final night, the night Sam Thomas had almost killed Kathy and her mother. They walked along the street toward a small Qwik Shop on the corner. As they strolled along Cindy Lou told Kathy about her home in Kentucky, of Stone Mountain and the wonderful Garrison clan. She told Kathy about the birds that sang outside the kitchen window, the squirrels that would eat popcorn right out of your hand, and about the stream that ran right through the Garrison's front yard.

Kathy held tight to Cindy Lou's hand, secure in the knowledge that the older girl liked her. More than that even. Cindy Lou cared deeply for her. Kathy wondered if her new friend would still feel that way if she knew about all she'd let her daddy do to her. *No!* She reminded herself that it was not her daddy. It was Sam. And, as Mrs. Jamieson had said, Kathy hadn't *let* him do anything. He was too big and too strong for her. But then, she wondered, why had he called her those dirty names and said everything was her fault?

Then Cindy Lou spoke and all the thoughts of Sam Thomas fled from the girl's mind. Her thoughts returned to Stone Mountain, Kentucky and a stream running through the front yard. They went into the Qwik Stop and purchased ice-cream bars.

Johnny Merit almost followed the two inside the store, but something held him back. Cindy Lou would never leave the kid alone on the street. She'd insist on taking her back to the house, and then the women would talk her out of going with him.

He slid into a phone booth two blocks from Northside and flipped through the Yellow Pages again. New Woman's bookstore. He dialed the number, pleased that he'd remembered seeing the ad in the *Kansas City Star*. Some new place in the Plaza area. He chuckled to himself. Those broads didn't know who they were dealing with. Johnny Merit was a player. And a damned good one.

"Hello, my name is John Jacobson. My wife recently passed away, and I want to set up a memorial in her name. She always wanted to give something to the Northside Center—and I was wondering if you could tell me the name of the director? Seems like I knew it at one time. Just slipped my mind. So much has happened—"

"Sure. It's Elizabeth Evans. She's usually there all day."

"You don't happen to have that number do you? The office number, not the hot line."

"Well, sure. Donations are hard to come by. And, uh, I'm very sorry about your wife."

Johnny wrote down the number, smiling. "Thanks for your concern. You'll never know what a help you've been."

He got back in the car and drove to the motel. He thought it over and scratched his original plan, which had been to call and ask for Cindy Lou. Suppose she didn't want to talk to him? Those broads had probably brainwashed her. He'd need to see her in person to put the old Merit charm to work.

Two days later a call came into the Crisis Center. The deep southern voice explained to the young operator that his name was Butch Garrison. He was in town to get his daughter, Cindy Lou, and was staying at the Starlight Motel. He brought her brothers along, and was having trouble with the city traffic—the old truck and all. Trouble with these pay phones, too. He guessed he'd just have to call back later. The line went dead.

Sue Kline was fresh out of college and had worked at Northside for about two weeks. She understood why the turnover rate was so high. Northside could barely pay people a living wage. Sue ran to find Cindy Lou with the good news.

Cindy Lou was stunned. "But I never asked him

to come for me. That old truck isn't any good. I told Pa I'd come on the bus just as soon as I could."

Sue beamed. "Well, he must have wanted you home pretty bad. He'll call back. Didn't seem to be having much luck with the K.C. traffic and the pay phones."

Cindy Lou went back to her room, knowing full well that her pa couldn't find Northside if he tried all day. She phoned the Starlight Motel and asked to speak to Butch Garrison. The motel clerk was puzzled about Johnny Merit's instructions, but he'd paid her ten dollars, so she followed them to the letter. Garrison and his sons were taking the truck to have some work done on it. It would sure help if his daughter could come there.

She changed into a freshly ironed shirt and a pair of jeans. She was too excited to wait until Sarah or Elizabeth Evans returned from lunch. Kathy helped her check the bus schedules, and the two planned the best route to the Starlight Motel. She promised Kathy that she'd bring Pa and the boys back to meet her, then Cindy Lou headed for the corner and waited for the next bus.

Kathy grabbed her jacket. What if Cindy Lou's pa wouldn't let her come back? She'd never see Cindy Lou again. Carefully, the girl slipped the heavy bolt out of its notch, looked around to see if anyone was watching, and stepped out. She wiggled through the back fence and raced after Cindy Lou.

• • •

Cindy Lou sat on the bus and thought about what had happened during the past few months. There was so much to try to understand. Johnny's love of hitting her, trying to get used to living away from her parents, the horrible bedroom scenes. Her ma had told her that she would have to grow up fast when she decided to marry so young. Well, she had done that all right.

Enough of that kind of thinking. There would be no more of Johnny Merit. If she'd learned one thing at the shelter, it was to get out of a bad situation fast. Before she was really hurt.

No, she wouldn't go back home to Johnny. Not even for the baby. She frowned. Especially for the baby. She didn't think he'd ever stop using his fists. The poor kids at the shelter were scared half to death from watching the beatings their mothers took. She didn't want her child to grow up like that.

"Here's your stop, girl." The burly driver growled back at her, putting on the brakes and squealing up to the corner. She thanked him and climbed down off the bus.

Kathy was ten minutes behind her.

Johnny sat alone in the motel room. Waiting. Surveying the drab room. He was meant for bigger things than a cheap motel room. He needed Cindy Lou with him. Hell, she belonged to him. No question about it. You'd think a stupid hillbilly would at least be able to figure that out.

He stared at the water-stained curtains and

brooded. Where the hell was she? It was just like that backwoods broad to keep him waiting.

Elizabeth Evans stopped by Sue Kline's desk.

"Want to take your lunch break now, Sue?"

"No thanks. I brought a sandwich. I'll have it later."

"Anything happen while I was gone?"

"No. At least nothing bad. Good news for Cindy Lou, though. Her father is in town. He drove in this morning to get her."

Elizabeth raised her eyebrows. "Really? I understood Cindy Lou didn't think their truck would make it to Kansas City."

"Well, it did. He's going to call back this afternoon, then come get her, I guess."

Elizabeth nodded. "Well, that's a relief. By the way, is Sarah here?"

Sue shook her head. "No. She had lunch with a friend of hers. Alison something."

Cindy Lou looked at the sign that read Starlight Motel. *Thank the good Lord, I've found it.* She walked around back, following the numbers to a door that read #8. The door was open a crack, and Cindy Lou hesitated, suddenly apprehensive. "Pa? Are you in there?"

She felt Johnny, more than saw him, as he stepped from the shadows and pulled her into the darkened room.

"Baby, I'm sorry." Johnny's voice had a touch of a whine. "I know it was a dirty trick, but I had to see you. Had to make you come back. I need you, baby. You have no idea what it's been like without you." He pulled her to him and roughly took her in his arms.

It took Cindy Lou a moment to comprehend. "Johnny—is my pa here?"

"No, baby. But your husband is. Now listen, honey, I promise I won't hit you anymore. Not ever. Just come back to me—I'm sorry about everything." Tears welled up in his eyes.

Cindy Lou looked at him with pity. Of course he was sorry. He was always sorry. But that was the end of it. He'd still hit her. There would always be the next time. If she overcooked his dinner, if she didn't help him cheat people. If—if—if.

"No. I don't think so, Johnny. I can't take any chances now. And you lied about my pa. That was wrong, Johnny."

"Please, honey. I promise. I love you—you know that. It could be so great, Cindy Lou. Just the two of us. I've got plans—"

She sighed and sat down in the big overstuffed chair. "I'm beat, Johnny. It took a long time to get here. And there's somethin' you gotta know. I'm pregnant. We're gonna have a baby, Johnny. That's why I can't let you hit me anymore. That's why I just can't take no chances. I don't want my baby hurt."

Johnny let out a roar. "Baby! How the hell could you be pregnant? Didn't you take those pills I got you?"

"They made me sick and I threw them out."

His face tightened angrily. "Well, you'll just

have to get rid of it. We sure as hell don't need a baby around. I'll see if I can find a clinic or something. That broad down at Mickey's probably knows one. How the hell far along are you anyway?"

She pushed the question aside impatiently. "It don't matter. I won't get rid of my baby—I want it. You hear me, Johnny Merit? I won't." She stood up and started for the door. "I don't want to be your wife no more, Johnny. I'm going home."

He grabbed her and jerked her back from the door. "Get this straight, you hick bitch. You're my wife and you'll do what I say. You're not having this baby!" He pushed her hard, knocking her to the floor. "If I have to I'll get rid of it for you."

She tried to stand. "Johnny, please—just leave me be. I'm just a dumb hillbilly. You said it yourself. Let me go. You don't need me."

"You're not leaving me, Cindy Lou. Get that through your stupid head. Not until I'm sick and tired of you. And then I'll do the leaving."

"My pa—"

His fist slashed through the air, furious at her intended threat. "Your pa isn't here. Nobody's here, you little bitch. He slapped her, and she fell to the floor once more. Johnny was on her instantly, pinning her under him. His lips found hers and he kissed her hard. His hands quickly tore the blouse from her shoulders, exposing ripened breasts. *God*, he thought. *She's beautiful.*

"Johnny, no. Please don't hurt the baby. Please—"

It was the wrong thing to say. Johnny smacked her in the face. "That's all you care about, isn't it? Well, there won't be any baby when I get through with you. You're mine, dammit. There'll be no damned brat in my house." He hit her again, harder than before.

Kathy huddled beside the door, trying to make out what the yelling was all about. Should she go inside? Was Cindy Lou's pa really mad at her? That didn't sound like the man Cindy Lou had described. Kathy bit her bottom lip and pushed on the door.

The first thing the girl saw was Johnny Merit's fist flying through the air, hitting Cindy Lou over and over again. Kathy let out a shrill scream and backed against the wall, cowering and emitting a strange little moan from her lips. Cindy Lou opened her eyes and gasped, "Kathy! Get away from here!"

Johnny Merit had just turned to see who was there when the first blow hit him. He staggered backward, a dazed look on his face. Suddenly he was spinning across the room, and away from the two girls. He opened his mouth to curse his wife, but an invisible vise tightened around his chest and rendered him speechless. *My God*, he thought. *I'm having a heart attack*. Then he heard a cracking sound and felt his ribs breaking. The pain in his back intensified and the noise in his head grew until it was a deafening roar. He slid to the floor. The last thing he saw was a young girl huddled against the wall of room #8 of the Starlight Motel, her hands over her eyes.

Chapter 9

Charlie Kaufman had a field day with Johnny Merit's death. His headline read: AVENGER STRIKES AGAIN, SECOND WIFE-BEATER DIES UNDER MYSTERIOUS CIRCUMSTANCES. Much to Jason Links' dismay, the article began with the question of justifiable homicide. Was this a case that could be prosecuted? In both cases, the avenger had saved lives. The letters to the *Star* were quick in coming.

TO THE EDITOR:

I think the police should stop investigating these wife-beating killings. Whoever is doing it is a hero in my opinion. It's about time someone started sticking up for battered women. The men who died got what they deserved.

Jan Cook
Shawnee Mission

TO THE EDITOR:

My old man started to work me over the other night, and I told him he better not hit me again, or he might be next. You better believe he stopped. Way to go, Avenger! Keep up the good work.

Name Withheld by Request

TO THE EDITOR:

This is an open letter to my husband. The next time you hit me I'm going to run an ad in the paper, telling the avenger who you are and where to find you.

Name Withheld by Request

"Read 'em and weep, boss," Max Killen said. "These women are out for blood now. Think we'll get any copycat action?"

"Those letters aren't even the worst of it," Links said, reaching over on Killen's desk for his first cigarette in years. "Alison saw a woman wearing a T-shirt that said, 'IF YOU HIT ME IT WILL BREAK MY HEART.' On the back it said, 'OR YOURS!'"

Max let out a yelp. "Shit! Why didn't I think of that? They'll make a million!"

Links narrowed his eyes. "Maybe you'd like another beat, Max. How about traffic duty. Shut up and get out of here. You've got a hell of a lot to do today, and making an asshole of yourself isn't one of them."

The captain was thinking back to that morning. He'd been sitting in the kitchen, listening to the radio and reading Charlie Kaufman's latest diatribe. "And now, K.C., we have a request for an oldie but a goodie. The lady wouldn't give her name, but she says she has a husband who likes to slap her around a little. Well, this one's going out to you, buddy. From your wife and her pal, THE AVENGER!" Nancy Sinatra's voice filled the airwaves with "These Boots Are Made for Walking." Links had turned the radio off in disgust.

He stared at the unlit cigarette he'd borrowed from Max, then threw it across the room to the overflowing trash can. "Damn," he muttered. "Damn it to hell."

The thing that was woefully lacking in his investigation was a suspect. Just as with the Simmons' killing, there was not a shred of physical evidence. The autopsy on Johnny Merit showed that the heart had been burst open, and although it was obvious he'd been beaten—not as badly as Jack Simmons, but beaten—there were no abrasions, no marks of any kind. Joe Turner was completely baffled. Now Jason Links knew where to start digging. Northside Crisis Center. He'd believed Cindy Lou Merit when she said she'd seen nothing. And after spending time with Mary Simmons, he'd decided she, too, was telling the truth. Of course, the Merit girl was too badly hurt to make much of a statement. But somehow he believed she was being straight with him. Mary Simmons and Cindy Lou Merit had never met. According to Dr. Evans, anyway. But there was still the Northside tie-in. Not that it seemed to be doing Links any good.

His men had checked out Northside's handyman who came around once a week, but the guy turned out to be sixty-four years old and suffering from arthritis. Furthermore, he was the only male that had anything even remotely to do with Northside. Links thought it was peculiar that they didn't have any security men, considering the men who had family staying there. But Dr. Evans had said their security alarms would have police there within minutes, and guards would just make the women more nervous. That left a huge number of possibilities. Family members of a woman who might have stayed there. He'd have to check out any former patients—whatever the hell they were called—who had since been killed. Anything that might cause someone to go on a rampage. Of course, someone might be living in the neighborhood and watching the house. *Someone had to know that Cindy Lou left Northside and met her husband.* Unless it was the biggest coincidence in the world. And Links didn't think so. Maybe the kid, Kathy, would be able to remember something. But she was still in shock, and from what Sarah Jamieson had told him about her background, Links didn't think she was going to be much help.

It didn't matter, though. Something would break. Links had a feeling about it.

The moans of the old man down the hall were getting on her nerves. She sat in her room trying to concentrate on the newspaper in her hands. It was getting harder and harder to keep her mind on what she was doing. "Lord knows, it's hard enough around here," she muttered, her hands shaking so badly she crumpled part of the paper. "What with these old people yelling and moaning." She never considered that she was also old, and did her share of crying and moaning in her sleep.

What she hated most about the nursing home was the smell. No matter how often the attendants scrubbed or the nurses cleaned the patients, there was always the smell of urine. It permeated the furniture, the drapes, and her clothing. It seeped into her pores.

"Incontinent." That was the word they used. Practically everybody around the place was incontinent. That, combined with the excessive heat and the strong disinfectants, accounted for the smell. A smell of urine, of excrement, of death.

If only I could get out of here, she thought for the hundredth time since she'd seen the first article. But her body was no longer under her control. She could manage on her feet only a short distance, and then only with the aid of a cane. Most of her time was spent in bed or in the wheelchair they'd issued her. She wore a diaper, as did most of them, and the cancer left her weak, barely able to feed herself. It was as though the poison that had eaten at her mind all her life had filtered through and was now destroying her body as well.

She was the single most hated person in the unit. She'd terrorized the nurses and patients for years; several nurses had revised their feelings about euthanasia because of her.

Long ago, she'd been given a private room. The families of other patients couldn't or wouldn't stand for their loved ones being subjected to her craziness. She insulted, badgered, screamed. She had no family or friends. But she did have one thing that kept her going.

She knew who was doing those killings in Kansas City. It was a little girl named Sarah Livingston. Oh, yes. She remembered that child from hell. That man from the newspaper should have had the letter by now. When had she sent it? A day ago? A week? She couldn't remember.

The phone rang at the nurses' station, and Mrs. Zimmerman picked up the receiver.

"Yes, this is the St. Charles Care Facility." She paused, frowning. "Yes, she is a patient here, Mr. Kaufman."

Mrs. Zimmerman was tired, and this news wasn't helping the ache in the back of her neck. She sat down in her chair with an air of disgust and indignation. "I cannot believe she bothered you, Mr. Kaufman. She's eighty, dying of cancer, and her mind is almost gone. She seems to think some child is running around killing people—she's been raving about it ever since she was admitted eight years ago. Please just disregard the letter. I'm sorry she took up any of your time."

Mrs. Zimmerman stared at the phone a few minutes before starting her nightly rounds. *Crazy old bitch*, she thought. *I won't even give her the satisfaction of knowing the man thought enough of her letter to call.*

Sarah felt as if she were sinking. As if she'd reached point zero. She read and reread the newspapers. Letters from women—and a surprising number of men—who believed the so-called avenger was a hero. Paul Jamieson was one of those men who talked a good game whenever the killings were brought up in conversation. She wondered what he'd have to say if the case wasn't just something in the newspapers. Cocktail talk. Jason Links didn't feel that way at all. Jason believed a sadistic killer was at large. An insane monster on a rampage.

Sarah's hands trembled as she lit another cigarette. There were two others smoldering in the ashtray. It was after midnight. The third night in a row that she'd awakened with what the psychologist in her knew was an anxiety attack. Knowing what it was didn't help much.

She had killed Johnny Merit quickly. There had been no time to think. She'd been having lunch with Alison when it happened. It was all she could do to excuse herself and run to the rest room. She'd locked herself in a stall and done what she had to do. Her only thought had been for Cindy Lou and the baby. She kept telling herself that she hadn't meant to kill him, just stop him. But she wasn't sure.

More and more her thoughts went back in time. Back to the days when Mrs. Carver would sit and have those quiet little talks with her. "You have to get control over the power, Sarah. Don't let the power control you—ever. If it starts to happen, just try to think of something else. Something wonderful and happy."

Sure, think happy thoughts when someone is

being beaten to death. Try walking away from that, Aunt June. Sarah seemed to hear herself as both child and adult lately. "But it's hard to do, Aunt June. Sometimes I get so mad I can't stop."

"I know, honey," June Carver had replied. "It doesn't seem fair, does it? It's not fair that you can't get mad and stomp your feet like other children. But when you get mad, people can get hurt." The old woman had pulled her on her lap. "Sweetheart, you have an incredible mind, an incredible gift. But you have to learn to use it wisely, or it will ruin your life. And the lives of people you love."

Aunt June. How lucky she was to have had her so close all those years. She tried to think back. It was all fuzzy. She guessed June Carver had no place else to live. Why else did she come to live with Sarah and her mother? It broke Sarah's heart to think of her mother. Alzheimer's. Years ago they'd have called it senility. It was all the same as far as Sarah was concerned. At first she'd visited every few days. Then it was every week. Now it was once a month. Her mother had no idea who she was. When she last visited, the nurse told Sarah that her mother was convinced her name was Mrs. Livingston. How strange. Maybe she'd had a friend by that name. It sounded somehow familiar. Sarah had even tried to read her mother's mind in the hopes she could understand what was going on. It was impossible. A kaleidoscope of people, bits of conversation. Nothingness.

She put out the burning cigarette butts in the

ashtray, lit a fresh one, and felt more alone than she ever had in her life.

Jason Links sat in his office looking over the evidence his men had gathered. On the top of the pile was the report from Northside Crisis Center. Links scanned the pages, absentmindedly drumming his fingers on the desktop. At last, he leaned back and jabbed at the intercom switch. "Max, will you come in here?"

Moments later Max Killen walked into the room, his face reflecting an uncharacteristic seriousness. Captain Links' mood was infectious. "Morning, Captain."

"Max, do we agree that these killings are somehow related to Northside Crisis Center?"

The younger man nodded. "I don't see any other tie-in."

Links studied the reports on his desk. "Here's what I want you to do. Go back over Northside's records. Compile a list of names—everybody who's ever had anything to do with the place. Check that list against police records, tax records, college records—anything. Somewhere out there is a father, a brother, uncle—someone with a screw loose. And don't overlook the men who were wife-beaters themselves. Especially them. One of those assholes might have found God. He might think this is his penance. Offing guys who haven't seen the light."

"Got any idea how many men this is going to take, Captain?"

"Yes, I do," Links said with a curt nod. "You'll

have all the manpower you need. All I can spare, anyway." He paused. "I'll tell you something. I've been in this bullshit business long enough to know that when a person starts killing in a pattern like this, he doesn't stop. Right now he's got the city on his side. The two guys he killed were animals. But what happens when the guy rips up some poor schmuck who wasn't beating his wife? Suppose they're joking around and this lunatic bursts in and crushes an innocent man? Then, Max, we'll have jokers like Charlie Kaufman asking for our heads on silver platters. He'll do a turnabout in a minute." Links looked wistfully at Max's cigarette sitting in the ashtray, smoke curling up toward the ceiling. "This guy thinks he's God, Max. We've got to bring him in and bring him in fast."

Elizabeth Evans looked at her watch, her face showing lines she'd never known existed before the past week. It had been nightmarish. Police were everywhere she turned, and now a call from that fool reporter. Charlie Kaufman was a muckraker as far as Elizabeth was concerned. If he thought he'd get a statement from her, he had another think coming. She was anxious to get home to her husband, to some peace and quiet. The noise level and tension at the shelter was always high. It was impossible to have that many women and children under one roof and have it any other way. The second murder had turned it into a three-ring circus.

Sarah walked into the office, a cup of coffee in

each hand. She put them both on Elizabeth's desk and sat down wearily.

"Need some caffeine before you head home?"

Elizabeth picked up the cup, then put it back on the desk. "My nerves are wound up so tight that I shouldn't have any more of this stuff. This investigation has me in knots."

"Well," Sarah said, her voice somewhat shaky. "I hate to be the bearer of more bad news, but Jason Links just called. He's sending more officers over here. They're going to check out everyone who has ever had anything to do with the Center."

"Oh, God." Elizabeth sank farther down in her chair. "I can't believe this is happening."

Sarah averted her eyes. "Jason said—" She hesitated. "He said it might be a man from one of our families. Someone who was fed up with the battering women take. So they're looking for"—she stopped again, faltering—"uh, an emotionally disturbed man that has some dealings with Northside. Maybe even a neighbor—someone who watches the house."

Elizabeth's eyes flashed. "The hell with that Captain Links and his theories. I'm sorry, Sarah. I don't think this person is necessarily crazy. My God, he saved Mary and her children. Saved Cindy Lou and probably Kathy. Would the illustrious captain rather have had it the other way around? I guess that would be cleaner, wouldn't it? He could just lock up Simmons and Merit, and all this extra work would be unnecessary."

Sarah shivered and said nothing.

Elizabeth stood up and took her coat from a peg

on the wall. "The latest news from the hospital is bad. Cindy Lou Merit lost the baby. They say they believe Kathy is no longer in shock, but she's having terrible nightmares—worse than ever. They've decided to keep her a few more days to see if she improves, but as of right now she's being sedated at night."

Sarah stared at the floor. "What do you think? Can she snap out of it?"

Elizabeth was grim. "I don't know. The child has been through so much, so fast. I just don't know."

Kathy lay in bed and waited for the nurse to come. She guessed it must be about time for dinner. They kept wanting her to eat, but the food seemed to stick in her throat. Later they'd bring a shot. The dreams would come anyway. Shots didn't stop them. Nothing would stop them. They were all mixed up. Sometimes she saw Cindy Lou's husband beating her, kicking her. But then he turned into her stepfather and he was after her again. Kathy bit her lip. Everything was her fault. She was the reason Sam Thomas had hurt her mother. If she hadn't been with Cindy Lou, maybe the man wouldn't have kicked her. She was just bad luck. It didn't matter. Somebody was out there waiting to get her. She knew it.

Tears were streaming down the child's face when Julie Thomas awakened. Sitting up suddenly in the chair next to Kathy's bed, Julie cried out.

"Kathy? Oh, honey—don't cry. I'm sorry I fell

asleep. I don't know what's the matter with me—"

She was sitting on the bed, her arms around Kathy, when Sarah came into the room.

Julie stood up and wiped her eyes. "Oh, Mrs. Jamieson. Thanks for coming. I feel so—I don't even know how to tell you."

Sarah nodded. "I understand. Don't try to talk about it now." She looked at her wristwatch. "Have you had anything to eat?"

Mrs. Thomas shook her head. "Nothing since lunch. I was just going to have a bite of Kathy's dinner. I—I didn't feel I should leave."

"Why don't you go down to the coffee shop. I'll stay with Kathy."

Sarah sat on the side of the bed, silent for a considerable amount of time after Kathy's mother left. When she finally spoke, she chose her words carefully.

"You're afraid, aren't you, honey?" Gently, she listened to the confused thoughts inside the girl's head. "You're afraid that your stepfather will come after you again. Those nightmares you're having don't make any sense, do they. Sometimes Johnny Merit is the same man as your stepfather."

Kathy looked at her in amazement.

"Kathy," Sarah continued, "in some ways they are the same man. They're both very bad. And you mustn't believe all this has been your fault. It's not. You've been thinking that what happened to Cindy Lou is your fault, haven't you?"

Kathy squeezed her pillow closer to her and nodded. Sarah stared off into the shadows of the darkened hospital room. She could offer the girl some words of encouragement, play counselor as she'd been trained to do. Or she could help her. Really help her. *God*, Sarah thought. *I feel like I'm on the edge of a cliff and the ground is starting to give way.*

She took a deep breath. "Kathy, I want to tell you something, and I want you to listen carefully. Nothing that's happened to you is your fault. You were a victim—and your stepfather is a wicked, terrible man. He's evil, Kathy. And what he did to you is unforgivable." Her eyes focused straight into Kathy's. "Do you understand me?"

Kathy's eyes opened wide. She could feel something in her head, something she couldn't understand. But for the first time since Sam Thomas had first entered her bedroom, she understood that it was he, not she, who was at fault. He was the bad luck. Not Kathy. Her mother had had the bad luck to marry a man who was crazy. The dark shadow that had dominated her mind for the past several years began to lift. She felt light-headed, almost giddy. She stared at Sarah Jamieson, and a strange understanding slowly came over her. This lady was somehow special. Not just that she was nice and kind. Kathy had always liked Mrs. Jamieson, had almost trusted her at times when she trusted no adults. It was more than that. Mrs. Jamieson was different from regular people.

Sarah spoke again, and her voice was firm. "Kathy, there is a very good chance that Sam Thomas will find you and your mother." The girl quivered. Sarah went on, looking deeply into the girl's eyes again. "If he does, I can stop him. All you have to do is cry out for me. You don't even have to say it aloud. Just call out in your head. I'll stop him. Do you believe me, Kathy?"

Kathy's eyes opened even wider. "I think you can, Mrs. Jamieson. I don't know how, but I think you can."

Sarah hesitated. *You're on dangerous ground.* "Kathy, sometimes there are people who can do things. Things you'd never believe they could do. It's a gift. I have a gift, and it tells me when someone I love is in danger."

"Do you love me?"

"Yes, I do, Kathy. Very much. And I'm not going to let anyone hurt you. No matter what. But, honey, you have to do something. If you see your stepfather, call for me at once. Otherwise, I won't know until he actually hits you or hurts you in some way. Will you do that? I can stop him before he ever touches you if you'll just call out with your mind."

Kathy understood. She had no idea why or how she did, but she knew Mrs. Jamieson was telling her the truth. A sense of peace came over her. None of it had been her fault. Her mother had said it, but she hadn't believed her. The doctors had said it, but she hadn't believed them. Now Mrs. Jamieson was telling her and she didn't have to believe her—Kathy knew it for a fact.

"There's one thing, Kathy. This has to be a secret. Even your mother can't know. If I help you, you must never say I was the one who did it. Do you understand?"

Kathy looked into the green eyes that could look right into a person's head and knew it must be the biggest secret she'd ever known. Mrs. Jamieson was magic.

Chapter 10

Max found the new address easily. The house was small, but freshly painted and well kept. There was a tire swing hanging from a large oak tree in front. He supposed it was a good thing Mary Simmons got out of the house on Green Street. It would have been hard to go back and face all the inquiring faces and nosy neighbors. Links had said that Paul and Sarah Jamieson were responsible for the move. They'd given the Simmons woman the money to find another place.

Mary had been waiting, and opened the door immediately. Max couldn't believe it was the same woman he'd questioned at the hospital. The only visible reminder of that night on Green Street was the large cast on her arm. Her curly red hair was shorter, more stylish, and she was wearing one of those long sweaters that werc the rage. But it was more than that. Her face didn't have that pinched look. She'd gained a little weight and she looked rested.

She led him into the living room, small but decorated in bright colors and filled with plants.

He remembered the place on Green Street. There'd been no plants there, no pictures on the wall. He wondered if Jack Simmons' death had caused this transformation or if it was something more. Like a man. If it was a man, Max hoped he was small and unfamiliar with karate.

"I'd like to go over your testimony one more time, if you don't mind."

"I want to help," Mary said slowly. "But I really don't know anything."

"Mrs. Simmons," he began. "I think you should know that even if you did know who killed your husband, I'd be in sympathy with you for wanting to cover up for him. For all I know the guy may get off. If public sentiment means anything, he'll be hailed as a hero. But I've got to have some information—anything you can tell me. I want you to go back over everything that happened that night. What we're trying to find is a common thread—anything that ties this in with the second killing."

Mary sat back in the chair and forced herself to try to relive the night it all happened.

"Well, Jack came in and started yelling at us. I called the police the minute I heard his voice—he was drunk, and I knew what would happen. He started in on me, like always, and Billy tried to stop him. He hit Billy and knocked him out." She stopped, her voice shaky. "It was awful. I thought he'd killed him. Then he grabbed me by the hair and pulled me into the kitchen. Made me call the police again. I hoped the woman would realize that I was being forced to make the call. Then he twisted my arm." She glanced down at the cast. "I knew he'd broken it. Then he knocked me down and started hitting me. He said he was going to kill us. I remember hoping that he'd forget that Ellen was in the closet. Then"—she hesitated— "then, I'm not sure. I must have passed out, because the only thing I remember clearly is the ambulance driver. I asked him about Ellen and Billy."

Max frowned. "You don't remember anything at all?"

Mary rubbed her temples. "I guess I was in shock. It was so strange—like a dream. You'd think I was crazy."

"I assure you, I won't think you're crazy, Mrs. Simmons. This whole case is crazy."

"I—I seem to remember Jack coming at me, and I thought, 'This is it, he's going to kill me.' He started choking me and everything started to get dark. Then all of a sudden he wasn't choking me. He was flying backward. I thought he looked like a puppet, dancing all alone. At the time I wondered if he was having a fit—from all the drinking, you know. Then he came at me again, raging. But he flew back that time, too. It—it looked like he was fighting with himself. You have to believe me, Officer. When the ambulance driver said Jack was dead, I thought he'd died of a drunken fit. I couldn't believe it when I heard someone had killed him."

Max wondered if she was blocking something from her mind. Maybe she did know the killer and just couldn't accept it. If she was lying she

was as good an actress as he'd ever run across.
Dancing around like a puppet. Links was going to
love that one.

"Well, if you think of anything else, will you
give me a call?" He handed her a card and flipped
his notebook shut. Just as he stood to leave, the
front door opened and Billy Simmons walked in,
accompanied by a middle-aged man. He was
thickset, stocky, and muscular. Not particularly
tall, but there was an air of power about him.

Mary Simmons seemed flustered. "Officer, this
is my son Billy. And this is his wrestling coach
from the school, Tom Novak."

Novak nodded to Max and put a bag of groceries
on the table. "Billy's going to be in great shape for
next season, Mary. I guess that head of his is too
hard to do much to," he said with a wink.

Max shook the man's hand and turned back to
Mary. "Thanks for your help, Mrs. Simmons. And
do call if you think of anything. Anything at all."
A wrestling coach. Christ almighty.

He drove straight to Truman Memorial to talk
to Cindy Lou Merit. She was off the critical list,
and according to the doctor she was making good
progrcss. He wondered why the hell they didn't
move her out of the obstetrics ward. Must be hard
on her, after losing the baby.

She was standing, looking out the window, her
back to him.

"Mrs. Merit?"

She turned and Max found himself looking at
one of the most beautiful females he'd ever seen.
She was taller than he'd expected, and she had

none of the defeated look he'd seen on some of the faces at Northside. The long silk dressing gown clung to her body. There was a large box with a department store label on it on the end of the bed. Max noticed that the card was signed, "Sarah." *Damn*, he thought. *Paul Jamieson's wife is some mother hen. Good thing he makes all that bread, because she seems to give a hell of a lot away.*

"I'm Cindy Lou. You must be the policeman they want me to talk to."

"Uh, yes." He was on the verge of stammering, and wished Sarah Jamieson had given the patient a flannel robe. Something a little less distracting. "I'm Max Killen, Mrs. Merit—"

"Please just call me Cindy Lou. I don't want no part of Johnny Merit now."

"Sure. Uh, Cindy Lou—can you tell me anything about the day your husband was killed? Anything that would help us?"

She smiled. "I'll tell you all I know. I didn't see anybody though. That day sure isn't something I want to think about. He killed my baby, you know." She looked at him square in the eye. "The doctors tell me the baby wouldn't have been right. Because of the beating. So I guess it's best he goes to heaven right now. But it still don't make me feel much better. It's best somebody killed Johnny, too. 'Cause if he'd killed my baby and then lived, my pa woulda shot him. Or me. I'da done it, too."

Max nearly choked. *God help this girl if she stood up in court and said something like that.*

"Cindy Lou, uh, do you mind if I give you some advice? Just between us? You might not want to say that sort of thing to anyone else. You wouldn't want anyone to think you had anything to do with your husband's murder."

Cindy Lou widened her eyes in surprise. "Well, I didn't. But if he'd killed my baby I guess I'd sure want to kill him. How'd you feel if you was me?"

Max nodded, relaxing a little. "I guess I'd feel exactly the same way. But let's keep it between us, okay? Just tell me what you remember about that day. From the time Johnny Merit called the Center."

She looked up at the ceiling a moment, then back at Max. "Yeah, I'll try. At first, when Sue told me about the call, I couldn't see how it could be my pa. My folks' old truck ain't much good. Plus, Pa likes to keep close watch on his liquor in case any government men are nosin' around."

Max stifled a snicker. *Christ, this girl was so charmingly honest.*

"So I first thought it must be a mistake. But, see, I'd written to Pa and told him about Johnny beating me up and how I went to the Center and all. Well, to tell the truth it did cross my mind that Pa might have come all this way to shoot Johnny. He does have a fearsome temper. Anyway, I got all excited, and Kathy and me looked up the phone number to the motel, and sure enough, the lady said my pa was there and so was my brothers. Then I figured Pa'd never find the Center so I got on a bus and went over there. Kathy and me looked up how to get there, too. But it was all a lie. Johnny's the one who called."

"How do you know that? Did he tell you?" He

hoped there was no mistake. That the girl's father hadn't been in town, too. Especially since Cindy Lou seemed so determined to tell the world he was perfectly capable of shooting Johnny Merit. Provided he could leave his still that long.

"Oh, sure. Johnny said he did it so I'd come."

"And you had no idea that thc little Thomas girl was following you?"

"No, I did not! I'da taken her back!" Cindy Lou paused and shook her head. "I guess I sound like a real hillbilly, don't I? Johnny said I was nothin' but a dumb backwoods hick. I been studyin' though."

She broke into such a sincere, open smile that it nearly broke Max's heart.

"You talk just fine, Cindy Lou. In fact, I kind of like the way you talk. I like it a lot. But tell me this, are you positive there wasn't anybody in the room? Maybe standing back in the shadows?"

"No. I can't say anything for sure. I didn't see anybody. But then, when he started hitting and kicking me, everything happened pretty fast. I remember seeing Kathy standing there and yelling at her to run. It's all so weird. One minute Johnny was kicking me, and the next minute he was flying back across the room."

Max looked up sharply. "Flying back?"

She nodded, looking perplexed. "Wild, ain't it? He jumped around like a chicken with its head cut off. Thought maybe he was havin' a fit. There's some folks up around home that do that. Get fits."

Fits. *Ha, maybe that's it. A disease going around among quick-fisted husbands.* Max thought he'd run it by Joe Turner. Sounded right up his alley. Max found himself siding with Cindy Lou. Johnny Merit had deserved to be shot—or worse. And worse was what he got. Anybody who could lay a hand on this girl deserved to get shot.

"Kinda makes you wonder, don't it?" She looked down at her hands.

"Wonder what?"

"How I coulda married Johnny Merit. Looks like between Pa and me, we'da seen it."

"From what I've seen of battering husbands, it would be hard to pick them out of a crowd."

She shrugged. "I guess. Well, it don't matter now anyway."

"You say you were already on the floor when Kathy came into the room?"

"I can't rightly say when she came in. I didn't see her till I was on the floor, though. Hmm." Cindy Lou frowned. "Like I said, it all happened so quick. Things were pretty blurry."

"Do you remember Kathy going to get help?"

"Oh, yeah. She kept crying and telling me not to die. Said she was running to get somebody."

"Were you still conscious when help arrived?"

She nodded. "I was tryin' to stay awake. I kept thinkin' that if I could just stay awake, the baby could make it."

Max's jaw tightened, and he felt a boiling rage inside him. *Johnny Merit was scum, and I'll be the first to shake the avenger's hand.*

"You didn't see anybody leave the room?"

"No. I'd of seen 'em. I was watchin' the door and waiting for Kathy. Prayin' somebody would get there in time to—" Tears welled up in her eyes. "Sorry. I guess I thought I was about all cried out."

"No, it's me who's sorry, Cindy Lou." Max felt like an intruder. Not to mention an asshole. "I shouldn't be bothering you with all this right now. I—uh, I'll go now."

He couldn't bring himself to walk to the door. "They tell me you're getting out of the hospital tomorrow. Do you have someone to pick you up?"

She smiled, wiping her eyes with the sleeve of the silk gown. "The Center's sending somebody."

He nodded, uncomfortable. "Well, I'll probably be at the Center quite a bit in the next week or so. I guess I'll be seeing you there. I'll, uh, stop in and see how you're doing."

Her face broke into a broad smile. "That would be great. Come by anytime. Lord knows I'll be sittin' around awhile."

He took one last look at her and left. He hoped he hadn't sounded like a fool.

He took the elevator to the Children's Ward, dreading the interview with Kathy Thomas. Links had told him her story, and he'd been amazed at the depth of emotion he'd sensed as the captain recounted the ordeal she'd been through. Max couldn't help wishing the avenger had started up a few months earlier. Fourteen years old, and the kid had already been through more than the average person goes through in a lifetime. The interview wasn't going to be easy. Links had told him the kid was terrified of men.

Dr. Evans had stayed with the girl while Links questioned her.

Julie Thomas was in the room when Max entered. "You must be Officer Killen. I know you have to talk to Kathy, but please remember that she's had a terrible shock."

"I know. I'll keep this short."

Julie's shoulders sagged. "God, this is all so— Oh, I don't know. I feel so guilty. This is all my fault. I may seem overprotective to you. But you see, I didn't protect her very well before."

Kathy stared at her mother. She felt guilty? Like things had been her fault? Kathy wondered if everybody always thought things were their fault.

"Now, Kathy," he began, all business. "I just need to know a couple of things. First, what made you go into the motel room? Did you hear Cindy Lou being beaten?"

She slowly nodded her head. "It sounded horrible. I couldn't think why Cindy Lou's father would be yelling. She said he was nice."

"You heard the yelling as soon as you got to the room?"

"Yes. She was already there—inside."

"Did anyone know you'd left? And that you'd followed Cindy Lou?"

She shook her head. "Nobody saw or knew Cindy Lou was leaving, either. I just—well, see, Cindy Lou trusted everybody. I didn't think she ought to go by herself. I love Cindy Lou."

A thought began to roll around in Kathy's head. Mrs. Jamieson loved Cindy Lou, too. Could she feel Cindy Lou getting hurt?

"Kathy," he continued. "Did you see anybody going into the room as you walked toward the door?"

"No. There wasn't anybody."

"What about inside the room?"

"It was dark. I covered my eyes. But—"

"Yes? Did you remember something?"

"He was rolling around on the floor." Kathy stopped. *No one had been there. Mrs. Jamieson had done it with her magic. She'd saved Cindy Lou.* Kathy closed her mouth. She would never tell.

Julie Thomas misinterpreted the abrupt silence. "This has gone far enough. Can't you see she's upset?"

Max felt like a shithead. "Kathy, you've been very brave to answer these questions." His eyes softened. "And you were the bravest girl I've ever known to go into that room to help Cindy Lou. You should be very proud." He coughed nervously. "I know you've been scared, but it's going to get better, I promise."

She looked puzzled. "I know that. I'm not scared anymore."

Hell, he thought as he left the room. *The kid probably thinks the avenger is going to be around to save her from the boogeyman.*

Charlie Kaufman couldn't believe it. Another letter from the old lady in the nursing home. Still insisting there was a little girl running around killing people. Only now she'd added a new twist. The kid did it with her mind. Kid had a name, too.

Sarah Livingston. Well, you could say one thing for this old bat, she was inventive. The letter was better than most of the ones he'd been getting. Every crackpot in town seemed to know who the avenger was. Charlie forced himself to read every one, though. You never could tell. He folded the letter and tossed it into the box beside his desk. "Don't they give old people anything to do in those homes," he muttered to himself. "Hooking rugs or something?"

Links went over the reports for the third time. Out of the four regulars and three part-time people at Northside, the only factor that stood out was that—with the exception of Sarah Jamieson—they'd all been victims of abuse of one sort or another. They hadn't tried to hide the fact, either. Everyone was up-front about her battering and abuse history. Three were married and four were single, all of them either divorced or widowed. Each had had a father or a husband with an explosive temper; none had any contact with the men at present. Only one woman's former husband even lived in the Kansas City area, and he'd been in the drunk tank the night Jack Simmons was killed. The husbands of Elizabeth Evans, Sarah Jamieson, and one volunteer, Jan Anderson, had all been cleared of any suspicion. Links knew he'd never hear the end of his having to ask Paul Jamieson his whereabouts on the dates and times in question. Paul had grinned and asked if he should have an attorney present. Links suspected that Paul was enjoying it all immensely.

Their greatest hope for a key suspect had surfaced a few days earlier. One of the part-timers at the Center was dating a professional wrestler, a huge man, and extremely protective of his girlfriend. The concept went down the tube, literally. Jungle Jim had been wrestling on nationwide live television during the Simmons' murder. Once Max met the man, he told Links the idea was ludicrous, anyway. Jungle was a bear of a man, but as mild-mannered as they came. It was one of the reasons the young woman had been attracted to him in the first place.

Jason picked up the report on Sarah Jamieson. Graduated from the University of Missouri in 1973. Met Paul Jamieson her senior year and married him soon after graduation. Honors diploma. Former high-school counselor in K.C. school system. Two children. Father died when she was an infant. Only living relative was a mother, confined to a nursing home. Sarah had been raised by her mother and an elderly aunt. The aunt died when Sarah was seventeen. He flipped to the next page. No uncles, no ex-husband, and no father who might be watching the activities at Northside. Links felt uncomfortable snooping through a friend's past. Not that she had much of one. He barely glanced at the rest of the pages marked "Jamieson."

He turned his attention to Elizabeth Evans. Again he ran into a brick wall. She'd been sexually molested as a child, by an uncle who was now too old and sick to be a suspect in anything. Her husband was a respected academic, small in build and certainly not a martial arts expert. No unexplained men in her life and no leads.

He turned his attention to the reports on people in the neighborhood. Most were low-income families, struggling to keep food on the table. Nothing unusual about any of them. No obvious psychotics, anyway. Most had little or no interest in the shelter, and many didn't even realize there *was* a shelter in the neighborhood. A few thought it was an alcohol rehabilitation unit.

Jason considered the man-hours it had taken to assemble the information on his desk, and he couldn't believe they still had nothing to go on. Not a decent suspect in the bunch. And that included Mary Simmons' new boyfriend, the wrestling coach. He was teaching a physical education class when Merit was killed and was at a poker game with several other teachers and a priest, of all people, when Simmons got it. Links jabbed at the intercom. "Max, get the boys in here. Let's go over all this one more time. Beginning to end."

Steve Jeffries entered first, handing Links a telephone message. "Came in while you were on the phone earlier, Captain."

Links glanced down and saw it was from Joe Turner. *Is it time to call in Edna?* Links scowled. "Oh, Lord. That's all we need. That, and for Charlie Kaufman to get wind of it."

Steve put his hand to his forehead. "I see something green. No. No. It's not green. I see something blue—wait—it's shaped like a square. The killer has something to do with a blue square! It's on his jock strap! No. I guess it's just the label. But wait—"

"All right, Steve. Give it up," Links interrupted, suppressing a smile. The imitation wasn't so far off. They'd used Edna Litvak before. Links was convinced that the woman had some kind of talent, a gift of some sort. But the information she could give them was always so vague it did little good. What usually happened was that the officers put in long hours solving the case, Edna came in and got one or two facts right, and the media went nuts over it all. Hadn't *she* told the police the killer would be found in a red house? Two people had already written letters to the paper suggesting Edna might be of some assistance.

Links had more faith in a psychic the newspapers had never heard of. Actually, no one but Links knew about her. Over the past fifteen years she had been responsible for saving three children and locating the bodies of two others.

The first time they had heard from her was in the kidnapping of the Brenner baby. Doctor Brenner, a heart specialist, and his wife had gone to a much publicized awards dinner in his honor. They left their five-month-old daughter at home with a sitter. The daughter was a miracle child to the Brenners, since they had all but given up hope of Mrs. Brenner ever conceiving. Then, at age forty-one, Louise Brenner gave birth to a bouncing baby girl, the answer to many prayers and dreams shared by the couple.

The Brenners returned home from their dinner and found the child's crib empty and the body of the sitter sprawled in the second-floor hallway. It was obvious the woman had not relinquished her charge without a fight. Three days later a former employee of Dr. Brenner's was arrested. The man had been fired from Brenner's clinic three months prior to the kidnapping. He had the doctor's home address in his pocket, along with a newspaper clipping regarding the awards dinner. The man refused to talk. He knew, and rightly so, that the evidence they had couldn't convict, and any admissions would seal his death warrant.

Six straight hours of interrogation changed nothing. Hope was fading fast. If the baby was still alive, and there had been no accomplice, the child was totally alone. The suspect stuck to his story. Until the arrest, the media had kept a lid on the case. By the six o'clock news on the day of the arrest, reporters talked of nothing else.

The Brenners begged the police to allow them to pay off the man, to let him go in exchange for the baby. The police refused, knowing full well he would never lead them anywhere. Then a call came into the station house from a Father Reiner. A woman had called his rectory and informed him that the baby was in an old abandoned farmhouse three miles off Highway 83. She had given him explicit instructions to the structure. The old priest figured it was a crank call; nevertheless, he called the police. A squad car was dispatched to the location, and the baby was located, hungry and disgruntled, but in stable condition.

The newspapers speculated that the call came from an accomplice. Links knew better, for once the child was found, and evidence gathered at the rural location, the kidnapper broke down. He swore he acted alone. Links believed him, and over the years he'd come to respect this anonymous psychic, though the woman never once admitted that's what she was. It happened four more times. In each case, the woman called and left her message with a minister. And in each case, the information was precise and on the money. Links had no idea who the woman was, but he understood that she wished to remain out of the public eye. Anyone else would have gloried in the free publicity. Jason Links no longer scoffed at the idea of using psychics. He just wished Edna Litvak had the same skills as his mystery woman.

Links looked at the group he'd assembled. All good men. All looked like they hadn't slept in days.

"All right." Links took a deep breath, inhaled the secondhand smoke in the room, and looked longingly at the cigarette dangling from Max Killen's mouth. His willpower weakened every day the case wore on. "Let's go over this shit one more time."

Sarah could still hear Paul chuckling about being questioned by Jason Links long after she hung up the phone. "I asked him if I needed a lawyer present," Paul had offered, obviously pleased with himself, and thinking that the affair was laughable. "Then I said," Paul had continued, on a roll. "Then I said, 'I guess I can just kiss off any hopes of being Attorney General, can't I?'" He roared.

When she had finally hung up the telephone, she'd stared at it for a long time.

Once again she looked over the files that had been copied by a young police officer earlier in the week. Her file told nothing. There was no item that might arouse any suspicion, or show she was any different from any other professional woman. She was married, had children, a college degree. Nothing odd about any of it.

A sadness overwhelmed her, and suddenly she wanted to see her mother more than anything in the world. It would be like always. The vacant stare, the blank smile. But Sarah needed the physical closeness. She telephoned the nursing home and received the usual report. No change. Her mother chatted with the other patients from time to time, but what she said was nonsensical.

She sat back in her chair and closed her eyes, practicing the same techniques she taught women at the Center.

I will remain calm. I am a good person. A decent person. I have nothing to be ashamed of.

Liar. You're a killer.

Good people don't kill. Decent people don't kill.

She felt her hands tremble as she tried to light another cigarette. *Why now? Why is it all happening now?*

Chapter 11

Nigel Phelps stepped out of his black Mercedes and handed the parking attendant his gold key ring. "I'll be in a meeting for several hours. See to it that nothing happens to my car." He pressed a twenty into the young man's hand, grabbed his thick briefcase from the back seat, and walked to the elevators. He stepped inside and pressed the second-floor button. When the doors opened on both sides, he scanned the hallway filled with hotel rooms, keeping his back to the side opening onto the parking level. The hallway was vacant. He stepped out and walked directly to the men's room located around the corner. He'd never understood why this particular floor had public rest rooms. There wasn't even a meeting room on the floor as far as he knew. Maybe there had been a remodeling. His primary interest was in the fact that the facility was seldom used, and that one of the stalls was completely encased. He entered the stall and unlocked his briefcase.

He placed the contents on the toilet seat: a pair of jeans, a red plaid shirt, sneakers, and a man's hairpiece. He removed two diamond rings, slipped them into the pocket of his suit jacket, and carefully undressed. Folding each piece of his suit neatly, he placed them in the case. Next, he opened his wallet, removed five hundred dollars, and placed the wallet on top of the suit. Satisfied, he snapped the briefcase shut and began dressing. A small, wiry man, Nigel projected a larger image than was the reality. He had a sharp-featured face, with piercing eyes that missed little. He zipped up the faded jeans, noting that he was already feeling a throbbing between his legs. Quickly, he stretched the hairpiece over his own thinning hair, removed a pair of dime-store eyeglasses from the pocket of the plaid shirt, stuffed the five hundred dollars in his jeans pocket, picked up the briefcase, and stepped out into the rest room. He gazed at his reflection in the mirror. He probably wouldn't need the glasses. Nobody would ever recognize him. But he was a cautious man and put them on anyway, ignoring the uncomfortable fit of the hairpiece. He looked in the mirror again. Even his own wife wouldn't recognize him now.

He felt in the pocket for the small black comb and carefully combed the hairpiece to his satisfaction. It was far better than the curly one he'd used a month ago. He glanced at his watch, then caught himself. *Shit!* He hastily pulled the Rolex from his wrist, opened the briefcase, and dropped it in.

Nigel pushed open the door to the rest room, stepped out, and casually walked to the elevator. He pushed the button for the tenth floor. Again, the doors opened on both sides. This time he entered the area leading to the parking level. An attendant approached him, took the ticket, and went back to his station, returning with a set of car keys. Nigel walked over to the 1973 Chevy, opened the trunk, and placed the briefcase inside. He tipped the attendant a dollar fifty.

He eased the Chevy into traffic and headed for Main Street. Sometimes he walked the twenty blocks, but more often than not he took the car, always parking it several blocks away. He'd purchased the Chevy from a kid who cleaned his swimming pool the previous summer. He paid cash, never bothered to change the registration, and kept it in a parking garage downtown.

As he drove, he felt the excitement mounting. The skirts got shorter, the makeup heavier, the sweaters tighter, as he neared his destination. He parked and went into a small bar, ordered a beer, and waited to be approached. He didn't have to wait long. The girl was friendly, young, and pretty—in a used-up kind of way. Too young for a policewoman, unless the cops were recruiting them out of the high schools. Nigel didn't think so. A man in his position learned to read people quickly.

"Lookin' for a little action, Pops?"

Nigel stopped himself from hitting her right then. "Sure. You live around here."

"Couple a blocks down."

"Alone?"

"What are you, nuts?" She rolled her glazed eyes. "Yeah, Pops, I live alone."

He pulled out the roll of money and paid for the drinks with a fifty. The girl perked up at the sight.

"I have some rather unusual tastes," he said frankly. "But I'm willing to pay for what I get. What will, say, two hundred get me?"

The girl blinked. She was lucky if she got ten bucks in this neighborhood. For two hundred the creep could get anything he wanted. Shit, she'd probably already done it earlier for ten.

The little one-room apartment was a pigsty, and it excited Nigel to be in such a place. He looked around, wanting to sink his face into the pile of filthy socks, underwear, and towels next to the bathroom door. He wanted to breathe in the odor. Suck the filth into his system.

"Get on the bed. I've got to tie you up to do it." He was starting to breathe heavier.

Shit, what an asshole, she thought. *He probably thinks he's the only cat in the world likes it that way.*

"First give me the bread. Then you got to stand outside the door while I put it away." She'd learned early on that when you're tied to the bed you can't always collect.

He agreed.

"Come on back in now," she purred, anxious to please. Maybe he'd become a regular. If she could get him coming in once a week, she could stay off the street damn near all the time. Just one two-hundred dollar regular customer could change her life.

He tied her to the bedposts, then looked around. A pair of nylons lay in the pile of dirty underwear. He picked them up, pausing to run his hand through the heap. He returned to the bed and before she could say a word, he crammed the pantyhose into her mouth. She squirmed and twisted on the grimy sheets.

He stripped quickly, neatly folding his clothes and placing them on a chair across the room. He stood there, looking down on the girl. Her eyes were wide, and she had almost succeeded in spitting out the nylons. Suddenly she looked grotesque. He slapped her hard across one small breast. With his other hand he twisted a nipple until it was purple and swollen.

"Keep those hose in your mouth," he said with a cold stare. He forced them back in place and straddled her. He was still limp, but it wouldn't be long now. He began hitting her.

Buried on the third page of the *Kansas City Star* was a paragraph about the latest murder in the City of Fountains. A young prostitute was found beaten to death in her apartment. She had been tortured and brutalized prior to her death, which had been caused by strangulation. She had choked to death on her own vomit.

Edna Litvak held the shirt that Jack Simmons had been wearing the night he was killed. Her brow knitted in concentration. Over and over she twisted the fabric through her fingers. Finally she stopped, handing the shirt back to Links.

"I feel nothing. I feel no other hands on this shirt."

Links looked blank. "Aren't you even going to try, Edna?"

"No," she said slowly. "I said I feel no hands on the shirt. But I do feel something. Something that tells me to stay away. I can't explain it, Captain. I just can't look any deeper."

Jason glowered at Max, obviously disgusted. Edna might not be the greatest psychic in the world, but she usually at least tried. Came up with *something*. Links felt like a fool for even calling her. He handed her the shirt Johnny Merit had worn.

"Try this one, Edna. Please. Maybe you can pick up something."

She handed the shirt back as though it were burning her fingers.

"It's no use. Something's blocking me. I can feel it. Another mind is at work, and it's far more powerful than mine."

Links sighed. "Are you trying to say our killer is psychic, too? And he's keeping you from helping us?"

"No—yes. I—I don't know." She frowned, stumbling over her words. "I don't get any feeling of evil, Captain. Maybe it's not the killer who is interfering."

Links looked skeptical.

"All right, then. Thanks for your cooperation, Edna. If anything changes and you can be of help, call me." He held out his hand and she shook it firmly.

"No." She looked him in the eye. "No, Captain. I wouldn't be able to do that."

The door closed behind her and Max slammed his open hand onto the desk.

"Christ! Why do we let the press coerce us into using her? What a bunch of garbage. I've never seen a psychic yet who was worth a shit."

Links shook his head. "I wasn't expecting any real help. But I at least expected her to *try.* She didn't even go into her routine. Maybe she's as taken with the avenger as you seem to be, Max."

Max hadn't known his feelings were showing through. "It's not that, Captain. I, uh—I just think that *somebody* saved the lives of some good people. I—"

"Especially the Merit woman, huh, Max?"

"All of them, Captain," Max snapped. Links knew he'd been correct in his suspicions. Everytime Max Killen began to go over the Merit report his face turned a faint shade of pink.

"Is your infatuation with this young lady going to affect your performance, Max?"

"Are you taking me off the case?" Max's eyes flashed.

"Not yet. But, Max. You'd better watch your step. If I think you're overlooking anything. Anything at all."

Max took a deep breath. "Well, then how about the obvious? How about what Edna just told us and what every one of the witnesses have said? You've got a psychic who says there's 'some mind' stopping her from seeing anything. The witnesses all say the victims 'flew across the room.' Maybe it's a case of witchcraft, Captain. Or flying saucers. Or magic of *some* kind." He glared at his superior. "I just don't want you to think I'm overlooking anything."

"Interesting thought coming from someone who doesn't even believe in psychics."

"Do *you*? Honestly?"

"Yes, I do. There have been too many times when Edna was correct on certain details. The *Star* had an article about the Hamilton Institute in St. Louis a few weeks ago. From what the piece said, the time for proving psychic phenomena is past. It's a scientific fact." Links sat down and crossed his arms across his slightly protruding belly. "The way I understand it, a true psychic picks up images and feelings from the items we give them. Some are better than others. There's one in Wisconsin that does a hell of a job. The police do not laugh at her, I guarantee you. She's led them directly to a killer. Directly. They've even issued her a badge number."

Max stared at the floor and grunted.

"And there's a woman in Kansas City who has helped us anonymously several times. I wish to hell *she'd* surface."

Max sighed. "All right, Captain. Let's assume Edna really can pick up things the rest of us can't. She said she couldn't do it this time. That another mind was blocking her. Could it be that someone is also causing Mary Simmons, Cindy Lou Merit, and Kathy Thomas to block out what they saw?

Unless *everybody's* lying, these people didn't see another person in the rooms."

Max began to warm to the subject. "These 'fits' the women thought Simmons and Merit were having—Mary Simmons said it looked like her husband was fighting with himself. 'Like a puppet.' That's how she described it. Suppose there was a psychic or somebody who could make all these people forget who was there? Like a hypnotist—" Max stopped talking, aware that he was running on. Wondering if Links thought he'd lost it.

Links sat quietly, his mind sorting through the information, classifying and filing. Finally he spoke.

"I don't know, Max. I just don't know. But we've drawn a blank everywhere else. I guess we need more information on the subject, and I know just where to find it."

Nigel Phelps parked his Mercedes in the four-car garage attached to his home. He shut off the motor and clinched the steering wheel, trying to stop the tremors in his arms. It was too soon. He had to get a grip on himself. He couldn't risk another trip to Main Street so soon. Even if nobody seemed very interested in the girl's death.

It frightened him that he was showing his violent side to Val. It was getting worse, too. In fifteen years of married life, he'd never let his problem spill over into his home life. The past year he'd felt his self-control slipping away. Crumbling. His carefully protected public facade was breaking apart. Sometimes he looked at his wife and imagined her tied to the bed, face contorted in fear. He couldn't get the picture out of his mind. But he had to try. Had to. If his family knew. His business associates. He hoped the aggression had been used up on the prostitute.

"I didn't mean for her to die," he whispered to himself, still gripping the steering wheel. "I didn't mean for it to happen."

But it had happened, just as it had happened with Mellie Howard when he was at Dartmouth. Mellie, who had taunted and teased him. Who had called him a little boy when he couldn't perform. *Well, Nigel, wait until after the girls find out the poor little rich boy's family jewels are only rhinestones.* She had laughed at him. Before the night was over she was screaming in terror, and begging him to stop. He had beaten her, raped her, and then beaten her again. Nigel's family jewels held out until the first light of dawn once he got them operational. And all it took was seeing her terror-stricken face. He didn't know if she was dead or alive when he ejaculated that final time. He took her limp body and dumped it into an abandoned well in back of his parents' lodge, still not knowing if Mellie was breathing. He couldn't allow her to say anything. Rhinestones. She'd been dead wrong about *his* equipment.

Luckily, Nigel had picked Mellie up outside a small bar on the outskirts of Hanover. Everybody knew about her. She ran with the college crowd, picking up spending money by showing wealthy young men what the world was all about. Mellie had taken one look at Nigel's Ferrari and readily agreed to drive the fifty miles to his parents' lodge. Somewhere along the way she'd taken a dislike to the boorish student, and when he couldn't perform, Mellie couldn't resist the taunt. It wasn't usually her style.

Mellie Howard had been Nigel Phelps' secret love. Sure, he knew about her. Knew she had had lots of his friends. But Nigel believed she was destined for him. Destined to make him a man and maybe even become his wife one day. She was his private dream.

Now he knew her for what she was. A whore.

He considered his options, then drove into Montpelier and picked up four bags of cement and some lumber. He chose the biggest and busiest lumberyard he could find to make his purchases. Then he returned to the lodge and meticulously mixed and dumped the wet cement into the well, boarded it up, and left.

Not a breath of scandal ever touched him, though the same could not be said for several of his Dartmouth classmates. Rumors about the young woman's disappearance circulated for a while. Several boys were questioned, but by the end of the term, Mellie Howard was forgotten.

Nigel never forgot. His most satisfying sex with Val had taken place on the ground beside the boarded-up well. Newly wed, Val thought she was the inspiration for his intense lovemaking that day. It excited her to think that she held such an attraction for her husband. Though both were in their mid-thirties, it was their first marriage. She knew she'd been right to hold out for Prince Charming.

Nigel entered the house, barely speaking to Val as he made his way to the upstairs bedroom. Usually a hot shower calmed him. He stripped carefully, some of the tension going with just the act of disrobing. He shut the door to his bathroom and looked into the full-length mirror. Mellie had been right about one thing. He didn't look like much of a man. He smiled, knowing that looks could be deceiving. He was a man all right.

The water cascaded over his body and he scrubbed furiously.

When he finally emerged he was serene. He crawled into bed and fell into a heavy, druglike sleep. Sometime later, Valerie Phelps crept to the door of the bedroom and peered inside. *Thank God, he's asleep*, she thought. *Thank God.*

Chapter 12

Links awoke early, eager to make the trip to St. Louis. It was an easy drive, interstate all the way. For Links, driving was a vacation. It relaxed him, gave him time to think. His father had been the same way. *Let's go for a little ride, boy. See some country and get the bugs out of our brains.* That's what driving did for Jason Links. It got the bugs out of his brain.

At 5:30 A.M., the traffic along I-70 was still light. By seven, when it picked up a little, Links had been on the road an hour and a half, and had reduced the murders to simple equations. Two men murdered. Both were wife abusers, violent men. Two wives left beaten. One connection between the two cases and that was Northside Crisis Center. No one admitted seeing another person at the crime scenes. Both women thought their husband was having some kind of fit. Most important: no physical evidence.

What if he stuck to his old belief? Looked strictly at the facts in the case? The facts all pointed to the fact that no one had been in either room. *Jesus*, Links thought. *Joe Turner and his plastic suit theory. Max and the hypnotist idea.*

Someone had to be watching Northside. He must have a way to get information, and a way to keep the women from identifying him. Both women had been hurt—could the killer have administered some sort of drug? No. Kathy Thomas had not been injured. She'd have known if someone attempted to give her a drug. The child was on shaky ground emotionally, but Links considered her the best witness he had.

Conclusion? Who the hell knew? Maybe hypnosis was the answer.

When Jason Links finally saw the Old St. Charles Rock Road exit, he was no closer to a solution. He pulled off and wound his way to the well-kept grounds of the Hamilton Research Institute. There had been a time when Links thought the place was probably a loony bin.

The name he was seeking was enclosed in a glass frame just inside the entrance to the main building. Emily Bronson, Room 207. He had spoken with the Institute director by telephone the previous afternoon.

Hamilton was now considered second only to Rhine in world prestige. If there was any validity to the idea of mass hypnosis, Links would find the answer here. He also planned to ask about Edna's 'stronger mind' comment.

"Come in—Captain Links, isn't it?" Emily Bronson rose from behind an enormous desk.

Links nodded. "Dr. Bronson?"

"Happy to meet you." She walked back to her

desk and sat down, motioning Links to a chair. "Now. How may I help you?"

Links wasn't sure how to start. He didn't want to appear a complete idiot. "Dr. Bronson, uh—I need to know some facts about hypnosis. Specifically, can a person by hypnotized without remembering it?"

She smiled. "Certainly. That's one of the most popular tricks a hypnotist does. It's nightclub stuff."

"And these people don't know they've been hypnotized?"

"Not necessarily. They are usually volunteers, though. So they know they may have been."

Links tapped his fingers on the arm of the chair. "Of course, these people know the man is a hypnotist. Could someone be hypnotized without ever being aware that he was even around a hypnotist? And could it work on a severely injured person?"

Dr. Bronson looked thoughtful. "Captain, why don't you tell me exactly what the circumstances are? The case in question. Then I may be able to help."

He frowned. "Do I have your complete assurance that the conversation will stay in this room? This is a murder investigation, and I *cannot* have any information leaking out. The press would have a field day with this."

"Of course. We occasionally work with the police here in St. Louis, Captain. When we do, I assure you it does not reach the newspapers."

Links relaxed. "Have you heard about the wife-beating murders in Kansas City?"

"Hasn't everyone? They call the killer the avenger?"

"Yes." Links smiled wearily. "It sells newspapers."

"How does this case relate to hypnosis, Captain?"

He took a deep breath and began to talk. When he finally finished, she shook her head solemnly.

"I don't believe what you are suggesting is possible. The chances of all these individuals being hypnotized is slim. Especially in the case of the two women who were terribly beaten. In that condition, it would be almost impossible to predict what the mind would do.

"What you are really talking about here, Captain, is mind control. Not just hypnosis. And contrary to what writers of fiction like to have us believe, mind control is simply not possible without extended 'brainwashing'—as some call it, or drugs. We have many gifted hypnotists here at the Institute. They could probably hypnotize you, Captain Links. But given the number of people you're talking about and the time frame, I doubt they could control thoughts in the way you are asking."

"Do you use hypnosis here often?"

"We've been doing experiments for years now. Sometimes it frees up a mind to go on to other psychic impulses. It works on some, and on others it merely impedes the flow. We find that it works best on people who have a hard time getting a clear picture. Subjects that allow outside factors to interfere. Like getting more than one channel on a television screen."

"I understand." Links nodded. "We work with a psychic who often has that problem. She has a hard time knowing what she sees."

"That would be Edna Litvak, wouldn't it?"

"Yes, do you know her?"

"Edna has been tested here numerous times. She has a great degree of psychic ability. But, like you say, she has a hard time interpreting what she sees."

"That brings me to the next point." Links leaned forward in the chair. "Doctor, we brought Edna in on this case, but she says she can't help us. She said that there is another mind, one much stronger than hers, and that mind is blocking her. What do you make of that?"

"Well, I don't know what to make of it," she answered truthfully. "I can't imagine it happening. Makes for good fiction, but that's about it."

She stood. "Captain, let me show you around the Institute a bit. It might help if you saw just what we do here. You can talk to some of our people—see the kind of testing we do."

They walked down the hall and stopped at a large window. Dr. Bronson flipped a switch and the voices of the two women inside could be heard. They were going through the Zener cards. When they finished, the woman was given her score. Fifteen correct out of twenty-five. An excellent percentage.

Dr. Bronson explained. "It was with the Zener cards that parapsychology was first put on a quantitative basis. In other words, with the scores on this test we can mathematically calculate the degree of clairvoyance a person has. By the way, Edna Litvak scores very highly on the cards."

The woman moved briskly down the hall. "I'm taking you to the T-wing now, Captain. We nicknamed it that because it's where we test telepathy—mind reading. It's simply a direct transmission from one brain to another."

She stopped by a door with a blinking red light. "We'll have to wait a few minutes. There's a test going on. The woman I want you to meet has been here about four months. She's quite a phenomenon. Jenny's tested higher in this area than anyone we have ever had at the Institute, except one. And believe it or not, the only one to have scored higher than Jenny was a little girl. She was about four or five, I believe. It was years ago."

Jason found the Institute fascinating, but he was beginning to think it held no clues to his current problem.

The red light stopped blinking and they entered the room. Emily Bronson walked to a young woman. About twenty-five, Jason guessed.

"Jenny, I'd like you to meet Jason Links." She deliberately dropped the "captain." "He's touring the Institute, and I wanted him to meet the prize pupil."

Jenny took Links' hand and shook it firmly. "I'm twenty-eight. What can I do for you?"

His surprise was obvious, and the young woman laughed.

"You won't have many secrets in this part of

the building, Captain." She studied him a minute. "You're wondering if Dr. Bronson told me you were coming. I assure you she did not. And you wonder if I could help you catch a murderer."

"How the devil do you know all that?" He was clearly astonished.

"I don't know, really. I've been able to read minds since I was about thirteen. I'd had a severe case of meningitis. My temperature soared to 106 degrees and stayed there for five days. I nearly died. When it was all over, I discovered I could tell what people were thinking. It nearly drove me crazy. Still does on occasion."

"Well," Jason said with a laugh. "I don't suppose you could send that mind of yours back to Kansas City. Pick out a murderer for me?"

"I couldn't find him. But I could probably tell you what he's thinking if you do pick him up."

Links laughed. "I'll bet you're a terror at a poker game."

Dr. Bronson led him back into the hall and into a lounge area. This wall was plastered with pictures of a small girl. "This is a combination lounge and 'mini-museum.'" The woman pointed to the photos. "This is the little girl I was telling you about. By far the most gifted subject we ever had—and probably the most gifted psychic who ever lived, as a matter of fact. She scored off the boards in clairvoyance, telepathy, and psychokinesis."

"What exactly is psychokinesis?"

"The ability to move things with your mind. Our little Sarah—Sarah Livingston was her name—could do it at the drop of a hat. Chairs, tables—you name it. And she never missed on the cards. Perfect score every time." She moved over to the wall where a twisted metal rod was hanging. "See that? Sarah did that. She was angry at one of the instructors and twisted the bar until it was red-hot. It actually burned into the floor when it fell."

Jason raised his eyebrows. "What happened to her?"

"No one knows. She never liked one of the instructors—the one that prompted her to twist the rod. But, you're not interested in all that. It all happened a long time ago. Ancient history."

"You'd think people would have heard of somebody who could do all that."

"Well, her mother wanted no publicity. No exposure to the outside world. I guess that's why they eventually left. She was a sweet little girl, though. I'd just been hired when it all happened.

"There had been another teacher—uh, what was her name—Mrs. Carver. Sarah adored her. When the old woman retired, the child never adjusted.

"One day she just didn't show up. Her mother had moved from their apartment and left no forwarding address. God knows, Mr. Hamilton moved heaven and earth to find her. But he never did. He was so angry about it he fired the instructor. Blamed it all on her."

Dr. Bronson paused and looked at one of the photos of a small, smiling blond-haired girl. "I've often wondered about her. I suppose her powers must have caused her problems. They nearly always do." She stopped, a faraway look in her eyes. Suddenly she frowned, irritated with herself. "Oh, I'm sorry, Captain. I'm just rattling on and on, aren't I?"

He smiled. "Rattle all you wish. I can't say when I've had a more interesting time. My wife will be envious—she'd enjoy this, too. I had no idea the human mind could do so much."

"Yes. Mr. Hamilton calls it the 'final frontier.' About the only thing left that's ninety percent mystery."

They walked to the entrance. When they got to the door Dr. Bronson extended her hand. "I guess I haven't been much help, have I?"

He laughed. "Anytime I get an education like that it's a help. If not with this case, then maybe down the road."

He climbed back into the car and started the engine. Interesting few hours. Wasn't going to do him a bit of good with the avenger, though.

Emily Bronson returned to her office alone, sitting behind the big oak desk. It was still hers, and would be for eight more months. Then it would be retirement, and the desk would belong to the new director. She couldn't complain though. The Institute had been good to her. She'd turned down a position at Rhine to come here. Tom Hamilton was nothing if not convincing. The gamble had paid off both in terms of money and job satisfaction. Her promotion to director was deserved, but it had come as a surprise. When he informed Emily that the position was hers, Tom Hamilton had made it clear that it was her handling of Charlotte Crawford that had been the deciding factor.

ST. LOUIS, MISSOURI
November, 1956

Emily Bronson sat in Tom Hamilton's office as he quickly scanned the latest reports on Sarah Livingston's progress. He smiled up at her.

"Emily, look at these test results. Sarah's abilities are growing on a daily basis. My God! Think what she'll be able to do by the time we go public!"

"I'd like to work more with her, Tom. I just feel like Charlotte is the wrong person. Sarah seems to hate her. Especially after that incident with the rod. And there's something, oh, I don't know. Something inherently bad about Charlotte. I have a gut-level feeling that she mistreats the kids. Never in front of anyone, though."

"Then let's get rid of her."

"Do you mean it?"

"Absolutely. I've been thinking along those lines for several weeks now. You're not the first to mention this."

"She's waiting in the outer office to see you, did you know that?"

"Well, let's have her come in. I'll terminate her employment right now."

Charlotte Crawford gave neither Tom nor Emily a chance to speak when she barged in the door. She waved a newspaper clipping in front of their faces and shouted.

"I have the proof I need now! The child is the spawn of the devil! Just look at this—she's a murderer. I'll have her put away. And I'll sue this place for making me work with someone who's so dangerous!"

She glared at the two astonished people. "You can't deny she tried to kill me. She sent that rod after me like a demon from hell! I'll have your precious Institute in ruins before I'm through. I told the girl that, too! I told her and her mother."

Tom's eyebrows shot up. "You did what?"

Her eyes narrowed into a smirk. "Yes. Your prize pupil. Your hopes for immortality. You shouldn't have hoped for immortality through a devil, Mr. Tom Hamilton. I told Mrs. Livingston today when she picked the monster up. I've been checking into their background. Now I know what she's done. I showed her the clipping. Told her what I knew."

Tom was so furious he couldn't speak. Emily seized the opportunity to say something she'd been wanting to say for months.

"Sit down and shut up, Charlotte."

Charlotte looked at her, stunned at Emily's sudden outburst.

"I said sit down! And don't open your mouth until I'm through."

Charlotte obeyed, more out of disbelief than anything else.

"Who the hell do you think you are coming in here with accusations and threats? You can just count your lucky stars the Institute doesn't sue *you!*" Emily took a shot not quite in the dark. "There are several parents ready to testify that you have abused their children, Charlotte. You want a fight? Well, by God we'll give you one. You'll be lucky if you don't end up in jail."

She walked over to Charlotte and grabbed the clipping. One glance and she shoved it back. You call this proof that a child killed someone? You're even more stupid than I thought."

Emily stood there, seething. "How dare you threaten this man? How dare you threaten this Institute? Now get out of here before I call the police. And if I ever hear you've done *anything* with that ridiculous clipping, I'll have you arrested for child abuse. I swear I will."

Charlotte gasped and backed out of the room. Her face was twisted into a mask of terror.

Tom Hamilton looked at Emily in amazement.

"That was the most astonishing thing I've ever seen. How did you know that approach would work?"

Emily sat down, still so angry she was shaking. "I wasn't sure. But that woman is a coward, and my father always said that when you deal with cowards, the best defense is a good offense."

Tom Hamilton grinned and picked up the phone. He dialed the number at the Livingstons' apartment. The phone rang and rang. Over the next few days he tried many times. To no avail. He could find nothing of Sarah and her mother. Nor could he elicit any information from old June

Carver. She, too, seemed to have dropped off the face of the earth.

ST. LOUIS, MISSOURI
May, 1990

Dr. Emily Bronson ran her fingers over the desk that would soon belong to someone else. The scene with Charlotte Crawford had taken place in this very office. They'd never heard from Charlotte Crawford again. Unfortunately, the damage had been done. Neither did they ever hear from the Livingstons.

A deep friendship developed between Tom and herself over the years. It was based on mutual admiration and identical philosophies. Then, ten years ago, when Tom's wife became yet another victim to Alzheimer's and was institutionalized, Tom gradually turned to Emily for more than friendship.

Emily knew Tom had loved his wife deeply, understood the pain he felt watching her turn from a lovely, gracious lady, into a zombielike creature who needed constant supervision. Finally Tom had had to admit he was licked, that he could no longer care for his wife at home. The countless experts and clinics had made no difference. His children finally convinced him, fearful that if he kept up his day and night vigil, they would lose both a father and a mother.

It didn't seem strange to Dr. Bronson that at age sixty-four she was relegated to the roll of mistress. She resolved that issue years earlier. She

and Tom were companions, lovers, and friends.
Even now, with his health failing badly, the two
were youthful in their feelings for each other.
When he felt up to it, they played chess, talked
through the night, and once in a while, they even
made love.

One of their favorite topics was Sarah Livingston. They speculated on what had happened to
her, what her life had become. Through the Institute, they kept track of all the major psychics in
the world. To their knowledge, she never surfaced.

Emily had forgotten the newspaper clipping. It
had all been so long ago. What exactly had it said?
Something struck a chord. Perhaps she'd better
speak with Tom.

Chapter 13

Valerie Phelps paced back and forth in the enormous kitchen on the first floor. Twice she picked up the phone with the intention of calling Northside and speaking to Sarah Jamieson. Each time, she returned the phone to its stand. It was both terrifying and reassuring to learn that this counselor was a member of Fountain Head. Reassuring, because it made her feel less alone. Terrifying, because Fountain Head members dealt with Nigel every day. Sarah Jamieson surely had no suspicions that she'd been the caller. Surely not.

What in God's name could she do? Nigel needed help, there was no doubting it. Professional help. Their marriage had never been particularly good sexually, but at least Nigel treated her with respect. As the years passed, she'd turned more and more inward, to her music. She played better now, even, than during her years at Julliard.

Her music lacked fire then. Now it was as though everything lacking in the rest of her life came to life in her music. There was fire now, and soul. Pathos. Many things.

Her parents would never believe her. They worshipped the ground Nigel walked on. And the Phelps family had been friends with the Williamsons for over a century. She'd been the plain daughter, the one her father feared would remain at home, an old maid. When his best friend's son began showing interest in Valerie at long last, R. D. Williamson had been overjoyed. And Nigel played the role of loving husband well.

She was startled when she heard the car pull into the drive. Nigel wasn't due home for another half hour. She forced a smile when he walked into the kitchen.

"Fix me a drink, will you, Val? I'm bushed." He put his arm around his wife's shoulder as they walked into the den and over to the elaborately stocked bar. She mixed him a Chivas and water, then poured herself a small glass of Chateau Y'Quem. *Maybe tonight will be all right after all.* She handed the crystal glass to Nigel and noticed the tremors in his hand as he took the glass from her. He downed the drink quickly and asked her to mix him another. She did so without commenting, knowing it would set him off if she criticized him. He took the drink and walked over to the ornate bookcases lining the east wall. He ran a finger over the tops of the leather-bound books.

"Jesus Christ, Val. Didn't I tell you I wanted

Mrs. Gates to remove all these books and dust? Look at this mess. I suppose the library hasn't been touched either."

Val chose her words carefully. "Yes, honey. I told her this morning. She said she'd have time Thursday. It will take most of the day to remove and clean all the books. She had too many other things to finish today."

Nigel yanked several books from the shelf, throwing them on the floor. "I decide what gets done around here, not Mrs. Gates. Don't you have enough sense to make the maids do what I tell them, Valerie?" He tipped his glass and drained the last of his drink, spilling part of it down the front of his shirt. Val set her wine glass down and walked behind the bar, putting a little more distance between them. *Please, God. Don't let him start up. I don't think I can take it.*

Nigel watched her as she moved and the sound of her heels clicking on the oak floor excited him in a strange way. He crossed the room quickly, grabbed the Chivas, and poured himself another drink. Valerie wondered if he'd become an alcoholic. He'd never been such a heavy drinker.

He could see the fear she tried to mask. *Serves the bitch right. I'm tired of doing all the work, making all the decisions.*

He whirled and threw the Chivas against the wall behind the bar, missing Valerie's head by inches. "Damn you, Valerie! It's time you learned there's more to life than spending my money and playing that damned piano. You have duties as my wife. It's high time you learned them." He knew he was irrational, and he knew that he didn't give a damn.

"I'm going for a swim. I want you to get on that phone and tell Mrs. Gates she can come in early tomorrow if she wants to keep her job. Tell her this room is a goddamned pigsty. Do you think you can handle that? Or is it too complicated for you?"

He stalked out of the room.

Valerie waited until she heard the back door slam shut and she knew he was on his way to the pool. She snatched the small phone from the table next to the Steinway and dialed Northside.

Sarah was gathering her things to leave for the day when Sue Kline informed her that she had a phone call. "The lady wants to speak with you personally. She's pretty upset."

She picked up the receiver and punched into the blinking line. "This is Sarah." She recognized the voice immediately. The woman whose presence she'd felt at the Country Club. The woman with whom she'd spoken twice before.

"Sarah. Mrs. Jamieson—I don't know what to do. He's acting crazy. Worse than usual. I'm scared."

Sarah spoke quickly. "Get out of the house. Do it now, before you get hurt. Do you have a car?"

"Yes, of course. But I don't know if I can get to it without him stopping me. He's in the pool right now—but I doubt if he'll swim long."

"Where is the garage in relation to the pool?"

"They are both in back. But if I went around behind the pool house I might make it."

"Good. If your purse is handy, bring it. You may want to have your credit cards or some cash. If it isn't handy, forget it. We'll take care of anything you need. Now, is there a restaurant or a hospital close to your home?"

"Yes. Antoine's is a few miles down the road. It's—"

"I know exactly where it is. Go there. I have blond—I don't think I need to describe myself, do I?"

Valerie gasped. "Do you know who I am? Did you know me at the luncheon?"

Sarah realized her error. "I—I just suspected you might be there. If you heard about it, I mean. Never mind that now. Just get out of the house and get to Antoine's."

Valerie returned the phone to the stand. The small light for the extension stayed on. She froze. The phone by the pool. He'd been listening to see if she called Mrs. Gates. Forget the purse. Run to the car.

She raced through the kitchen, down the hall, and out the door. She yanked open the door to the garage. Nigel was waiting for her. The expression on Valerie's face pleased him. It registered stark terror.

Sarah felt something was wrong as she drove to Antoine's. When she arrived and found no one waiting, she was certain. The woman should have been here before she arrived.

No one had been there asking for her. In fact, the restaurant was almost empty, and waiters were busy setting up for the dinner crowd.

Sarah sat down and waited. Maybe the woman changed her mind. They often did. Sarah couldn't think what to do. She didn't know the woman's name or where she lived. Just knew it was in this area. Without any close contact, Sarah didn't think she could find her. Would the incident at Fountain Head be enough?

She walked over to one of the hostesses. "Could you direct me to the rest room?"

Valerie huddled in a daze on the bed. She couldn't believe it. Nigel was a raging lunatic. Whatever thin string of sanity he'd been holding on to had snapped; the man was totally mad. He didn't even seem to know who she was.

"You whore, Mellie! You won't ever laugh at me again!"

He was going to kill her. Why hadn't she asked for help months ago? Why hadn't she insisted Nigel get help? She knew the answer to that one. *Because nobody insists Nigel Phelps do anything.*

He had raped her twice and his teeth marks covered Valerie's breasts and stomach. She'd finally stopped screaming, because the screams only seemed to spur him on. He was crying now. Caressing her face gently.

"I'm sorry, Mellie. I never meant to hurt you."

"Nigel, please. Listen to me. I'm not Mellie. I'm Valerie, your wife. Nigel, please remember!"

He looked at her with surprise. "Val?" His face

twisted into anger. "Val! You were going to leave me! You called and told someone about me! You're just like Mellie! She was going to tell people, too. And she paid for it." He paced around the room. "Just like you're going to have to pay now, Val. You can't be trusted."

He picked up a crystal candlestick from the dresser and smashed the long end against the wall. Valerie watched in horror as Nigel looked longingly at the jagged edge.

"Spread your legs, Val. You want a man? I'll show you how good it can be." He smiled. "You'll love the feeling, Valerie. You'll be completely satisfied." His expression changed once again to fury. "You'll die a whore's death—"

Valerie screamed in terror and blacked out into a blessed unconsciousness.

The force of Sarah's first blow knocked him off his feet and the crystal candlestick flew across the floor. He scrambled up, staggering toward the bed, his hand outstretched. The pain in his chest was unbearable.

"Val—" He fell to the floor, understanding that he was going to die. He welcomed it.

Sarah leaned back against the stall. The woman was hurt, but there was nothing she could do. She couldn't call an ambulance—she had no address. She hoped the woman could do it herself.

Valerie slowly regained consciousness and stared at her husband's lifeless body. Carefully, she crept from the bed and edged toward him. His chest was crushed in. *My God! What happened?* Someone must have come into the house and heard her screams. Someone killed him.

Her mind sped in a hundred directions as she reached for the phone to call 911. She looked at the crusted blood on her breasts and stomach. Generations of breeding stopped her. She couldn't bring herself to do it. To muddy his name now.

Valerie Phelps put the phone down. *This is one last thing I will do for you, Nigel.*

She limped to the bathroom and showered. Painfully, she dressed in a long-sleeved shirt and pants. She combed her hair and applied fresh makeup. Then she stripped the bloody sheets from the bed and replaced them. From one of the guest bedrooms, she brought a suitcase and placed the soiled sheets and the candlestick inside, careful to pick up the shards from beside the dresser. She carried the suitcase to the storeroom and put it behind a stack of boxes. Then she went back and surveyed the room. One final thing.

She swung back the oil painting from the wall and opened the wall safe. There was almost a thousand dollars in cash. She wiped the safe clean and left it standing open. Downstairs, she picked up one of the leather-bound books and stuck the hundred-dollar bills between its pages. She replaced the rest of the books and swept up the broken crystal glass.

She sat down at the Steinway and began to play. She'd have to say she was here, playing her piano. Nigel had been swimming, and he must have come up the back stairs to dress. Someone must have broken in and surprised him. *Why would anyone want to kill my husband? He was such a good man. And for what? A thousand dollars? That's about what was in the safe. He'd have given them the money. They didn't have to kill him.*

The music calmed her. She took a deep breath and picked up the small phone. This time she made the call.

Jason Links and Max Killen walked into the kitchen of the Phelps' home. They could hear the sounds of the growing crowd of reporters and curiosity hounds outside the house.

"It's all over the radio now," Jason said. "I'm going to have to make a statement soon. What do you think? Is she telling the truth?"

Max hesitated. "I get the feeling she's holding something back. Did you see how she kept clinching her hands?"

"Well, that would be natural. She just found her husband murdered. But her story sounds a little forced. Almost like she rehearsed it."

"There's no doubt that this is the work of our pal the avenger?"

Links grunted. "Not as far as Joe's concerned. He says the body is in the exact condition as the others."

"Maybe she's afraid to finger the guy. Scared he'll come back for her."

"The thing that bothers me is that she denies that Phelps was ever abusive. If that's so, we have a whole new ballgame on our hands."

Max nodded. "I guess you were right, Captain. The avenger has gone off on his own now. He's really on a rampage."

Links stopped himself from saying "I told you so." Instead, he said, "Let's bring her into the kitchen. Maybe she'll open up more if it's just the two of us." He sat down at the huge glass-topped table and looked around the room. It was disconcerting to find himself in one room that would encompass his own living room, dining room, kitchen, and downstairs bath. Big money. It reminded him of the coming furor. Nigel Phelps. Killed by the man an inept Kansas City police force seemed unable to catch.

Max returned with Valerie Phelps. *She looks tired*, Links thought. *Tired and just about at the end of her rope.* He noted her face. It was blotched, swollen. As if she'd been crying for hours. He tried to remember if she'd broken down during her statement. He thought not.

"Mrs. Phelps," he began. "I hate to make you go through all this again, but I need it to be fresh in your mind. Uh, would you like me to make you some coffee? You look like you're about ready to collapse."

Her voice shook. "Yes, Captain. I'm sorry. I should have thought of coffee for your men. They've been here for a long time now. They probably need some, too."

"Don't worry about them. It's you I'm concerned about. Just show me the percolator, and I'll get some coffee started."

She walked over to the cabinet and opened a

door, exposing an elaborate coffee-making system. She pushed a button. "Coffee will be ready in a couple of minutes."

He heard the soft whir of a grinder and knew the coffee would be fresh, too.

She sat down at the table, her hands shaking violently.

Links decided the questioning could wait until she had a cup of coffee and settled down a bit. "Mrs. Phelps, is there anyone you need to call? Family? Friends? You really should have someone with you."

"Yes. I guess I should call my parents. They're in New York on business. Probably staying at the Plaza. And Nigel's mother and father—that's going to be difficult. They're on a cruise. I have the itinerary somewhere." Her voice broke. "This will kill Nigel's father. He's in poor health—" She covered her face with her hands. "I can't believe this. What could have—" She stopped. *What could have caused him to go crazy?* That's what she'd been about to say. "What could have killed him? Who could have done such a horrible thing?"

Links knew she'd somehow shifted gears, had started to say something else. "Would you like me to call your family doctor?"

She was obviously startled at the suggestion. "No!" She recovered her composure quickly. "No, Captain. That won't be necessary."

"I'll leave an officer here tonight, Mrs. Phelps. Unless you want to stay with a friend."

"No. I have no—" She stopped. Links knew what she'd been about to say. *I have no friends.*

She continued, shifting gears once again. "I think I'll go to a hotel."

Links felt sorry for the woman. All the money in the world and she didn't even have anywhere to go, any friend she could stay with on the night her husband had been brutally murdered. It didn't seem right.

Valerie located Nigel's parents' itinerary and wrote down her own parents' names. She stared at the papers, trembling. "I don't know if I can do it. Call them, I mean. I just don't know."

Links took the papers and handed them to Max. "Have Steve make the calls. Tell him Mrs. Phelps' parents are probably staying at the Plaza in New York, and the victim's parents are on a cruise." He glanced down at the itinerary. "Somewhere in the Northwest Passage." He turned back to Valerie.

"Steve Jeffries is a good man, Mrs. Phelps. He'll break this news as gently as possible."

She went to the counter and poured three cups of coffee. "Are you sure your men wouldn't like some coffee, Captain?"

He was amazed at her control. This was finishing-school training at its height. "When we're finished talking, Mrs. Phelps. Then we'll go back in the den, and they can serve themselves."

She nodded and took a tentative sip of her coffee. "I'm really feeling much better now. Go ahead and ask me whatever you need to know."

Links glanced at his notebook. "Just start from the beginning. Approximately what time did your husband get home?"

"About five, I believe. It was a little earlier than usual."

"Did he seem out of sorts? Worried? As if anything was unusual?"

"No." The answer was too abrupt.

Links watched her fumble with the coffee cup. "What did you do when he got home?"

"Oh, we had cocktails—then Nigel wanted to swim. He liked to unwind that way."

"How many drinks did you have?"

She shrugged. "I don't really remember. I had a glass of wine and Nigel had scotch. Two, maybe three."

"And how long did you both stay there in the den?"

She frowned. What had she told them before? She couldn't remember. "I don't know for sure. Maybe an hour." In reality, it had taken Nigel less than thirty minutes to down the drinks. But she didn't want them thinking he was a lush. She had extra time to account for, anyway.

"Then what happened?"

"He decided to take the swim. That's the last I saw of him until I went upstairs."

"He didn't have any phone calls? Nothing to indicate he might be expecting someone?"

"No. There were no calls. He wasn't expecting anyone. Nigel would never have greeted a guest in swim trunks."

"You didn't accompany your husband to the pool area?"

"No. I stayed in the den. I wanted to practice my piano."

"And you heard nothing? Nothing at all?"

"The den is soundproof, Captain. Nigel had it done because of the piano. It—" She stopped. *It drove him crazy.*

"Yes?" Links urged her to continue.

"It helps me to have no outside noise when I practice."

"Mrs. Phelps, I'm going to have to ask you something personal, and I hope it won't upset you." Links sighed, knowing full well it would upset her. "Did your husband ever abuse you? Harm you in any way? Specifically, did he harm you tonight?"

Her hand flew to the high-necked shirt she wore. *God! How could they know?* "Why, no," she stammered. "Why would you think such a thing?"

"Because the man who killed your husband is without a doubt the same man who has killed two other men recently. Both men were wife-beaters. Violent men who landed their wives in hospitals." He leaned forward. "Have you ever had any contact with Northside Crisis Center?"

Her mind whirled furiously. Had she ever given them her name? A telephone number? *No. Never. Not even tonight when she talked to Sarah. They could never prove she'd made the call, even if Sarah Jamieson said so.*

"Captain, surely you don't think a woman in my position would have need to call a women's shelter?" *The check stubs. She'd given Sarah a check for a hundred dollars.* "I—I donated some money to one of the centers. The Country Club women are interested, you know."

He nodded, noting her agitation and nervous hands. "Well, why don't you go back in the den, Mrs. Phelps. I know how exhausted you must be. I'll have my men out of there in a few minutes."

She put her coffee cup on the counter and slowly, as if she were in physical pain, walked from the room. Links looked at Max.

"What do you think? She seemed pretty upset that we might suspect she'd been abused." He shook his head. "I can't help feeling sorry for the woman. You'd think she'd have *some* friend she could call."

"It reminds me of something Sarah Jamieson told me, Captain. She said abused women cut themselves off from their friends."

Links rubbed his chin and stared at the door where Valerie Phelps had just disappeared.

Chapter 14

Sarah sat alone in the living room. She'd some-how made it through the evening meal, sent Paul off to a political meeting and the kids off to bed. The normal evening chatter had nearly driven her over the edge.

Mom, we have a game tomorrow. Did you wash my uniform?

Mom, we're having an art show next week. Mrs. Lindquist wants you to make cookies.

Hon, have you seen my files on the Edgemont case? I thought I left them on the desk.

Sure you don't want to come along? Might be some interesting people there. Not like the usual social bullshit.

Couldn't they see what was happening? Couldn't anybody see that she was in trouble? She sat with her long legs curled up in the chair. She pulled the robe tightly against her in a gesture that seemed to indicate she could keep everything from touching her if she could form a small enough ball in the large chair.

Why haven't they been here? Why hasn't Jason

called? Surely he knew Valerie Phelps had called her.

The story had dominated the ten o'clock news. There were no details of the actual death, just the statement that he'd been brutally murdered. Then extensive footage of Nigel Phelps and his many good works. Films of his family's far-flung financial empire, interests that ranged from cosmetics to car manufacturing. "Tonight," the anchorman said, "America has lost one of its giants."

Bullshit! The man was crazy! He was coming at her with a broken candlestick!

Maybe Jason was already putting together a case against her. Maybe that's why he hadn't called and asked any questions. Wouldn't they at least call to verify that Valerie Phelps had called her? Unanswered questions went round and round in her head.

When Paul came home she listened as he told her of his nearly assured political future. She followed him to bed, and felt the heat from his body wash over her as he pulled her close. Sarah pushed tighter against the haven of his warm body, a haven that might be short-lived.

She slept fitfully at first, waking several times with disconnected dreams she couldn't quite remember. Fragments, leaving her with the uneasy feeling that it was important to remember. At last she fell into a deep slumber.

She was in a yellow room. A yellow room with blue lace curtains covering the windows. The curtains were blowing gently from air circulated by a large brown floor fan in the corner. There was music, a man's voice singing, ". . . when whip-poorwills call, and evening is nigh." Sarah stood looking at the naked yellow walls and watched as red flowers began appearing on the yellow paint. She walked over and put her hand on the wall. The flowers were warm and wet. She looked at her fingers. They were covered with blood. Some-one was screaming. A woman. Then a man screamed. Sarah covered her ears, but she could still hear the screams. The man sounded in agony. The music kept going on and on. ". . . my blue heaven, my blue heaven."

Someone was shaking her. "Sarah. Wake up! Listen to this. Northside is off the hook."

Sarah forced herself out of the nightmare and opened her eyes. Paul was standing over her, newspaper in hand. "Wh-what are you talking about?"

He spread the newspaper in front of her. "Read it for yourself. Nigel Phelps was killed last night. They know it was the avenger, but this time there's no connection. Jason must have been right in the first place. This guy is no good Samaritan. Phelps' wife was not an abused woman. So maybe now the police will be off your backs."

"What?" She was fully awake now. "Let me see the paper." Her eyes flew over the front-page article. There was no mention of Valerie Phelps' call for help. No mention that she'd been beaten. According to the article she'd been in another room during the attack, playing the piano. The killing had the same M.O. as other avenger killings. Only this time robbery was a factor.

How did she do it? And why? Why would she lie to the police?

Sarah's eyes filled with tears as she reached for her husband. "Oh, Paul. Hold me. Just hold me. Make everything go away."

Surprised, he took her in his arms. "Hey—don't let this upset you. You won't have to put up with Max and his crew any longer. That's good news." He stroked her hair. "Listen, I know you felt the avenger was just out there protecting women. I did, too. We were wrong, that's all. He's nothing more than a serial killer."

Paul climbed back in bed with her. He pulled her close and began stroking her arm. "This will all be over soon, honey. Jason will get this guy. You know him. Jason never gives up."

The thought didn't comfort her.

"Well, what do you think, Joe?" Links had finished reading the Medical Examiner's report and phoned the man at his office in Truman Memorial.

"Just like I said in my report, Jason. Body was in more or less the same condition as in the other killings. Burst heart. Crushed chest. But there's a couple of big differences. Phelps had had sex shortly before he was killed. Christ, did he ever have sex. There were traces of semen from his knees to his upper chest. Could have been smeared during the fight, I guess. But I doubt it. This was quick as hell."

"How do you figure that?"

Joe Turner cleared his throat, and continued. "Well, the body wasn't battered as badly as Simmons or Merit. Actually there has been a pattern developing ever since Simmons. Merit was obviously killed quicker than Simmons. Phelps was killed quicker than Merit. Looks like the avenger is killing more and enjoying it less." He snickered.

"Don't go out boozing with Charlie Kaufman, Joe. Your attempts at humor would leave the Kansas City newspaper readers cold."

"There's something else, Jason. I didn't have this information until this morning, but I think we have a blood type on your man. Phelps had blood on his hands, not his type, either. In fact, the odd thing here is that it looks like the financial mogul put up a better fight than even Jack Simmons did. Interesting considering he was kind of a lightweight. The little guy must have been a hell of a scrapper. He even had traces of blood in crevices between his teeth. Strange that the avenger didn't break him up worse than he did."

"You're sure this *is* the work of this so-called avenger?"

"Oh, yeah. Not a doubt. Chest crushed exactly the same. Heart. Everything matches. Except that the killer got hurt this time. And Jason, uh, want some advice?"

Here it comes. Links sighed and settled back for a theory. "Sure, Joe."

"Your boy just may require medical attention. Human bites are the worse kind of bite there is.

I'd take a Doberman sinking his teeth into my arm over a human being. The chance for massive infection is strong. I've seen people on intravenous antibiotics because of human bites. You might check with emergency-room personnel."

Links thanked him and hung up.

So where the shit does that leave us? Phelps had sex just before he was attacked? *Jesus.* Either the guy was one brazen son of a bitch, or Valerie Phelps was lying. What a guy. If he did entertain someone in his own house, in the bedroom he and his wife shared, then fought the avenger hard enough to get blood between his teeth, Nigel Phelps was a dark horse indeed.

Max listened with growing interest. "But why would she lie, Captain? So what if she did have sex with her husband earlier? And believe me, considering the reports we've got on Nigel Phelps, he would not entertain some broad in his wife's bedroom. He was one conservative character. A card-carrying stuffed shirt.

"I have no idea why she'd lie, unless she knew the killer."

Max frowned. "Is Joe absolutely sure this was the work of the avenger? Could it be a copycat killing? Somebody wanted Phelps dead and used the avenger's M.O.?"

Links shook his head. "I don't see how. The papers never got wind of the fact that the chests were all crushed with equal pressure applied on all sides. According to Joe, that's damn near an impossibility. And Phelps' chest was exactly the same. But somehow he hurt the guy. Who'd have figured that?"

"Well, you sure pegged one thing right, Captain."

"Yeah? What was that?"

"Public sentiment. The same folks who thought we should deputize the avenger day before yesterday want our heads on a platter this morning."

They drove to the Plaza, arriving at The Alameda only to find that Valerie Phelps had checked out early. The desk clerk had no information, but the bell captain told Links that an elderly couple had arrived in a limousine and whisked Mrs. Phelps away just before eight o'clock.

The door of the Phelps mansion was answered by a woman in her mid-fifties. She identified herself as Mrs. Gates, the housekeeper.

"That poor dear woman. I felt so sorry for her. Looked like she hadn't had any sleep at all. I don't care how fancy that hotel is—nothing beats sleeping in your own bed." She hesitated. "Of course, after what happened—"

Links nodded. "Have Mrs. Phelps' parents arrived?"

"Oh, yes. They're all upstairs. Over in the other wing, of course. Not—" She stalled again. "I hope you catch that monster who killed the Mister. It's not safe to be in your own home these days."

Links assured her that they were doing everything possible.

"It's always a shock, ma'am," Max began. "When someone you know is killed suddenly—and if it's murder, well—"

Links was glad he had Max accompany him. He could see that Mrs. Gates was warming to the young man.

"It certainly was. I lived right here with them for almost five years. Then Mr. Phelps decided they didn't need me so much of the time. I moved in with my daughter and her family. But you know, the Mister never cut my wages at all. He was so generous."

Real generous, Links thought. *Took away the room and board and didn't even cut your wages.*

Mrs. Gates wiped a tear from one of her red-rimmed eyes. "I just can't believe he's dead, God rest his soul. Poor Mrs. Phelps. I don't know how she'll get along without him."

She opened the door wider and asked the men to step inside. Once again the two found themselves sitting at the enormous glass-topped kitchen table with cups of freshly brewed coffee in front of them.

"Mrs. Gates," Links began the questioning. "What time did you leave yesterday?"

"Four-thirty. Mr. Phelps is real insistent that the help arrive on time and leave on time. Punctual, that's what he is." She stopped short. "Was. I can't get used to it."

"Are you the only help they have?" Max smiled and took a sip of the delicious coffee.

She shook her head emphatically. "Land no. There's Mrs. Josephs. She comes in a little later.

I'm in charge though. Mr. Phelps likes—liked— things just so. He trusted me to see to it that things were like he wanted them. Very particular, he was."

Links picked up on the comment. "So Mr. Phelps pretty much ran the house? Not Mrs. Phelps?"

Mrs. Gates stopped, startled. "Well, I guess you could say that. The Misses is kind of artistic, you might say. Could have been a concert pianist I think. She's not as fussy as the Mister. So I make sure everything's done proper, for him." She shook her head again. "Poor dear. I just can't imagine what she'll do without him."

Probably breathe, Links was tempted to say. "Is Mrs. Phelps able to talk to us this morning, Mrs. Gates?"

"The sooner we can get all the facts the sooner we can catch this guy," Max added.

"Oh, yes. I understand. Of course, I'll go get her right now. She's holding up real good considering."

Valerie Phelps entered the den with a couple Links took to be in their late seventies. Both were well preserved, as the rich very often are.

"Captain, this is my father, R. D. Williamson. My mother, Anne."

R. D. Williamson immediately took charge. "Captain, I hope you have some ideas as to who might have done this. I can't believe that someone could break into a house in this neighborhood and murder a man in his bedroom."

"We're trying, Mr. Williamson—"

"A man like Nigel Phelps. I've known him since he was a boy, Captain. The Phelps family is one of the most respected in this country." The elderly man was adamant. "God knows how Nigel's parents will take this. Conrad Phelps is one of my closest friends. Our families have been in business together for almost two hundred years."

He paced over to the Steinway and back again, shaking his head. Links was watching Valerie Phelps and the odd expression on her face. He couldn't peg it. R. D. Williamson continued his eulogy. "We couldn't have asked for a better son-in-law. Kind. Considerate. Gave Val everything." He cleared his throat. "My daughter was a lucky woman to have had Nigel Phelps pick her for his wife."

This time there was no mistaking the expression on Valerie's face. It literally screamed, *Bullshit.*

Links got down to business. "Yes, I'm sure that's true, Mr. Williamson. Now, we need to speak with your daughter. I'm sure you understand this has to be private."

"But, I see no need—" Mrs. Williamson fluttered.

"It's perfectly all right, Mother." Valerie was soft-spoken, but firm. "I'll be just fine."

Reluctantly, the Williamsons left the room. Valerie's mother took a fearful last look at her daughter, as if she thought the officers were going to shine a light in her eyes and hit her with rubber hoses.

"They're just concerned about me," Valerie

explained, sitting down in one of the Chippendale chairs and motioning for the two men to do the same. Her hands no longer trembled.

Links opened the file folder and glanced over it. Finally he looked up. "Mrs. Phelps, there are a few discrepancies I've got to get cleared up. I'm afraid I'm going to have to ask you something that is of a very private nature." He glanced over at Max, who continued to keep his head turned toward a window. "Mrs. Phelps, according to this report, your husband had engaged in sexual intercourse shortly before his death. Yet—"

"Oh. I guess I forgot to mention that, Captain," she said, cringing inwardly. "Though I can't imagine what that has to do with the killing."

"It probably has nothing to do with the killing, Mrs. Phelps. That is, if the person he had intercourse with was you."

"Well, of course it was me." She was abrupt, sitting a little straighter in the chair.

Links nodded and made a notation. "One thing puzzles me. You said you didn't see your husband after he went swimming. Any traces of semen should have been washed off his body if that's true."

They know. They know I'm lying. She stood up in what she hoped was a haughty enough manner. "Gentlemen, I have no idea what you're talking about. I consider it inappropriate and crude, as a matter of fact. Perhaps Nigel didn't actually take a swim. Maybe he changed his mind. Or maybe he never even got to the pool. What difference is it anyway? You say this man has killed two other men—I should think you would have better things to concern yourselves with than whether or not my husband and I had—marital relations."

Links started to speak, but she quickly interrupted. "Now, Captain, I really am feeling quite tired. I don't think I can answer any more questions now. Mrs. Gates will show you out."

She was out of the room before either man could issue a protest.

Jason Links pulled his car into the parking lot at the Rusty Scupper and stretched as he got out. "It's after 2:00. Hopefully, we've missed the lunch crowd."

They entered the dimly lit building and found a quiet table in the rear. Max started talking first.

"You know, Captain, she's right about one thing. Phelps probably just didn't go swimming. Either he changed his mind, or he never made it to the pool. I don't see that it makes any real difference. Mrs. Phelps couldn't have known the killer. I just don't buy that. She'd never know the same people who might know Simmons or Merit."

"I know, I know," Links agreed. "But the woman's holding something back—" The waitress arrived and his train of thought was broken. Later, as Links was contentedly sipping his iced tea, he picked it back up again.

"I know Mrs. Phelps is covering up something. It seems to me that it's got to be the battered-wife angle. I keep going back to that. Of course, there's no tie to Northside that we know of. Except the donation she made. That might mean something. But did you notice the amount of makeup she's worn every time we've seen her? That lady doesn't strike me as a woman who slathers on pancake. And I've noticed she wears long sleeves and high-necked blouses. Might not mean anything, and it might mean she's covering up bruises. I want her medical records checked for unexplained injuries." He paused and narrowed his eyes. "Also, for blood type. I'm going to have Joe try to match it with the blood on Phelps. Maybe he didn't fight the avenger after all. And if he did inflict injuries on his wife, according to Joe, she may need medical attention very soon."

Max stirred more sugar into his tea. "She might be trying to shield her old man. Publicity and all. If so, I guess you know what that means. It means the avenger is getting a bad rap. He—"

"Hello, boys. What's this about the avenger getting a bad rap? Are you keeping something from the press?" Charlie Kaufman was standing by the table, a menu in hand. "Mind if I join you," he said with a quick grin. "I hate dining alone."

Jason forced a smile. "Why no, Charlie. The Kansas City police always welcome members of the press."

"Sure, Links." Charlie settled in and waved to a waitress. "So what's this about the avenger getting a bad rap?"

"Maybe we don't know Phelps' killer *is* the avenger, Charlie." Links' voice was cold. "Maybe we don't even know there is such a person as the avenger. Maybe that's a Charlie Kaufman fantasy."

"Shit." Kaufman snorted. "It's a bitch, all right. 'Course, I personally know who's doing the killings. Got a hot tip a few weeks ago."

"Is that so?" Links scowled. "And you've been keeping this choice morsel to yourself, huh? Maybe we should run you in for withholding evidence."

Charlie laughed. "You wish. Nah, I got this great letter though. Two of 'em, actually. This old bat in a nursing home. Says she knows exactly who's doing the killing and she can prove it." He accepted a Budweiser from the waitress and took a quick swig. "Hold on to your hat, Links. It's a little girl. Old lady swears it. And get this. She says the kid does it with her mind. A real witchcraft deal." He chuckled. "There you have it, boys. Scoop of the year. Hop out and find—let's see, what's the kid's name? Uh, Livingston. Sarah Livingston. Find her, Captain, and you've got your 'avenger.'"

Links slowly set his sandwich back on the plate. *Sarah Livingston.* He knew the name. Dr. Bronson's miracle child. He could hear Emily Bronson's words. *Sarah did that. She was angry at one of the instructors and twisted the rod until it was red-hot.*

Links forced himself to bite into his sandwich again. Edna Litvak. *Another mind is at work. It's far more powerful than mine.*

"That's quite a story, Charlie," Links said casually. "I'm surprised you haven't followed up on it."

"Yeah, well, I did just that, Links. When I got the first letter. That's why I'm a good newsman. Never discount a lead. I figured, 'What the hell?' Worth a phone call to St. Louis. So I call this nursing home, and they tell me this old bag's off her rocker. Been screaming about this kid named Sarah for years. I figured that would be the end of it. But I heard from the old broad again. Loony as a tune."

Jason kept his voice natural. "So who is this old woman, our star witness?" He forced a chuckle. "We may get her here to testify."

Charlie took another swig of Bud. "Uh, Crawford. Charlotte Crawford. Yep. Loony as a damn tune."

Links was silent as he drove back to the station house. Max finally spoke.

"What is it, Captain? That tale Charlie told?"

Links shook his head. "I don't know," he said slowly. "I just don't know."

He sat down at his desk and tapped a pencil on a blank legal pad, then started to write.

1. No physical evidence—Simmons and Merit. (Check with Joe—blood samples on Phelps' hands and teeth.)

2. Witnesses swear they saw no one. *Are they lying!*

3. What could crush a human being the way these men were crushed?

4. Edna.

"Shit!" Links crumbled the paper and tossed it into the trash can. *I'm grasping at straws. There's no damned way I'm going to suck into this bullshit theory.* Jason Links thought about the facts in the case and wished he still smoked.

The nurse led him down a wide hallway, warning him as they walked along. "Now, Mrs. Crawford is a handful, at best. She's gone downhill badly these past few years. I don't think she even knows what she's saying half the time. Are you a relative?"

"No," Jason Links answered. "Just a friend."

"Charlotte?" The nurse stuck her head in the door. "Charlotte, you have a visitor."

Links looked at the withered body bent over in the chair and once again wondered what the hell he was doing at this place. It hadn't taken many calls to track her down. *To track down a wild goose chase*, he thought. He closed the door and walked over to the old woman. "Mrs. Crawford? I'm Jason Links. Captain Links, with the Kansas City police force. I was wondering if I might talk with you for a few minutes."

She turned her steely eyes toward him. "It's about time. I've been waiting for weeks. Is that devil child behind bars yet? Ought to be—" She raised a shaky hand and shook her finger at him.

"*Ought to be!* Put the brat away, where she can't hurt anybody anymore."

"Why don't you tell me about her, Mrs. Crawford. You say her name is Sarah Livingston?"

"That's right. Sarah. She's the one who's doing it. Killing everybody. Wicked. That's what she is." She closed her eyes.

"How do you know that, Mrs. Crawford? How do you know this Sarah Livingston is killing people?"

The old woman opened her eyes. A bony hand went to her head. She ran her fingers across a faint scar. "See this? She did this. She put her devil mark on me. I'm lucky I'm not dead, like the others."

Links began to think it was useless. He'd been stupid to come. "Like what others, Mrs. Crawford," he asked wearily. "Anyone else besides the men in Kansas City?"

She narrowed her eyes and spoke in a hoarse croak. "Her father, of course. I've told you that a hundred times! She killed her father. Just like she killed those others. The police couldn't figure it out. But I did. She did it with her wicked little mind. Work of the devil, I tell you! Just like the devil's mark she put on me." Once again her pale hand, road mapped with knotted veins, brushed across her forehead.

"When did this happen, Mrs. Crawford? Exactly when did Sarah Livingston kill her father?"

"It's been weeks ago! If you'd come when I told you to, you might have caught her! Now she's run away. If you get her, be careful. You'll be like the others—think she's not evil because she's just a child. She'll fool you, too."

Links shook his head in despair. Charlie Kaufman had been right. The old woman was senile. Still, the name Sarah Livingston had popped up twice in relation to the case. Why? Damned if he knew.

"Well, thank you for your help, Mrs. Crawford. What you've told me is very valuable." He turned to leave.

"Wait!" Her gnarled hand reached out for his. "You haven't seen my evidence. My proof." She opened an old Bible on the nightstand and removed a worn, yellowed newspaper clipping. Her eyes turned shrewd. "You'll see."

Jason carefully took the clipping, which appeared on the verge of disintegrating.

No Clues in East St. Louis Killing

Police are still baffled over the condition of a man found beaten to death Wednesday in an East St. Louis apartment. Glenn Livingston, 28, of 2538 W. 15th Avenue, was apparently the victim of a brutal assault only a short time after he had beaten his wife, Beatrice Livingston, 25, into a state of unconsciousness.

Livingston, who had two previous arrests for abuse, was found with the upper torso crushed, heart ruptured, and jaw broken in three places. Chief Medical Examiner Wallace Kelly cannot account for the complete lack of abrasions found on the victim's body. "I've never seen anything like it," Kelly commented at the crime scene. "The man had been beaten as badly as I've ever seen, but there's not a scratch or a cut on him. It beats me."

Livingston's body was discovered by police after a neighbor heard sounds of violence coming from the apartment. Officers broke down the door only to find the unconscious Mrs. Livingston, her husband's battered body, and the couple's three-year-old daughter, Sarah. Unharmed, the child was found sitting on the floor next to her mother's body.

Homicide investigators suspect the assailant knew the family, since the door to the apartment was locked and showed no signs of forced entry. An unidentified informant has told the Post Dispatch that police are further puzzled by the lack of physical evidence found at the scene.

Mrs. Livingston remains in critical condition.

Links stood transfixed. There could be no mistaking the similarities. Not that he believed that a three-year-old child had killed her father with her mind, then gone on to a career of killing wife-beaters.

But there was a connection somewhere.

"Mrs. Crawford, would you mind if I took this clipping with me?"

Her face twisted into an insane snarl. "No! You mustn't take it! It's my only proof. I have to have it—show the world what a wicked child Sarah is.

She'll come after me now. I know it. I have to have the proof." She was fully roused now. "You've got to find her. She'll do it again. She's a killer."

Charlotte pulled her shawl tightly around her shoulders.

Links removed his notebook from his back pocket and jotted down the information. He could stop by the *Post-Dispatch* and get another copy. Then he'd pay another visit to the Hamilton Institute.

It took him almost an hour to drive into St. Louis proper and find the offices of the *Post-Dispatch*. Links parked the car and headed for the records department. The young woman punched the data into the computer and Links soon had a printout. Glenn Livingston had died on May 12, 1955. The daughter would be around thirty-eight years old now. There were several more items regarding the Livingston death, but they all boiled down to one thing. The crime had gone unsolved.

Links paid the woman for his copies and asked for directions to the Bureau of Records. Mrs. Beatrice Livingston had dropped from sight in 1956. She had been employed as a domestic and had received her late husband's Social Security benefits. Those benefits had not been touched since November, 1956.

Jason Links was anxious to return to the Hamilton Institute. He couldn't remember exactly what Dr. Bronson had told him about the child. They'd lost track of her. Moved heaven and earth to find her. Little Sarah Livingston just might have a powerful enough mind to hypnotize witnesses. To block Edna Litvak. And she might carry a burning hatred for battering men. Could the person who killed Glenn Livingston still be living? No. If he was still alive he'd be far too old. But someone knew how he'd done it. How he'd pulverized a man and caused his heart to explode.

Links crossed town and headed west on I-70. He hadn't called for an appointment with Emily Bronson, thinking it might be better to catch her unaware. Maybe she was holding back something. Might be afraid of making the Institute look bad.

Once again, he drove up the winding, tree-lined road that led to the Institute. He parked the car and went inside. This time he didn't go directly to the director's office, but wound through the halls until he located the lounge where the Sarah Livingston shrine was located.

His eyes immediately went to the steel bar, twisted like a paper straw, hanging in the showcase. A chill went up his spine as he examined the bar more closely. An inch and a half of solid steel. Could this really have happened? Would an Institute with the reputation of Hamilton stage something like this? Links' eyes narrowed as he read the account of the child's feat.

The subject, Sarah Livingston, age four, twisted this solid steel bar on November 17, 1956. In one of the most amazing examples of psychokinesis ever recorded, Livingston forced the bar into the air, twisted it until the object was white-hot, and sent it sailing across the room. The subject never duplicated this feat while at the Institute. Witnesses to the incident were Dr. Samuel Peterson, Assistant Director, Hamilton Institute, and Mrs. Charlotte Crawford, Chairman, Children's Division.

Links didn't think any hoax had been perpetrated. He looked at the many pictures of the child. A sweet, innocent face surrounded by a mass of blond hair. There were other articles in the various showcases. In one case was a Raggedy Ann doll and an account of the child's bringing a doll from one room to the other simply by willing it to come. Another case held a set of dice and an account of her psychokinetic powers in moving them to specific numbers. Yet another story told of the child's ability to hold a table off the ground for an indefinite time period.

"They've documented her well," Links said to himself. But there was nothing that helped him learn what he needed to know. Nothing that led him to a giant of a man who crushed people he didn't like. Links wasn't buying the psychic killer theory. It was too farfetched. Not even farfetched. Impossible.

"Well, Captain, I see our little Sarah haunts you." Emily Bronson spoke from behind him. "What brings you back so soon?"

He turned and smiled. "Dr. Bronson. Good to see you."

"Have you made any progress with the hypnosis theory?"

He shook his head. "I'm not sure if I'm talking about hypnosis or just what. I want some information on Sarah Livingston." He took the plunge. "Did the Livingston girl ever injure anyone while she was here?"

Dr. Bronson hesitated. "Uh, no, Captain. What makes you ask that?"

He knew the signs. The forced smile, the averted eyes. She was lying.

"I'm not at liberty to say. But I need to know anything you can tell me about Sarah Livingston. Please don't try to cover up anything that might have happened here years ago. I can tell you this much. I have reason to believe someone she knows is involved in several murders. Sarah Livingston may or may not be involved. Doctor, I don't want to have to ask you these questions at police headquarters."

She nodded resignedly. "Of course. I'll tell you everything I know. Give you any help you need. Let's go back to my office."

He followed her down the hall.

"Now, Captain," she said, waving him to a seat. "The reason I said Sarah had never hurt anyone here is that there is no actual proof that the child meant to cause harm. The chairman—we say 'chairperson' in this day and age—of the Children's Division, Charlotte Crawford, insisted Sarah meant to hurt her. Dr. Peterson, who witnessed the incident, believed the metal bar just got away from the child.

"You see, Captain, we try to screen our staff thoroughly. But once in a while, well, a teacher turns out to be unsuited for the job. Charlotte Crawford was one. She was unsatisfactory, a very disturbed woman who took out her frustrations on the children. Unfortunately, we didn't realize it before she and Sarah tangled."

"Obviously a mistake on Mrs. Crawford's part," Links said quickly. "What did the child have to say about it?"

Emily Bronson thought back to those first months when she arrived at Hamilton. "I wasn't really involved with Sarah then, Captain. But from what Mr. Hamilton said later, I believe Sarah was very upset. It's difficult, you see, with children. We couldn't know if Sarah *directed* the bar at Charlotte, or if she just 'wished' something would happen to the woman. Every small child has had similar wishes—but when a child like Sarah—well, I'm sure you understand. According to Dr. Peterson, Charlotte kind of lunged at Sarah. I'm sure the girl thought she had to protect herself."

"What do you think, Dr. Bronson? Do you think the child had the potential to specifically injure someone?"

She put both elbows on the table and lightly massaged her temples. At last she spoke. "Yes. I do believe she had that potential, *if* she felt threatened. And there's something else . . ." Her voice trailed off.

"Yes?" Jason's voice was crisp, insistent.

"Well, I once overheard Sarah's mother reminding her about her temper. Telling her she must watch herself. It seemed to me that the woman was terrified."

"Afraid of her own daughter?"

"No. Not exactly. It was more like a mother reminding an unruly child to watch his table manners in public. Like the conversation had been held many times over. Sarah's mother seemed scared, but not of the girl."

"How long after the incident did Sarah stay here?"

"Not long. You see, Charlotte got hold of some ridiculous story and threatened Mrs. Livingston with it. She took Sarah away and we never heard from them again. I guess the woman was afraid someone might believe Charlotte's story. I don't know."

"And no one here has ever heard from them again?"

"No. Tom Hamilton has never given up hope that someday she'll come back. She would have been the greatest psychic the world has ever known, Captain Links."

Links nodded in agreement. "No doubt. Now, Dr. Bronson, I'm going to need your records on Sarah Livingston. I'll want to know all about her relatives, any friends of her mother's—everything."

Emily looked at Jason in surprise. "But there was no one. Mrs. Livingston had no family, no friends—we checked into all that. The father was dead. It was just Sarah and her mother."

"How did Mr. Livingston die, Doctor? Did you ever check into that?"

She took one look at Jason Links and knew that he was fully aware of the manner in which Glenn Livingston had expired. She spoke evenly.

"I think you already know, Captain. Mr. Livingston was murdered. They never found out who did it."

"I understand he'd beaten his wife badly prior to the killing."

"I believe so. Mrs. Livingston never confided in me, of course. I barely knew her. But she did talk to one of the teachers, and Mrs. Carver mentioned it to Tom—Mr. Hamilton. In fact, at one point, June Carver said she believed Sarah may have felt physical pain herself when her mother was beaten. I've never seen the journal Mrs. Carver kept on Sarah, but Mr. Hamilton did and—"

"I'll want to make a copy of this journal, Dr. Bronson."

"I wish I could oblige you, Captain, but I'm afraid that's impossible. The journal isn't here at the Institute. When June retired, she must have taken it with her."

"Isn't that unusual? For an employee to remove records potentially valuable to the Institute?"

"Certainly. I can't imagine why she would do it. She moved away from St. Louis some months after she left the Institute. No one checked through Sarah's files until later. Several things were gone. We assumed June took them with her, possibly thinking she might write a book. Luckily, the film we had of Sarah was still there. It hadn't been removed. A fascinating film, too."

Links nodded. "Certainly not very professional. Taking records like that."

"And highly unusual for a woman like June Carver. She was a thoroughly professional and loyal employee."

"Unlike this Mrs. Crawford?"

"Absolutely. Charlotte was a spiteful woman, on the verge of paranoia. Yet her credentials had been excellent. I always wondered if she wasn't having a mental breakdown."

"Did she have any real reasons to dislike Sarah Livingston? Or was that part of her paranoia?"

"Sarah was a threat to her, Captain. According to Sarah, Charlotte shoved one of the children. Sarah pushed her—with her mind. She knocked her back, away from the child. I think Charlotte started to understand what the rest of us had failed to see—that pain inflicted on those close to Sarah affected her. Charlotte later used this information in a particularly sadistic way. She learned of Glenn Livingston's death and accused Sarah of being the killer. That's how she frightened Mrs. Livingston so badly."

"Dr. Bronson, do you think the child had the ability to kill someone with her mind? To do to a human being essentially what she did to that steel bar?"

She sighed. Tom Hamilton had asked her to be completely truthful regarding Sarah. As much as he felt a fondness for the memory of the child, a curiosity about her present life, he also felt a loyalty to his Institute. There would be no cover-ups if the police returned.

"Yes, Captain. I believe Sarah could kill some-one. I mean, she had the ability. It would be far easier to mangle flesh and bone than a steel bar. But the real question is whether or not she *would* kill another human being. And that, Captain Links, is something I can't answer. I knew her for a short time when she was four years old. What she's become now—"

"But according to this story the Crawford woman told, Sarah had already killed a man. Her father."

"That story was ridiculous. Sarah would have been three years old when Glenn Livingston was killed."

Links didn't like where it was all leading, but he pressed forward. "What if she could feel her mother being beaten, Dr. Bronson? Wouldn't she have protected herself?"

Emily stared at the desktop and shrugged. "I don't know. I think it would be a natural reaction."

For the first time since he'd heard Charlotte Crawford's story, Jason Links began to entertain the idea of a woman who could kill with her mind. It was ludicrous, he knew that. But with all he'd learned about the child, he could not ignore the possibility. It would answer everything. The lack of evidence. The pressure that had been applied with even distribution. The witnesses who swore nobody was there.

"What normally happens to psychics as they

mature, Dr. Bronson? Do their powers intensify, or do they sometimes grow weaker?"

"Both," she said simply. "More often than not, a child grows out of his psi awareness. Most subjects do far better before puberty. That's where Hamilton, Rhine—institutes such as these come in. We try to help the children retain their abilities, to develop them as they grow older. Now, if you're referring to Sarah, I'd have to say that there was very little chance of her losing any powers. In her case, I believe it would go the other way. Her powers seemed to increase every day."

Links glanced at his watch. "Well, Dr. Bronson, it's late. I need to get started back. I'd like to take your files on Sarah Livingston. The ones you still have. And a copy of the film you mentioned. I'll have the files copied and sent back to you immediately. I think you understand the urgency of this."

Emily nodded, grimly. "Yes. I understand you believe Sarah has committed some particularly grisly murders." She stood and walked around the desk to Links. "I sincerely hope you're wrong, Captain."

Links headed west on I-70. He drove slightly below the speed limit, having no desire to hurry. A massive amount of information had to be digested. Information he could share with no one. *Take this to the D.A. See how fast they pull your badge.* It all worked, though. Everything fit. Livingston's body had been in the exact condition as the Kansas City victims'. But was it logical to believe a baby could do that? Even a baby with extraordinary abilities? Three years old. How much reasoning power does a child that age have? Can they distinguish right from wrong? Probably only on a very basic level. A baby would not want its mother hurt. It would most likely react to pain inflicted on itself. What if the child had only to *think* and the person inflicting the pain was stopped?

Fighting with himself.

Thought he was having a fit.

Sorry, there's absolutely no evidence to show anyone else entered the room.

There's another mind.

He glanced back over his shoulder to the large cardboard boxes that contained Sarah Livingston's files. The answer was there. He stepped down on the gas pedal, suddenly anxious to get home.

Chapter 15

Sarah gripped the receiver and listened to what Alison Links was saying.

"—so anyway, I don't know if we'll be able to make it tomorrow night or not. This Crawford woman is probably a wild goose chase, but you know Jason. If he comes home with any lead at all, he'll want to follow up on it. Why don't I give you a call when Jason gets back from St. Louis?"

Sarah slowly replaced the receiver. *Charlotte Crawford wrote a letter to the newspaper! To Charlie Kaufman! She remembered her after all these years. But how would she possibly know anything! Could she!*

She sat down at the kitchen table and lit a cigarette, inhaling slowly and deeply. A knot was beginning to form in her stomach.

She hadn't thought of Mrs. Crawford in years. The woman was part of the memories her mother and Aunt June told her to erase. Mrs. Crawford hated her, that much she remembered. And she'd hated Charlotte Crawford. *Why! Something to do with other children. Shoving them. Sarah had done something. What?*

What in God's name had she done?

Alison had said the old woman was in a nursing home. *What was the name?* She tried to think back, to reconstruct the conversation. *St. Charles.* That was it. The St. Charles something-or-other home. She picked up the telephone.

NEAR FARRELL, MISSOURI
May, 1990

Sam Thomas looked out the window of the one-room cabin that had been his home for over three months. He watched as Luke Barnes brought the ax down on the neck of the chicken. A revolting way to get meat for supper, as far as Sam was concerned. God, how he hated it when the chicken ran all over the yard, flopping around and sloshing blood everywhere. He turned away from the window, disgusted. At least it wasn't squirrel or rabbit, which were the other alternatives. He'd sell his soul for a Kansas City Strip.

He needed to get away from this place, but his car was almost out of gas, he had but a few dollars, and there must be a warrant out for his arrest in K.C. He had no choice but to stay put. It was just pure luck that he'd remembered this place anyway. He'd first met Luke Barnes when he and two of his friends were deer hunting a few years earlier. He'd zeroed in on a huge buck when a giant of a man grabbed his gun. Sam had nearly messed his pants when he looked up into the apparition's curiously vacant face.

"Don't shoot Fred, mister." The giant looked down at Sam and shook his head. "He's my deer. Me and him are friends." Sam had looked up at all six feet eight inches of the man and decided not to argue the point. He could live without Fred on his living-room wall.

But Luke had turned out to be a bonus. He showed the men exactly where to find the most and the biggest deer, helped them gut and bleed the animals. Luke Barnes knew the woods better than anyone Sam had ever known. He lived alone in a small cabin he and his father had built when Luke was a small boy. The big, slow-witted man survived off the land, raising chickens and tending a small vegetable garden. He had no electricity or plumbing, and had no idea that anyone else did.

The day Sam got his buck he watched Luke hoist the animal on his back and carry it two miles to the cabin. Sam watched and thanked his lucky stars he hadn't shot Fred before Luke Barnes got to him. The man probably weighed 350 pounds, and there wasn't an ounce of fat on him. Luke was gentle, soft-spoken, and had the mental capacity of about an eight-year-old. But the man was knowledgeable about the countryside and grateful for company, two qualities Sam had remembered the night he'd run from the police. He'd headed straight for Luke's cabin and had been there ever since.

Sam thought of his wife and stepdaughter often. He missed them more than he cared to admit. He was sure he could get Julie to drop the charges if he could just talk to her. Julie had always obeyed him. Twice, he'd driven into Farrell to call her, but there had been no answer.

He wanted his family back. He thought back to nights he'd crawled into Kathy's bed when Julie had been at work. Kathy was five when it first happened. She'd been crying from a nightmare and he'd gone in to comfort her. He lay on the bed and patted her arm, aware of how beautiful the child was. He began stroking her hair, and suddenly felt a stirring between his legs. He'd eased his hand under the cotton nightgown she wore.

"Hush, baby. It was only a dream. Daddy's here. Daddy won't let anything hurt his baby."

His hand found her crotch and he began rubbing. Kathy had pulled away at his touch.

"It's all right," he'd told her. "Daddy will make you feel better. You won't have any more nightmares, because Daddy loves you." He pulled her to him and began kissing the child.

Kathy pushed at his chest. "Don't, Daddy. I'm okay. I'll go back to sleep now."

Sam was not to be put off. He was feeling a thrill he'd never experienced with an adult woman. She shoved him again, and he slapped her. Kathy lay back, stunned. No one had ever hit her like that. Her real father had never even spanked her. She burst into tears. "I'm going to tell my mommy on you," she cried out.

Sam removed his belt and stood over her, doubling the leather. "If you tell your mother anything, I'll spank you so hard you'll not walk for a week. Your mother doesn't want to hear your stories."

"She—" Kathy was sobbing.

"She nothing! Do you want to see me hurt her bad? If you tell your mother and upset her, that's what will happen!"

Kathy was terrified. She lay frozen to the spot, positive that Sam would do just that.

He looked down at her, then relaxed. He began removing the thin cotton gown. "That's Daddy's good girl. Daddy's going to make his little girl happy. He's going to make her feel so good."

Over the years he'd turned to Kathy often. Sex with Julie seemed dull, without any excitement. Kathy often struggled, and he enjoyed the thrill of overpowering her. When she began to develop small breasts, Sam's lovemaking began to take even more violent twists. It was on one such night that Julie had surprised him. Still, if he could just explain to his wife about how Kathy had teased him, got him worked up, he thought she'd come back. If not, maybe he could just take Kathy and leave the state. Surely the child missed him. He sure as hell missed her.

He was thinking back on it all when Luke entered the cabin.

"Here's a nice fat chicken, Sam. We'll eat good tonight." The big man opened the front of the stove and threw in some kindling wood. He put a pot of water on to boil. Sam knew what was coming next.

"I got to pluck the chicken now, Sam. Do you want to help?"

"No, you go ahead," Sam answered. "You're a lot better at it than me."

Luke brightened at the remark. "My daddy taught me, Sam. He said I was the best chicken-plucker he ever saw." Luke smiled broadly, proud of himself.

Sam was sick to death of hearing Luke's childish prattling. His entire range of knowledge centered on what his daddy had taught him about survival. Luke had a vocabulary of perhaps three hundred words, and he used them constantly. If he would just shut up, Sam figured he might be able to take it.

Sam thought he'd try once more to elicit the information he sought from the big man. He smiled and started talking.

"You know, Luke, if I had a little money, I could drive into town and get us some candy. Don't you like candy, Luke?"

Luke nodded enthusiastically. "Daddy used to bring me candy. But I haven't had any for a long time."

"Well, you have money from the eggs you sell. I've seen people come every few days. And the hunters sometimes give you money, don't they?"

Luke nodded. "That's real nice of them, Sam."

Sam sighed. "Well, now, why don't I take a little of that money and go get us some candy? Wouldn't you like that?"

Luke tried to think. "No, Sam. I don't think so. I have to save that money. Daddy told me not to ever go to town, and not to spend any of the money, and not to tell anybody where I put the money. He told me that over and over, Sam. He said I would need it sometime."

Sam forced a grin. "But, Luke, your daddy wouldn't care if you got a little candy. That wouldn't take very much money. Come on, let's do it."

Luke hated to say no to Sam. He'd been a good friend and Luke liked him. But his daddy wouldn't like it. His daddy had told him to save every penny he could in case someone came about . . . what? What were they going to come about? Oh, yes. Taxes. His daddy had said somebody might come someday about taxes. That was what the money was for. His daddy had been dead for five years now and no one had ever come. But if they did, Luke would be ready. He had promised his daddy.

Luke walked over and picked up the pot of boiling water. "No, Sam. I can't use my money for candy. There's only one thing I can use the money for, Sam. I can't break my promise to my daddy." He went outside to dip the chicken.

"Damn! Damn it to hell." Sam spoke the words out loud. He'd already tried to pry the information from Luke. To no avail. Luke just buttoned up. He crossed over to Luke's bunk. He had looked through the bed a hundred times and come up blank. Out of desperation, he tried once more. Nothing. He looked around. Over the past couple of months he had literally taken the cabin apart. If Luke Barnes had any money here, he'd hidden it well. He kicked the bed hard. "God damn him," he swore.

He went once again to the worn Bible where he knew Luke's father had placed several legal papers. He'd glanced over them before. They didn't say much. He pulled out the slim sheaf of documents. As near as he could figure out, Luke's father had known the boy would be unable to handle anything past his personal survival. The old man had left him the land free and clear, along with the cabin. An account had been set up in a Farrell bank, and it was from this account that the ycarly taxes were to be paid.

"Yeah, yeah." Sam scowled. The bank account wouldn't do him any good. Even Luke couldn't get to that. He was about to put the papers back when he noticed a small piece of paper he'd overlooked. It was stapled to the back of the others.

In the event that the monies deposited in the Farrell State Bank are depleted to the point they are insufficient for tax purposes, it is hereby agreed that bank personnel will contact Luke Barnes. At that time he will be given the opportunity to pay said taxes. Due to the man's limited mental capacity, the bank shall be instructed to send not less than three representatives to the Barnes home, to assure that his rights are not violated.

Sam stared at the addendum. Luke's father had been concerned about the bank account running dry. Perhaps not until Luke was an old man himself, but it was feasible. By the time it happened, Luke would have enough cash to handle the payment. The old man had understood his son well. Luke would never spend a dime until contacted about taxes.

Sam checked the initial deposit information. Old man Barnes had deposited just over twenty thousand dollars. It had been put in Certificates of Deposit, and with the going rate of interest, there would be sufficient funds to pay the taxes for years to come.

The only other document in the package was a will stating that Mr. Barnes believed Luke capable of living on his own, unassisted. It was the father's wish that the young man not be institutionalized. If, the will stated, it was ever decided that an institution was necessary, all monies in the Farrell State Bank would immediately be transferred to a bank in Blue Springs, and new executors would be appointed to the estate.

The old man was shrewd. That much was obvious to Sam. He protected his son as best he could. That stipulation removed any temptation on the part of a bank official to have Luke committed.

Sam's list of problems was reduced to one: how to convince Luke it was time to pay taxes. *That might be tricky*, he thought, *no matter how simple Luke is*. Too many times, he'd brought up the subject of money. Sam thought long and hard until it came to him. He replaced all the documents in the chest and walked out to the yard where Luke was still plucking his chicken.

"By the way, Luke," he began. "I've got to leave tomorrow for a few days—"

"Leave?" Luke looked like a child who had just been told his best friend couldn't play any longer.

"Yeah. Can't be helped, Luke. You see, I own a house in Kansas City, and tomorrow is the day taxes are due. I wouldn't want to lose my house, Luke."

Luke was startled. "Taxes? You have to pay taxes tomorrow?"

"Sure, Luke. Everybody does. A friend of mine forgot to do it one year, and now he doesn't have anyplace to live. They took away his house, his land, everything."

Luke was visibly agitated. "I have to pay taxes, too, don't I, Sam? Is tomorrow the day I have to pay?"

Sam answered slowly. "Luke, *everybody* has to pay taxes tomorrow, or they lose their houses, whatever they have. Look, do you need some money to pay yours? I have money in Kansas City. I could give you what you need." He stopped and waited for the offer to register.

Luke smiled. "That's real nice, Sam. But I got the money. Daddy told me to save for taxes. He made me promise, Sam."

"Well, that's fine, Luke," Sam said smoothly. "If you want me to, I'll take your money with me tomorrow and pay your taxes when I pay mine. There isn't any need for you to go clear in to Kansas City."

Luke thought that over, rubbing his forehead in concentration. Finally the big man/child spoke. "No. I better pay the taxes myself. Can you take me?"

Jesus Christ. Sam tried to smother his scowl. *Don't tell me I'm going to have to lug this half-wit with me.* He argued the point with Luke, stressing the point that it would leave the cabin unguarded. But Luke remained steadfast. His daddy would want him to pay the taxes himself.

Sam considered the shotgun and rifle in the trunk of his car. Luke would have to be asleep. He couldn't take the chance of merely injuring him. Sam shuddered at the thought. The .22 would be worthless. It would have to be the shotgun. On the other hand, hunters had been through, and someone might remember the car. Better to take him to Kansas City, have him keep his money in a safe place—the glove compartment—then drop him off somewhere. By the time he ever was in the position to tell the authorities anything, Luke would be so confused he'd probably just be taken to an institution.

Sam bit his lip. If Luke was institutionalized, that would leave the cabin empty. He could use it if he needed to do so. He just wished there was a way to get the money out of the Farrell State Bank. Maybe if he could forge some documents that proved he was a relative.

It was worth thinking about.

Early the next morning, Sam lay in bed and pretended to sleep later than usual. Luke went to the fireplace and reached up inside. He carefully removed five blackened bricks, and then brought out a good-sized metal box. Sam waited until Luke had replaced the bricks and believed his hiding place was secure. Then he began to stretch and yawn.

"Oh, Luke. I must have overslept."

Luke was looking at the pile of bills and change on the table. "Come here and look, Sam. Is this enough for taxes?"

Sam crawled out of bed and casually walked to the table. He figured Luke must have well over three thousand dollars in the heap. *Holy shit!* Sam had to hide his excitement.

"Is this enough, Sam?" Luke appeared worried. "Is this enough for taxes?"

"Yeah." Sam patted Luke on the shoulder. "Don't worry, pal. That's enough."

All right, have it your way, Sam thought. *We'll see how well you get along in the city.*

Chapter 16

Sarah looked down at the withered, emaciated form of the woman who had caused her so much childhood trauma, and felt nothing but pity. She was dying, of that Sarah was sure. The old woman's eyes were starting to glaze, and she talked in rambling, disconnected sentences. Sarah tried to reach her.

"Mrs. Crawford, I'm Miss Johnson, a reporter for the *Kansas City Star*," she lied. "I understand you have some information about the killings we've been having. Could you tell me about it?"

The old woman turned to her with blurry eyes. "Sarah did it. She killed them all. I'll be next. She'll come after me now. She's the devil. Wicked. Wicked . . ." Her voice trailed off.

The room was unbearably hot and beads of perspiration broke out on Sarah's forehead. *How could she know?* She felt light-headed, and wanted to run out of the room. Maybe she didn't want to ask the next question. She didn't want to know.

"Mrs. Crawford, how do you know this woman killed those men?"

The old woman roused. "Woman? What woman? Sarah is a little girl. Haven't you been listening? She's a vicious little girl. A bad seed. She kills people with her mind. Just like she killed her own father." She pointed to the Bible on her nightstand. "It's in there. All the proof you need. She killed her father and now she's killing people in Kansas City."

Waves of nausea shook Sarah's body as she reached for the worn Bible. She opened the book and saw the clipping. It was as if the headline reached out and knocked her in the face. Her legs began to buckle as she read the account of Glenn Livingston's death. *Livingston.* Her mother had said her father's name had been Glenn Jones. But now her mother called herself Mrs. Livingston. And so it must have been.

It can't have happened that way. I couldn't have killed my father. He couldn't have beaten my mother like this. She said he was a kind man. A good man.

Sarah reread the article. There was no mistake. The body was in precisely the same condition as Jack Simmons. As Johnny Merit. Phelps. Her father's name had been Livingston. He had beaten her mother and Sarah had killed him. *May God have mercy on me.*

Charlotte Crawford groaned, obviously in great agony. "Stop her. Stop that child of the devil. Don't let her kill me, please." The old woman's face was contorted in pain and fear.

Sarah leaned over her and smoothed her hair back from her forehead. "I'll stop her, Mrs. Crawford. Sarah Livingston won't ever hurt anyone again. You have my word on it."

She turned and left the room, numbed by her newly gained knowledge.

Jason sat at his desk in the warm, comfortable den Alison had created for him when she remodeled the old West Port house. There were papers and file folders scattered throughout the room and on Links' desk was a reel-to-reel tape player. He'd already viewed the film, and as Emily Bronson had promised, it was amazing. The child was as close to magic as anything Links could have dreamed up. She could make objects fly through the air, read minds, direct the throw of dice, call out the Zener cards correctly twenty-five times straight. It was pretty heady stuff. But it was nothing compared to an old tape that Links had found stuffed down between several old file folders. He didn't think even Emily Bronson had listened to it, knew what it surely must be.

The speaker had identified herself as June Carver, formerly an experimental psychologist at Rhine Institute, currently the director of the Children's Division of the Hamilton Institute. Links knew that the tape must have been preliminary to June Carver's written journals. He also knew that much of the information on the tape had been kept secret even from Hamilton Institute.

On the tape, June Carver stressed the importance of complying with Mrs. Livingston's desire for anonymity. There were, the woman emphasized, vital personal reasons for Mrs. Livingston's request. Mrs. Carver explained in academic detail experiments done with Sarah Livingston that involved the use of distance as the variable factor. She had started by putting objects in other rooms and having Sarah move them. Ultimately, June Carver documented cases where Sarah moved objects in Mrs. Carver's house, over twenty miles away.

Links listened to the entire tape, then switched off the player. So Sarah Livingston could move objects twenty miles away. Did that mean she could also kill from such a distance?

June Carver. The name seemed vaguely familiar. Like he'd seen or heard it, yet paid little attention. Maybe it was that first visit he'd paid to Hamilton. He frowned. No. It was something here in Kansas City. Had Elizabeth Evans ever mentioned the name? It had something to do with Northside, he decided. He picked up the phone and dialed headquarters.

"Max? I need a favor. Could you get the files on Northside from my office and drop them by the house?"

"Sure, Captain. I'm off duty in twenty minutes, anyway." Max hesitated. "There's something I want to talk to you about. Uh, what are the chances of my getting a couple of days off next week?"

"In the middle of a murder investigation?" Links barked. "Are you going nuts?"

Max laughed. "No. I'm going to get married."

Links sputtered. "You're what? Surely not that Sally what's-her-name."

"No, Captain. I'm marrying Cindy Lou Merit."

Links' answer was swift. "Jesus Christ, Max. You hardly know her!"

"I know everything I need to know about her. I know she's the best woman I ever met."

"Not to mention a sexy-looking one," Links said wryly.

"That's just it, Captain." Max was adamant. "Her looks are just about the least important thing about her, now that I've had a chance to get to know Cindy Lou. She's a wonderful person, Captain. Nothing like any woman I've ever gone out with."

"Look—"

Max interrupted him. "The decision's made, Captain. I just feel like the luckiest man alive that she said yes. And you know what? She thinks I'm wonderful, too. I don't have to act cool or hip or any of that shit around Cindy Lou. God, I love it. And I love her." He smiled to himself, understanding that Links was perfectly justified in his concern, but also knowing that what he was doing was right. "Cindy Lou wants to ask Sarah Jamieson to stand up with her, Captain. And if you wouldn't mind, I'd appreciate it if you'd stand up with me."

Links sighed and leaned back in his chair. "Well, of course, Max. If this is what you want to do, I'd be happy to stand up with you. How many days off do you need?"

Max paused before answering. "Uh, if it's possible, I'd like to take a week or so. We'd, uh, like to drive to Kentucky and see Cindy Lou's parents. And, we're—we're going to take Kathy Thomas with us. She's dying to meet the Garrisons, see Stone Mountain. Cindy Lou thinks it will kind of, well, restore Kathy's faith in men. The Thomases are going back to their old house for a couple of days. I guess they'll be moving to a new location soon—but Mrs. Thomas wants to pack up some things. Kathy is a little nervous about it. The less time she spends there, the better."

Jason was flabbergasted. "You're taking a fourteen-year-old along on your honeymoon?" He whistled. "I stand corrected, Max. This is obviously true love." Links shook his head in disbelief.

"Tell you what, Max. I'll try to give you all the time I can. Who knows, maybe the case will be wrapped up by next week, anyway. Right now I need those files."

"You got 'em, Captain." Max hung up the phone, still smiling.

The drive back from St. Louis was the longest five hours Sarah had ever spent in her life. She still couldn't believe it. She had killed her own father. Her flesh and blood. Had she killed others? Others that her mother had covered up? Had she killed anyone while she was at Hamilton? Was that why her mother had changed their name and moved?

Hiding is a terrible thing. She'd said that to

Mary Simmons. Yes, she'd been hiding, too. Hiding from the fact that she was a killer long before now.

Like before. She'd thought that once. *Just like before.* Somewhere in the crevices of her mind, she'd known that she was capable of extreme violence. She'd known it could start again.

She looked at the rolling hills along the interstate. Everything looked green and fresh. Lovely farms with people going about their business in a rational way. People driving by in cars, laughing, talking to each other. Having fun with their families. *Why me? All I want is a normal life. I want my husband and my children. I want to work, to do something productive. I want to be happy. Why has it all turned out so wrong?*

When Sarah was about sixteen, June Carver had mentioned a theory about the powers. It was probably the electrical shock, June had said. A shock Sarah had received as a baby. One side of her hair had blackened, so the charge had gone out through her head. June had been convinced that the charge affected her brain capabilities. She'd told Sarah of other psychics who had been in accidents of one sort or another. Edgar Cayce had fallen from a tree and landed on his head. Peter Hurkos had had a head injury. *But there was a big difference*, she thought.

Those men hadn't killed anyone that she knew of. They'd used their great powers for healing, for helping. She had no ability to heal. She'd tried it once, when Dan had been sick. Tried to pull the fever from him, into her own body. It hadn't worked. There were other things she couldn't do. She had no powers of precognition, as far as she could tell. The future was as uncertain to her as it was to anybody else. She sometimes felt uneasy, like something was wrong. But so did lots of people. Once something had happened, she could help. But she couldn't predict it.

You've done just what they were afraid of. You've used your powers for hurting. Not helping.

She tried to shake the thought off. After all, she'd helped the police several times. The Brenner baby. Once she'd seen the television reports, she'd been able to zero in on the child's location. Other times, too. She always called a church. Afraid she'd be recorded, and Jason would recognize her voice. And even now, she'd killed to save lives.

If even one of those men could have been rehabilitated, then you were wrong.

And Jason Links now had the same information she had. He knew. It would only be a matter of time until he tied it all together. She assumed he'd gone to Hamilton, since Charlotte had worked there. What would they have told him?

June Carver. The name was somewhere in her files. Buried in the back, probably. But she knew it was there. *What will happen to my children? To Paul?* Paul could forget his political ambitions. But that wasn't the worst of it. They'd all be branded as freaks. Their lives would never be the same. *What if I go to prison?*

Could that happen? Could they really make a case against her? It didn't matter. Once it was public knowledge, everyone's lives would be drastically altered. Paul would never look at her the same. He'd wonder if she was reading his mind. If she suddenly might lose her temper. *No wonder I was told to keep my temper in check at all times.*

Would Jason prosecute her? Yes. She knew he'd have to at least try. He couldn't let it go on.

She knew there was one way to stop it. It would have to stop if she were dead.

Suddenly, she had to see her mother. Even if the old woman didn't know who she was again. Sarah drove through Kansas City to the Bonner Springs exit.

Chapter 17

Stunned, Jason Links sat reading the report compiled on Sarah Jamieson. Maiden name, Jones. Mother's first name, Beatrice. Father's name, Glenn. And at the very bottom of a back page, the name of her aunt. June Carver. It was all there and it fit. Mrs. Livingston had done what so many people do when they change their names. She'd retained the same first names and simply changed the last.

Sarah Jamieson. The wife of his best friend. The one person at Northside he hadn't scrutinized. *Fool.* Everyone should have been checked thoroughly. *Sarah.* Even when he kept hearing the name, he'd never once connected it with Sarah Jamieson. *Sarah.* Shit, she was more than the wife of one of his closet friend. *She* was one of his best friends. There had to be some mistake. How could Sarah Jamieson have that sort of power and he not know it? There was nothing. Or was there?

Links thought back over the years. There was that time when they were playing cards. Sarah had jumped up and run outside. Dan had fallen from a tree. She'd told them she just had a feeling something was wrong. He'd passed it off as mother's intuition.

There was another incident. Sarah and Alison had gone shopping in the Plaza area, and Alison's purse was snatched. The two women came home laughing about the thief, how he kept tripping and falling down. When a policeman had come along, he'd retrieved the purse and arrested the thief. The man was flat on his face. The arresting officer had also laughed about it later. He said the petty thief swore something invisible had grabbed him.

It was mind-boggling. Could the Sarah Jamieson he knew have killed three—no, four—men? Including her father? Could she have projected psychic waves from the safety of her own home? Waves that were capable of crushing a man's chest?

A woman had called an ambulance for Mary Simmons. A woman who wouldn't identify herself.

He thought back. Sarah had been having lunch with Alison when Johnny Merit had been killed. What had Alison said about that lunch? Sick. Sarah had become ill. She'd doubled over at the table, then excused herself. Told Alison she'd had a touch of the flu. Alison had been worried about her. She said Sarah returned from the rest room pale and shaky. Could Sarah have felt the blow to Cindy Lou Merit's stomach? Gone to the rest room to kill him?

God almighty. He guessed a good attorney would call for a verdict of self-defense. Pure and simple. How could it be proven anyway? He'd be busted if he went to the D.A. with this.

There was one unanswered question. Nigel Phelps. If Valerie Phelps was not an abused wife, how did that murder fit in? There was nothing to connect Nigel or Valerie Phelps to Northside. Nothing except his and Max's gut-level feeling that Valerie Phelps was holding something back.

He prayed that was the case. If not, his friend Sarah Jamieson had gone over the line. He decided to pay Valerie Phelps another call. He wanted everything clear in his mind before he approached Sarah. And he would approach her. He'd have to, for everyone's sake.

Links went into the kitchen and got a bottle of beer. He sat down and watched the 6:00 news, knowing Alison was there somewhere behind the scenes. She'd be home soon.

He took a sip of the cold liquid and sighed. *I'm sorry, Sarah. I'm truly sorry. God help us all.*

Beatrice Livingston smiled vacantly at her daughter.

"Yes, dear," she went on. "My daughter's name is Sarah, too. But she—" Her smile turned to a frown. She began fidgeting with a handkerchief in her lap. "Haven't they come with lunch yet? I haven't had anything to eat for weeks now."

Sarah bit her lip and swallowed hard. When she'd entered the room an orderly had been removing food trays. "I'll see if someone can bring you something to eat."

"My daughter used to come," Beatrice said,

staring at the window. "She must have died. I never see her anymore."

Tears filled Sarah's eyes. "I'm Sarah. Mother—" She forced her mind once again into her mother's confused mind. "I'm your daughter. *I'm your Sarah.*"

Mrs. Livingston's eyes cleared a bit. "Oh. That's so nice. I thought you died. Didn't the bar hit you?"

"What bar, Mother?"

"Well, I can't remember. It was a big bar. Twisted." She looked puzzled, then brightened. "The one you twisted, Sarah. But then," she paused again. "Oh. It was the other lady. She died."

"What other lady?" Sarah felt weak.

"At the school. That's when we had to go. We had to go away."

Sarah took a deep breath, trying to stay calm. "Did I hurt someone at the school, Mother?"

Beatrice became agitated. "Oh, I can't imagine where they are with my food. They try to starve us. I'm so hungry." Tears filled her eyes. "Do you know where I am?"

Sarah very nearly blacked out with grief. "You're safe, Mother. You're in a nice safe place, where people love and care about you."

She smiled broadly. "I'm so glad. I was afraid I was lost."

"There's something I want to know, Mother. It's something I *have* to know." Again, she forced her mind into the disconnected thoughts and images in her mother's head. "Tell me about my father. I have to know." She stared at her mother's confused face and concentrated.

Pregnant. Shouldn't have married—had to. Bad. Always bad. Hitting me. Hitting my baby. Where is my food! Why doesn't someone come? Bad. Glenn. Very bad. He was going to kill me. But my baby stopped him. She stopped him. Help. Got to have someone help her. They can't find out. What did you say, June? Yes. Go away. We have to. Can't let them take Sarah away from me. Oh, why doesn't somebody turn on the television? Is it time to fix dinner for Sarah? Why is she so late from school? Drinking. That's when he hits me. If he comes home drinking, be careful. Is that you, honey? Is that you, Sarah?

"Yes, Mom. It's me."

Sarah sighed. Zombielike, she picked up her purse and took out her car keys. "I'll be back soon, dear. And I'll have someone bring you something else to eat."

Her mother smiled. "I don't need anything. I hide food, you know." She grinned like a naughty child. "They don't know about it. Over there." She pointed to her trunk in the corner. "Go and see."

Sarah went to the old trunk and opened the lid. There were a few half-rotted apples and a withered orange. *God.* She picked the old fruit out. "I'll get you some fresh—"

"No! I need it. In case they forget." Her mother shook her finger as Sarah had seen her do so many times through the years.

"All right. I'll put it back, but I'll have them

bring some more, anyway." She reached in the trunk, hoping to find a towel or something with which to wrap the apples and orange. The fruit had been placed on a thick ledger. Sarah took it out and wiped the stains from it. Curious, she opened the first page.

Journal. June Carver. Subject: Sarah Livingston. 1955.

"Would you like to have the book?" Her mother's words startled Sarah.

She slowly nodded. "Y-yes. Could I take it?"

"Oh, yes. It's not mine. It belongs to my daughter."

Sarah replaced the fruit, kissed her mother on the cheek, and walked to the nurses' station.

"Could you please bring Mother a snack? I think she's hungry again." She clutched the journal to her chest and hurried out the double glass doors.

NOVEMBER, 1956. Beatrice and I have both determined that to leave St. Louis is the only answer. Charlotte will certainly take her information to some authorities, unless, of course, Tom Hamilton stops her. I have soul-searched this matter and decided not to go to Tom. He would, as usual, try to help Sarah. But it would most definitely compromise the Institute. I do wish I could ask his advice. He has an innate shrewdness about psychics that even the scientists at Hamilton do not seem to have.

Sarah had skimmed over the early notes. She knew about the Zener cards, the dice tricks, all of it. What she did not understand was the references June Carver had made to Charlotte Crawford. *The incident.* That's all she'd written. Sarah sat in her bedroom, hoping Paul would be at his meeting late. He'd wanted her to attend. The Democratic Party Chairman was to be there, as were several financial backers and two county chairmen. Sarah knew it meant Paul had the nomination sewn up. More politics. Nothing could have forced her to go. She'd lied. Told him she had to be at Northside until nearly 10:00 P.M.

She looked at her watch: 9:22. Running her finger down the handwritten notes, she searched for key words or phrases. *Sarah's father.* She stopped.

JANUARY, 1957. Kansas City has proven a perfect location. Between my savings and Beatrice's weekly salary, we make out fine. It would have been nice to have been able to continue the retirement, but impossible under the circumstances. We have heard nothing of Charlotte Crawford's doings. Hopefully she will keep quiet as long as she knows nothing of Sarah's whereabouts. I find it hard to believe, even after seeing Sarah's powers demonstrated so many times, that she could have killed Glenn Livingston. Sarah's father was an extremely violent man, according to Beatrice. Makes me appreciate my own Eldon so much. Women don't know how lucky they are to find the good men. He must have been an alcoholic from the beginning. Beatrice says he was seldom sober. The more he drank, the more abusive he was. For my research purposes, however, the primary point of concern is that Sarah began to feel the blows when Glenn hit Beatrice. That is why he ultimately died.

Sarah put down the book and lit a cigarette. So it had always been this way. No wonder her mother and June had been so overprotective. So concerned about the kind of boys she dated. In her entire teenage years, her college years, she'd never once come in contact with a boy who had been rough with her. It was as though she could sense violence and kept her distance. Now she understood why it had been of such importance.

She looked up at the ceiling and exhaled, almost chuckling. *So that explains my mother's and June's warnings about boys who tried to push girls around. I thought they were trying to protect me. Wrong. They were actually protecting the boys.* She shook her head, knowing in her heart that they'd been protecting everybody, and especially Sarah. She continued to read. Her heart quickened, as she realized she was reading the account of her father's death.

. . . He'd come home extremely drunk, according to Beatrice. He had had some sort of altercation with a man at work, and was highly emotional. Beatrice had put some money aside for necessities—Glenn evidently had spent most of their money on liquor. He happened to find it in Beatrice's purse. He began screaming obscenities and hitting her. Sarah toddled in just as it started. She was physically knocked down when her father first hit her mother. The child began crying and Beatrice tried to reach her. Glenn hit her over and over, with Sarah's cries becoming hysterical screaming. Beatrice said all of a sudden Glenn flew backwards. He appeared surprised, as if he thought Beatrice had hit him. She was afraid he would kill her, then. He took another step forward, his fist in the air, and then fell to the ground. Beatrice likened it to a puppet. He jerked up and down, in a blind rage. It was then that she saw Sarah, sitting on the floor and clinching her fists. Staring straight at Glenn. Beatrice must have passed out. When she came to, a neighbor was leaning over her. Sarah was sitting content-edly on the floor. The police arrived soon there-after. That was what convinced Beatrice that Sarah had to be exposed to an environment such as Hamilton. A place where the powers could be controlled.

Sarah heard the front door open. She hurriedly closed the journal and put it in the bottom of her sweater drawer.

"Hon—I'm home. Come on down. There's a couple of people I'd like you to meet."

Great. She stubbed out her cigarette and looked in the mirror. *Just damned great*. Sarah ran a

brush through her hair and went downstairs to
meet her husband's political cronies. Her husband, who still believed he'd be the next Attorney
General of the state of Missouri.

Chapter 18

The following morning, Joe Turner chewed on the end of his pencil and checked his watch. It was almost 11:00 A.M. He had phoned five doctors' offices so far. In an effort to get back in the good graces of the Medical Examiner, his young college intern had taken on the task of contacting every emergency facility in the city. So far, no cases of infection due to a human bite. Joe wanted to find the avenger. And he was convinced this was the way to do just that. He flipped through his medical directory. *Dr. Leroy McClinton.*

"Hmm." Joe wasn't sure. McClinton was a society physician, primarily. Probably wouldn't come up with anything there. On the other hand, Jack the Ripper had been a member of British royalty, or so they thought. He dialed the phone.

Links was just preparing to leave for the Phelps home when the Medical Examiner phoned.

"Want an inside tip, my man?" Joe Turner was thrilled with himself.

"What kind of tip, Joe?" Links smiled to himself, waiting for the newest theory regarding plastic suits or out-of-state criminal activities. He wondered what Joe would say if he told him exactly how the avenger operated.

"I've been calling around, Jason. Checking on the infection idea. I knew damned well whoever Phelps bit would get into some trouble. The bacteria level in his mouth was very high."

"Yeah?" Links' interest perked up. "So what did you find?"

"Just this. Last night Dr. Leroy McClinton was called to the home of one of his patients. Severe infection. Problem is, the patient wouldn't give him much information, certainly didn't admit the infection was coming from any bites. Just insisted on being given high-powered antibiotics. Real high-powered. Leroy's scared as hell he did the wrong thing—not making the patient check into a hospital."

"I didn't know doctors still made house calls, Joe. That's a hell of a tip right there. And what makes you think this particular infection has anything to do with human bites?"

"Same explanation on both counts, Jason. Leroy wouldn't make a house call on a bet unless it was somebody important. Somebody like Mrs. Nigel Phelps."

Links sat forward in his chair. "You're sure? Severe infection?"

"You got it. She wouldn't admit shit to him. But he's one of those assholes who'll prescribe anything to a blue blood. I scared the hell out of him. He finally admitted he'd taken a blood sample.

Ten to one it'll prove out the theory. Nigel Phelps didn't bite the avenger. He was working over his wife."

"Thanks, Joe. I'm on my way there right now."

Mrs. Gates opened the door and looked at Links with suspicion. "The Misses isn't feeling very good this morning, Captain. You better come back another day."

"I'm sorry, ma'am. That would be impossible. I'm going to have to insist on seeing her right away."

Mrs. Gates glared at him sullenly and opened the door. "Wait in the kitchen." She motioned him back through the house much as one might shoo a dog. Links shook his head. He decided to call Sarah from the Phelps' home.

"Mind if I use the phone a minute?"

She narrowed her eyes and nodded. "I guess it will be all right."

When she'd disappeared around the doorway, Links flipped open the phone book sitting on a shelf in the telephone stand. He thumbed through the Yellow Pages until he came to the listing Crisis Intervention. He hoped Sarah was at Northside, because he was going to have to meet with her as soon as possible. He looked at the general hot line number and realized he'd need the private line listing. He glanced down at the bottom of the page and stopped short. There was a phone number written neatly in pencil, with the name "Sarah" printed beside it. He dialed and the voice on the other end of the line said, "Northside Crisis Center. May I help you?"

Links phoned Joe Turner's office.

"Joe, just how serious did you say a human bite can be?" He listened a moment and nodded. "You'd better call your pal Leroy, and tell him to get his ass out here and check on Valerie Phelps. And, Joe—tell him I said so."

Links let himself out the back door.

He drove directly to Northside, opting to confront Sarah in person. Links had no idea how to begin. *I shouldn't have to say a word*, he thought. *If this is all true, she'll know exactly why I'm there and what I'm thinking.*

He didn't have to worry. Sarah Jamieson had not come to work. She'd called in and taken a personal day. Links phoned the Jamieson house and no one answered. That left tonight's bridge game. *Shit. Where the hell can she have gone off to?*

Sarah was stopped by the security guard standing by massive iron gates.

"Yes, I'm expected," she said carefully. "Tell Mr. Hamilton it's Sarah. Sarah Livingston." She was starting to know I-70 like the palm of her hand.

The old man sat propped up in bed, obviously ill. Even advancing years and heart disease couldn't destroy the force of Tom Hamilton's personality. His eyes sparkled, moist with excitement, as he greeted her.

"Sarah. Little Sarah. You have no idea how

much I've wanted to see you again. To talk with you." His voice nearly cracked. "You have no idea what this means—when Emily told me you'd called the Institute this morning . . ." He shook his head, then quickly composed himself. "Now, you must tell me everything. Where you went, what you've done." A shadow passed over his face. "Above all, Sarah, tell me about this situation in Kansas City."

Sarah told him everything she knew. Everything she'd done.

Tom Hamilton sighed when she'd finished. The answer was so obvious. The core of the problem was so self-evident. He reached over and took her hand.

"My dear, dear girl. June predicted it. She could see what might happen." He swallowed hard. "Not the killings, of course. If she harbored any such suspicions, she kept them to herself. She saw the potential power. You could launch a space shuttle, Sarah. God only knows, that mind of yours might be able to force a devastating hurricane back away from a coastline. Cause the sky to open up and rain on a drought-stricken area. There's really no telling. But it could also set off a bomb. It could cause a fighter plane to explode." He sighed. "She was right, of course. They'd hound you to death. And your family. Your mother and June—they did the right thing. Kept you protected."

"But *was* it right? What about now? Maybe if I'd stayed—learned to hold back—"

"We'd never have permitted it, Sarah. I'm afraid

our exuberance would have outweighed our logic and ethics. The real problem is that they didn't explain why you had to stay away from battering situations. These women—they are causing you to revert to an old stimulus. Your brain is producing alpha waves that cause you to feel another's pain. You should never have taken this particular job, Sarah. The very thing that caused you to feel empathy for the women is causing you to reach out and protect them. And unless—unless you want to continue to do so—"

She lowered her eyes. "Yesterday I came up with a solution, Mr. Hamilton. A permanent one."

He sadly shook his head. "Suicide? I wonder how many of our psychics have used that as an escape. It's no solution, Sarah. It's a very permanent answer to what I see as a temporary problem. The problem is your job."

"I'll have to quit." She frowned. "It won't stop, even though I understand why it's happening."

"I'm afraid that's true. In the meantime, you must rid yourself of these guilt feelings. Much the same as soldiers who return from war. Put it behind you. And be careful with whom you associate in the future."

"Mr. Hamilton, did I ever injure anyone at your Institute? Anything connected with a bar?"

"Ah." He raised his eyebrows. "So you know about that. Yes, I'm afraid you did. You were protecting yourself, Sarah. As to how much damage you intended to inflict—well, that's not for me to say. Dr. Peterson believed the power just got away from you. Personally, I don't think you should worry about it. You certainly didn't kill Charlotte Crawford, and God knows there were people at Hamilton who would have liked to do just that."

She stood, feeling in some kind of control for the first time since Jack Simmons had tried to choke the life out of Mary.

"Mr. Hamilton, thank you so much. I—I don't know what to say."

The old man smiled. "It's me who should be thanking you, Sarah Livingston. Even though I know we can never record this case, never let the world in on it, *I know that Hamilton Institute once taught the greatest psychic mind in the history of the world.* That is quite enough for me." He sat up a little straighter in bed. "There is one thing you can do for me."

"Yes, of course."

"Come back to see me. Will you do that?"

She smiled. "Absolutely. If I'm not in jail."

She arrived back at her home only moments before Paul walked in the door.

"Where in God's name have you been?" Paul put his briefcase down and hugged her. "I called Northside and they said you never came in. Nobody answered here. Northside said Jason had been there looking for you. Christ, I was worried sick."

"I spent the day at the library, Paul. I had some research to catch up on. I'm sorry—I thought I told you." She looked exhausted.

"Look, do you feel like this game tonight? We can beg off."

"No." She shook her head emphatically. "No, I think we'd better play just as we planned."

"Well, let me call out for some food. You don't look like you need to be cooking."

Sarah looked at him with watery eyes. "Have I told you lately how lucky I was to have found you?"

He pulled her close. "I'm the one with the luck, honey. Don't forget that."

Chapter 19

Sam and Luke pulled into a gas station and filled up. Sam gritted his teeth, furious that he was having to spend his last four dollars on gasoline when his companion held over three thousand in a metal box on the floor of the passenger's side of the car. *Just wait*, Sam thought as he counted out the wadded up money. *Just fucking wait.*

He climbed back into the car and tried to formulate a plan. Luke wouldn't even get out to go to the bathroom without taking the damned box of money. He'd drive around awhile and get his bearings. If worse came to worse, he'd take him to the house.

Sam was thinking of Kathy and her little white nightgown.

Steve Jeffries signed his name to the report and started clearing off his desk. He was still reeling from Max's news. *Who'd have figured Killen would take the plunge?* But, on the other hand, Steve had seen Cindy Lou Merit. What a doll.

Nice, too. His thoughts were interrupted by another young officer.

"Say, Steve. Got a minute?"

"Sure, Richie, what's going on?"

"You know I've been working on those hooker killings. The ones over around Main?"

Bill nodded and put the last of his papers in the drawer.

"Well, I've come up with the damnedest thing. We've had a line on a 1969 blue Chevy Impala. It's been seen in the vicinity of four of the killings—couple of regular girls in the area say they think the last girl, Maretta Anthony, got into that car the day she was murdered." Richie looked down at his notepad. "We've been checking the downtown area, put out feelers. Yesterday, a parking lot attendant calls and says he thinks he's got the car. Turns out there's a briefcase in the trunk. It's got some clothes and—get this—a wig in it."

Bill raised his eyebrows. "Whoa. Who's it registered to?"

"Kid over off Broadway, close to the Plaza. Tracked him down easy enough. No phone, but he was there when I finally found the address. Here's the wild part"—he stopped and shook his head—"kid says he sold the car quite a while ago. Sold it to a guy he used to work for. Cleaning the swimming pool. Got fired immediately after he sold the car, too."

"So who's the guy?"

"Nigel Phelps."

Steve's mouth dropped open. "I'll be a son of a bitch."

Richie nodded. "I'd sure like to track down Captain Links. He's been hot as hell that we haven't made much progress on these Main Street killings. Plus, there's the connection—"

"Right," Steve jumped in. "I'll try and track him down for you. Jesus. He's going to flip out."

Sarah busied herself in the kitchen. She took the deli tray Paul had picked up, and rearranged every slice of pastrami and Swiss. She added extra black olives to the condiment tray. She removed all the ice cubes from the ice maker and put them in a plastic bag in the freezer. Then she sat down, as though she was waiting for the ice maker to fill up again.

"Sarah, they're here." Paul walked into the kitchen and opened the freezer. "Where're the ice cubes?"

She pointed to the bag. "I—I was afraid we'd run out."

He appeared confused, but nodded as if he agreed. He filled the ice bucket and stood watching his wife. Finally he sat down. "Hon—what's wrong? You've been distracted for days now. I've kind of been wondering if you're upset about the Attorney General race. Is that it? Don't you want me to run?"

She smiled and sadly shook her head. "I want you to do whatever makes you happy, Paul. You know that."

"What is it, then? All this mess at the Center?"

"Oh, I don't know. Things sometimes get confusing, you know? Like you know what you have to do. You just can't decide how to go about it."

"Tell me. I probably don't have any answers, but I can at least be a sounding board."

She took the plunge. "Paul, I want to quit my job at Northside. Maybe go back to school and work on my Ph.D. Do research of some kind."

He was clearly surprised. "I thought you loved Northside. Working with Elizabeth, and the women. What brought this on?"

"The violence, Paul. I can't take any more of it. It's getting to me." She reached over and took his hand. Hers was trembling. "I worry about the women all the time. Elizabeth warned me it might happen that way. I just can't do it any longer. Bring all that pain home with me."

He squeezed her hand. "Then quit. Look, if working there has caused the change that's come over you these past few weeks, then you should get out. Do you think I haven't noticed the middle-of-the-night absences from bed? The over-flowing ashtrays? The long silences? I thought the killings were getting you down. Then lately I wondered if it was the political connection. I don't want to put you in a position you can't live with, Sarah."

She stared at his strong hand holding hers. "Nor do I, Paul. God only knows, I don't want to do that to you either."

"Hey!" Alison Links' voice called from the other room. "Are you bringing ice in here, or are we drinking straight tonight?"

Jason carried two glasses into the kitchen. "I,

uh, thought I'd give you a hand, Paul." He wondered how he could approach Sarah, or when he might have the opportunity to talk to her alone. Maybe it would have to wait until tomorrow. *Christ. What a mess.*

Sarah heard him clearly. She knew he wanted her to wait while Paul carried a tray to the living room. *Sorry, Jason,* she thought. *I've got to do this my way.*

Aloud, she said. "Here, Paul. Let me take that. And then let's get started. I'm hoping to be lucky tonight."

Links opened his mouth, then closed it abruptly. He shrugged and followed Sarah through the door.

Alison had just started dealing when Paul spoke. "So, Jason, how goes the investigation? Any closer to an arrest?"

Jason picked a few of the cards in front of him and tapped them on the table in an unconscious habit. He glanced at Sarah, then said simply. "I'm fairly sure I know the identity of the killer, Paul."

Paul had no chance to reply when Alison spoke up. "Jason! You didn't tell me that! I can't believe you've kept this sort of information from me!"

"Now, don't get excited. I have a lot more work to do before I make an official arrest. Before I can prove out the theory."

"And do you think you can?" Sarah inquired quietly. "Prove it, I mean."

"Yes," he said deliberately. "Yes, I think I can."

"Well, that's terrific, Jason." Paul interrupted the moment. "It looks like we have a celebration going tonight. You've got the avenger—excuse the Kaufmanesque terminology—and Sarah's on her way back to college."

Alison was startled. "You are? I don't understand. Are you going to go part-time, or what?"

Sarah looked squarely at Jason, then back at Alison. "I'm quitting my job. I'll be going back for a Ph.D. starting the summer term, if I can make the arrangements."

Alison was confused. "But I thought you loved Northside! What brought this on?"

Sarah put her cards down on the table. "I can't take the pain anymore." She again looked directly at Jason Links. "I don't know if you can understand this, but I feel pain every time a woman at the Center gets hurt." She picked up the cards and slowly began sorting them. "Sometimes things happen, and then I react the only way I know how. It's got to stop."

Paul began nodding. "These past few weeks have been hell for her. You wouldn't believe it."

Links looked at Sarah. "I don't know. I might."

Alison frowned as though she had missed something. "Well, is it because of these killings, Sarah?"

"Yes. That's a good part of it. But it started long before. A long, long time ago."

Jason watched her closely.

Alison quickly picked up the conversation. "Oh, I know. I wouldn't be able to take it either. To look at a woman with her face beaten to a pulp, and know the son of a bitch who did it will be out walking the streets in a few days. No offense, Jason. I know the police can't control the courts." She picked up a huge pastrami on rye and took a generous bite. "God, that's the best sandwich I've ever tasted!"

Links still looked at Sarah. "But the courts are where justice has to be determined. I can't do it, my men can't do it. It has to be decided in the courts, no matter what."

Sarah felt a twinge of peevishness. There were a few things she'd like to have said. As it turned out, she didn't have to.

"Well, now, Jason," Alison replied irritably. "The courts seem to be just a little lenient on men who abuse their wives. In case you didn't notice, both those men—Simmons and Merit—had been in jail for abuse before. And if it wasn't for the avenger, they'd now be murderers."

Sarah noticed Jason Links' neck turning a deep red. "So what's your answer, Alison? Chalk all these killings up to what?"

"Oh, the hell with it." Alison slammed her cards down on the table and glared at her husband. "We've been over this a thousand times." She picked her cards back up. "I bid a club."

Sarah was in such a state of nerves she couldn't count her points. She passed. Jason Links glared back at his wife and bid a spade.

"You'd better have a legitimate spade bid, dear," Alison said. "You know I never bid a short club."

Paul bid a no trump, and Jason passed. Sarah offered a weak two no.

Paul took the bid to game, and Sarah put her cards on the table, thankful to be the dummy. She excused herself and went back in the kitchen. She sat down at the table and put her head in her hands. It wasn't going right. Jason Links wasn't going to give it up. He would prosecute her to the full extent of the law.

Sam pulled up in front of the house. "We'll stay here tonight, Luke. It's my house—and the tax men will come here tomorrow. Better bring your box inside where it'll be safe."

Luke appeared disoriented.

Dumb son of a bitch will never remember where he was, even if he gets a chance to try to explain anything to the police.

"Okay, Sam. I'll bring it. Will the tax men be here for my taxes, too?"

"Sure. They'll be here." Sam had it figured out. He'd talk to Julie, explain everything. Then he'd get Luke to hide the money in the spare room, where he'd be sleeping. He'd try to get one of the guys to stop over tomorrow, pretend to be the tax man. Give him a hundred or so for the trouble. Then he'd simply take Luke downtown and lose him. That was the best way.

Sam unlocked the trunk and pulled out his shotgun. Just in case Julie started anything. If she did, he'd take care of her and Luke at the same time.

Sarah came back just as Paul was sweeping the final trick off the board.

"Made it. Two over." Paul looked self-satisfied. Sarah looked miserable.

Sarah picked up the shuffled deck and started dealing. Twice she faltered and nearly misdealt. Jason looked at her from the corner of his eye. "So, Sarah," he finally began. "What makes you think you can just turn your back on the Center? Walk away from it."

Walk away from the next beating, you mean, don't you? The next killing.

"Jason, you have my word, that when I walk away it will be for good. The moment I realized what—what was happening, or, more precisely, *why* it was happening, I felt the weight of the world off my shoulders. Don't think for a minute I'd let it happen again."

"My God, Sarah," Alison said with eyes wide. "I had no idea it was getting to you like this. That's terrible."

"Terrible is a mild word for it, I'm sorry to say." Sarah looked squarely at Jason. *Please understand me. I didn't have any other choice.*

Links picked up his cards. He could see what was happening. What he was allowing to happen. He was letting Sarah explain herself, without an actual confrontation. She knew that he knew, of course. He supposed she'd read his mind. *So now what? What do you do now? This is one of your best friends. But even that wouldn't save her, unless—unless she really hadn't had a choice in the matter. If she had to kill or be killed.*

What if you'd been there? Seen the men beating their wives to death. Wouldn't you have shot them if that's what it took? The damage to Simmons' body kept surfacing in his mind. He tried to visualize Sarah concentrating on squeezing a man to death.

Did he even have a case in the first place? That was the question. He thought about it. Doubtful. Glenn Livingston's death could be brought in, but it wouldn't matter. Even the records from Hamilton wouldn't actually prove anything. All it would do was wreck lives.

Was there any justice in any of it?

A more powerful mind. More powerful than Edna. As powerful as the woman who saved the Brenner baby. His anonymous psychic! It must have been Sarah.

He stared at her and she nodded imperceptibly.

The phone rang, and Paul Jamieson answered it. "Jason, it's for you. Richie, from the station."

Links picked up the phone and spoke into it. He paused, listening, suddenly alert. "You're sure? There's no mistake." He gripped the telephone receiver hard. "Get me a full report in the morning. And, Richie, thanks. I needed to know."

He sat back down and the three others looked at him expectantly. "Just got a break on those prostitute killings on Main, that's all."

He rubbed his forehead, then spoke again. "I think you made a wise decision in quitting, Sarah. All you can do is try to do what's best and right under the circumstances." He smiled for the first time that evening. "There's not a court in the land that'll hang you for that." He looked back at his hand. "Now let's get on with the game. Sarah's not the only one who feels lucky tonight."

• • •

Sarah felt almost giddy as she walked Alison and Jason Links to the door. It was over. No more killings. Paul would run for, and hopefully win, the seat of Attorney General. She would go back and finish her doctorate, concentrating on research. The only time she would ever think about her past was when she visited Tom Hamilton. And she would do that. Somehow he'd put her existence into a better perspective.

They stepped out onto the back patio.

She gave Alison a hug. "Thanks for coming. It's the best evening I've had in a long time." She turned to Jason, hugging him, too. "And Jason, thanks for—for everything."

"Oh, just a minute," Alison said. "Paul is making me a little doggy plate. In case I feel the urge for another pastrami sandwich later." She disappeared into the house.

Sarah felt the presence of Jason Links as she'd not done at any time previously in the evening. He appeared solemn, thoughtful. Finally he spoke.

"Am I making the right decision, Sarah? Have we seen the last of our so-called avenger?"

She answered softly. "You won't regret it, Jason. I guarantee you, Kansas City has seen the last of it."

"I hope so, Sarah." His eyes were piercing even in the dark night. "I sincerely hope so."

She stood in the doorway, waving good-bye until they'd long since passed from her sight. It was starting to sprinkle, and the air was filled with a clean, fresh smell. She felt good. Alive. She was going to change into the pink negligee Paul loved so much, then she was going to seduce the future Attorney General of the state of Missouri. She smiled as she walked back into the house, anticipating the rest of the evening.

Suddenly a scream cut through her head like a lightning bolt ripping through the sky. There was the sound of a gunshot, then more screams. She recognized the voice in an instant. It was Kathy.

"Help me! Mrs. Jamieson! He's killing Mama!"

Sarah felt the blood drain from her face as she slid down the wall until she sat crumpled on the floor. She drew her hands together.

"Forgive me, Jason. Just one more time."

Chapter 20

KANSAS CITY, MISSOURI
May, 1990

Avenger Dead in Bloody Swan Song
Charlie Kaufman, Staff Writer

Kansas City homicide detectives confirmed last night that the serial killer known as "The Avenger" is believed dead after a rampage that left yet another wife-beater/child-abuser dead.

Sam Thomas, 41, sought on assault and child sexual abuse charges by the K.C. police force for several months, broke into his former home to confront his estranged wife, Julie, 37. Thomas' stepdaughter, Kathy, 14, was also present, still wearing an arm cast from a previous attack by Thomas.

According to the Thomas child, her mother was saved by an unidentified intruder who, after taking two shotgun blasts in the chest, still managed to crush Thomas to death before lapsing into unconsciousness.

The identity of the Kansas City Avenger remains a mystery, but according to police, he was nearly seven feet tall and weighed over three hundred pounds. Thus we come to the end of a saga reminiscent of Charles Bronson's "Death Wish," the story of a one-man battle against crime. How the Avenger located his victims is still undetermined. Every woman whose life was saved had at one time been connected to Northside Crisis Center. Ironically, young Kathy Thomas' life was twice saved by this giant of a man. Just two weeks ago, Johnny Merit, a transient who attacked his pregnant wife, Cindy Lou, causing her to miscarry their child, was also killed by the Kansas City Avenger. Kathy Thomas had followed Mrs. Merit to a local motel, where the attack took place. The child did not see Merit's attacker, but following the incident in her home, she has stated that the Avenger is a man she had seen near Northside Crisis Center several times.

In a related story, Valerie Phelps, widow of industrialist Nigel Phelps, has issued a statement from a private nursing facility, where she is listed as being in serious but stable condition. Mrs. Phelps has admitted that her illness is a result of injuries inflicted on her by her husband prior to another Avenger killing. She had previously denied allegations that her husband had been abusive.

A portion of the prepared Phelps' statement read: "Earlier, I withheld information concerning my husband's mental condition from the police. I did so in a foolish attempt to protect his name and his family. In fairness to the man who saved my life, I feel required to now step forward with the truth." Mrs. Phelps went on to say that she believes it is possible that her husband was suffering from a brain tumor.

Captain Jason Links, Homicide, made the following statement from the crime scene. "The Medical Examiner has completed a preliminary report on the condition of Sam Thomas' body. It is in precisely the same condition as the other victims of what the press has dubbed 'The Avenger.' I am satisfied that the man now dead of gunshot wounds is the same man who has eluded us in three previous killings. We will make a concentrated effort to identify this man, but as far as the department is concerned, the case is now closed."